White Dragon

Regina A. Hanel

Yellow Rose
by Regal Crest

Texas

ISBN: 978-1-61929-142-3

First Printing 2014

9 8 7 6 5 4 3 2 1

Original cover design by Donna Pawlowski
Final cover design by AcornGraphics

Published by:

Regal Crest Enterprises, LLC
229 Sheridan Loop
Belton, Texas 76513

Find us on the World Wide Web at
http://www.regalcrest.biz

Published in the United States of America

Acknowledgments

I'd like to thank Cathy Bryerose and the entire Regal Crest Enterprises team for their continued support and invaluable assistance, allowing my second manuscript to become a joyful reality.

Special thanks to my editors, Mary Phillips and Mary Hettel, and to Pat Cronin, Editor-In-Chief, for their much appreciated comments, suggestions, careful scrutiny, and eyes for detail. Editors have a special way of seeing what we don't see and elevating our work.

Loving thanks go to my partner Veronica for being my sounding board and first-line editor, and for dealing with my "time away" when I'm lost in thought, writing.

And thanks to the readers. I wasn't sure I'd be able to create a second book, but many of your comments and interest have made it possible. I'm grateful for your support and hope the words keep coming. If you get a chance, stop by to visit my website or contact me at www.rhanel.com. I'd love to hear from you.

For Veronica — the warmth within my heart and
the inspiration in my soul.

Old European Riddle

"What flies without wings, hits without hands, and
sees without eyes?"

Chapter One

THE EXPEDITION SWAYED as Ranger Samantha Takoda Tyler pulled into the gravel, hole-strewn parking lot. Scant minutes passed since the call from dispatch. She stepped out of the vehicle, hefted her EMS bag, and started along the zigzagging path that overlooked Phelps Lake in Grand Teton National Park. About twenty yards from the bottom of the trail, Sam spotted a man in a navy blue shirt and tan fishing vest sitting a short distance from the water's edge. He waved her over.

Before she reached him, he yelled, "I twisted my ankle between the rocks. I can't put weight on it."

Sam set her bag on the ground. "Okay, let's have a closer look. I'm Ranger Tyler, and you are?"

"Toby Hodgeman — Senior," he said.

Sam reached for his ankle and undid the laces on his hiking boot. "How was the fishing earlier?"

"Fine," he replied between gritted teeth as Sam removed the heavy boot and his sock.

"What were you fishing for, whitefish or trout?"

"I don't see why that matters, but mackinaw, if you must know."

"Trout it is then."

His eyes widened. "You fish?"

"I stay away from eating fish or meat, so I have no reason to, but I'm familiar with the fish and wildlife in the area, and in the park." After a few seconds she added, "Your injury appears to be a fracture. I'm going to immobilize your ankle and call for backup to help get you out of here."

Sam called dispatch, then extracted an orange brace and several other items from her EMS bag. With a gentle touch, she wrapped the flexible, foam covered aluminum splint around Toby's lower leg and ankle, then secured it with an Ace bandage wrap.

Twenty minutes later, she helped carry him along the trail to the ambulance waiting in the parking lot. As she turned to leave, he called to her.

"Uh, Ranger Tyler," he said. "Thanks again for everything. Sorry I was a bit gruff earlier, it's just that the pain — "

"Not a problem," Sam said. She stood still for several seconds uncertain whether his less than friendly tone had more to do with his injury or instead centered on something else. Rather than make assumptions, she added, "Don't worry about it. I'm glad I was able to help."

"Still, thanks."

"You're welcome. Now get out of here and take care of yourself," she said. Sam spoke in a firm, yet friendly tone as the medics lifted him into the ambulance. "And watch where you're stepping next time."

SAM WISHED THE call from dispatch hadn't come at the end of her shift. Her original plans were to leave work early, pick up a bouquet of flowers, and surprise Halie with dinner. Since Sam's promotion to Sub-District Supervisor last fall, the increased administrative duties often added a minimum of an hour or two to her day.

Sam placed a quick call to Halie, letting her know she'd be late. Not far from her favorite florist, Sam headed south on Moose Wilson Road, thankful the traffic was lighter than normal, speeding her trip. At the florist, she lingered, selecting their finest and most fragrant flowers. After placing the bouquet on the seat of her vehicle, she eyed the arrangement one more time with satisfaction. Halie was sure to like them.

Sam traveled along Gros Ventre River Road, past familiar picturesque mountains and wide-open expanses of grassland. She slowed the Expedition to a near crawl in front of their sprawling ranch house. The property was flat and level, separated from the road by a four feet high, white, wooden fence. The lawn was well kept, but needed mowing. Pink, white, and red impatiens lined the walkway leading from the driveway to the house, which was set back about a half-acre from the road.

Sam parked the Expedition in the driveway as close to the garage door as she could, out of the line of view from the living room windows. She gingerly shut the SUV's door and snuck around the rear of the house. Sam entered through the heavy wooden back door that led into the mudroom, excited to surprise Halie. Momentarily placing the flowers on top of the wash cabinet counter, she unlaced her work boots and straightened out her uniform. Sam then tiptoed into the alcove from the garage, holding the flowers. She grinned from ear to ear thinking about the verbal lashing she would have gotten from her feisty partner had she not crept up on her wearing only socks.

Halie stood in front of the dark green, granite kitchen counter, an elegant sight to Sam, even though she was only preparing salad for dinner. Halie's curly, flowing blonde hair caressed her narrow yet sturdy shoulders. The sleeveless purple blouse she wore hugged her torso. Her petite frame modeled her designer blue jeans and firm buttocks, causing Sam to catch her breath as her heart beat several times faster.

Sam inched closer, but before she was able to move against Halie from behind and reach the bouquet of flowers in front of her, Halie spun part way around, intercepting her.

"Oh my god, you startled me," Halie said. She brought her right hand up to her chest, and in the next breath added, "Hey, wait a minute. What've you got there?" At which point her face lit up in the manner Sam imagined earlier.

"These are to say I love you—I'm glad it's finally the weekend—and I'm doubly thankful to be spending it with you."

Halie took the extensive bouquet of flowers, wrapped in cellophane and tied with a dark purple ribbon, in both hands. She sniffed deep, then moved them to the side and kissed Sam on the lips. "These are beautiful. You didn't have to do this. I thought we were celebrating tomorrow."

"We are, but I wanted to get a head start today."

Halie slid the salad bowls to the side and set the flowers on the counter. "I should have known you'd do something like this. That's so sweet. I'll put these in water right away."

"Good idea. They've been in the car a while. The traffic wasn't too bad, but still, I'm sure they're thirsty enough. Where's Jake?" Sam scanned the kitchen. Jake, her dog, wasn't one to miss meeting her at the door, especially when coming home later than usual. "I mean, I'm glad he didn't give me away, but at the same time, I can't remember the last time I outsmarted him."

"He's exhausted. I let him out when I got home and he flushed a rabbit from under the mountain ash in the back and chased it full speed around the yard. The two of them ran in circles, and then the rabbit ran into the woods and he took off after it. I don't think he caught up to it though. I watched him slog his way back across the lawn, tongue hanging out and panting. When he reached the deck and came into the kitchen, he didn't stay around for his usual treat."

"Sounds like you've got him pegged," Sam said. "He's all brawn but no bite. I wouldn't want him any other way. God knows enough innocent animals are killed every day, and not all for good reasons."

"I wouldn't want him any other way either," Halie said. "I don't know what I would've done if he walked up to the door with that cute furry critter in his mouth."

Sam took a step toward Halie and hugged her. "You probably would've called me."

"Darn right," Halie said, as the clanking of Jake's nails on the tile flooring and the jingle of his tags when he shook himself, echoed from the dining room. "Speaking of our devilish pooch, it sounds like he's on to you."

"Hey there buddy," Sam said, bending at the knees as Jake entered the kitchen. She pet Jake on the head and scratched him behind the ears. "How's my good boy doing? Huh? How's my good boy? Didn't hear me come home today, did you? You're losing your touch, mister. Did you have a fun time chasing that rabbit?" she said, ruffling the hair around his neck.

Jake's tail wagged so hard his whole butt moved back and forth several inches in each direction before banging with force against the cabinet face. When Sam stood, he pranced all around her legs, pushing up against her like a love-struck cat. "Hey, watch it. Don't step on my toes with those nasty claws of yours," she said in jest, though in truth, getting stepped on by an eighty pound Rhodesian Ridgeback was not at the top of her 'fun things to do' list.

Apparently oblivious of Sam's ribbing, Jake continued his happy dance around his mistress and best friend.

"Did he eat dinner yet?" Sam asked.

"Yeah, that he found energy for."

"That's a good boy. Then I've got a treat that'll make you forget all about that elusive little rabbit," Sam said. Although she enjoyed teasing Jake, she loved having him around, and in the same way with Halie, she couldn't get enough of his company or imagine her life without him in it. He had been her rock when she went through tough times, and she'd always be grateful to him for that and all the other loving things he did.

As Jake's nose pushed firm against her hands, she held out the raw knuckle bone she'd bought him. Without hesitation, he snapped up his prize, plopped down where he stood, and chewed rigorously.

Sam grabbed an old towel from the closet by the mudroom. As she drew near, Jake lifted his bone and once the towel was in front of him, placed the bone down and continued eating.

"That should keep him busy for a while," Sam said. "Do I have time to take a bath before dinner? I feel so grungy from work."

"Please do," Halie said, "but hurry up, because I'm starving already."

"No surprise there," Sam said before she hustled through the dining and living rooms. As she made her way up the stairs, she unbuckled her leather gun belt and carried it and its contents into the bedroom with her while her free hand began undoing the buttons to her uniform. She couldn't wait to relax in the warm water and catch a second wind.

SAM DRIED THE dishes as Halie washed. Sam's eyes continually found their way to Halie, though her stolen glances appeared to have gone unnoticed by her partner. If it were only the glances that went unnoticed, Sam wouldn't have minded, but the lack of attention dove much deeper.

Even during moments of alone time, Halie appeared preoccupied to Sam, and Sam missed the intimacy they hadn't shared for several months. With each day that passed, Sam's lips longed more and more to feel the softness of Halie's lips and the gentle caress of her hand against her skin. Sam wanted to breathe in her scent. Her body ached to feel the warmth and tenderness of her touch. She wondered if Halie felt the same desire. If she did, she wasn't showing it.

"How about another glass of wine?" Sam suggested. "We could sit out on the deck and watch the sun set, just the two of us, away from any distractions."

"That sounds good," Halie said. "We haven't done that in a long while."

Jake squeezed past Halie as she opened the sliding glass door, and bolted out across the deck, down the steps, and onto the grass. After refilling their glasses, Sam met Halie near the railing, the wood still warm from the sun as she leaned against it. As they watched Jake roll around on his back and kick his feet in the air, the sun began to set in a fire-like orange hue, letting the cooling night air settle over them. Sam rested her hand on top of Halie's and stroked the smooth surface with her thumb. Warm, tingling sensations ran up Sam's arm and her heartbeat quickened.

Sam first met Halie in Chief Thundercloud's office fourteen months earlier. From the start there had been something special about Halie Walker. There was gentleness and comfort in her chestnut brown eyes. Sam never imagined how special. Halie had visited the park to do a cover story for a wildlife magazine she'd worked for in Boston. The chief had partnered Sam up with Halie to help in that endeavor. Though initially bullheaded and reluctant to change her routine and assist Halie during her stay, Sam's view of her softened as their connection to each other grew. With each passing day and unique experience, their bond blossomed into a relationship beyond both their expectations.

Much had transpired since that day. Sam glanced into Halie's eyes, hoping to see the desire and anticipation behind them, hidden these past months for reasons unknown to Sam, but she couldn't read them. Wanting to ask the reason why, but afraid of the answer, she instead asked, "Are you cold?"

"A little chilled," Halie said, rubbing her arms.

Sam reached her left arm around Halie and pulled her close. The warmth between them spread. "I can get your sweater if you like."

"No, this is fine, thanks."

In the quiet, Sam ached to be closer to Halie. She wondered if this night would be like so many recent others, her desire left wanting, or if it would be as it had in the past, where Halie wasn't able to get enough of her, and vice-versa. Nervousness of the unknown crept in, replacing hopeful anticipation. Sam tried to shake it loose, but she couldn't. She took another sip of wine, convincing herself not to self-prophesize. The past isn't always representative of the future, she told herself. Eventually their lives would get back to normal. God knows they had many wonderful days and nights where passion burned wild in them both. Why Sam now toyed with the idea that Halie didn't want or need her as much as she wanted and needed Halie was unclear. She was certain Halie loved her, and if she loved her, Sam shouldn't worry so much.

As Halie pressed against Sam, Sam's body relaxed along with her jumbled thoughts, comforted by Halie's apparent desire for closeness. After a few seconds, Sam angled her body to face Halie. She brushed her lips against Halie's cheek and kissed the side of her face with tenderness. As Halie shifted and faced Sam, Sam's eyes contemplated Halie's lips, the heat within her rising as swift as a mild blowing breeze. When the line of sight from Halie's eyes lowered to Sam's mouth, Sam moved closer and kissed Halie with soft passion, waiting for her lips to part and their tongues to find one another. Sam's breaths shortened. Yet as quick as the intensity between them rose, it vanished in an instant as Halie pulled away with an abruptness that startled Sam.

"Shoot, I almost forgot to tell you," Halie said. "I picked up the flyers for the gallery opening from the printer today. I should get them and show them to you. They came out great."

A sharp sting of disappointment shot through Sam's heart as if Halie plunged a dagger straight through it yet again. At first, no words formed in Sam's mind. A cloud of dejection engulfed her, its cold tendrils replaced the heated blood that flowed through her veins moments before. "Now?" she managed in a whisper.

"Yes, now. Why not?"

Sam felt as though she was watching a stranger. Halie's words erupted so matter of fact, that Sam could not reply. Her throat constricted as her chest tightened around her heart. She stood baffled, unable to answer. Was she doing something wrong? Was Halie not physically attracted to her anymore? Was there someone else? No, she didn't believe someone else was involved, but then what? Why was she acting so strange? Sam understood Halie had been pre-occupied to the point of near obsession with getting her career back on track the past few months, but she couldn't reconcile this matter as the only reason for Halie's distance. There had to be something more. Why wasn't Halie talking to her about what was wrong? Didn't she deserve the truth? This was supposed to be a weekend of celebration, the one-year anniversary of when Halie had agreed to stay with Sam and start building a life together, but it now felt like nothing joyous. A dark chasm filled the space between them. Sam could barely look Halie in the eye, but she knew she had to answer her. She strained to find the words to a question she couldn't believe had been asked. In a near whisper she said, "Because although I eventually do want to see the flyers, since I'm excited for you about your gallery opening too, but I was more excited about spending some quality time with you—for a change. I thought you wanted the same thing tonight, but I guess I misread you—again."

"No, you didn't, and I do, it's just that I've been so tired lately. I'm burning the candle at both ends and it's catching up to me. I don't have the energy and I didn't want to disappoint you, so I thought I'd show you the flyers instead."

"Unfortunately, I only see the candle burning from one end," Sam said. "And as for the disappointment, you managed that better than you realize." All she wanted to do at that point was retreat to bed and hope against hope for sleep to overtake her, knowing instead, she'd spend another sleepless night trying to figure out what was wrong with Halie. Tears felt as though they were welling behind Sam's eyes, but she held them back. Before she could excuse herself, Halie spoke.

"I'm sorry. I don't know what to say. I've upset you. I didn't mean to. I've been so busy. I don't think about much else except getting on my own feet again with work. I know you're there to support me and all, but it's important for me to do this on my own. I need to feel I've accomplished something in my life and I may have let that need control everything. I promise I'll make more of an effort to pay attention to us."

Sam waited for a deeper explanation, but nothing else came. She wished she could believe the words her partner spoke, but she knew better. "You've told me this before, but here we are again. I love you. I need to know what's genuinely going on with you. It's only fair to the both of us. There's got to be more to this than you're telling me."

"No, that's all there is."

"I don't believe you. Is there someone else? Have you found someone else?"

"No — I *haven't* found someone else. Why would you even ask me that?"

The shocked expression on Halie's face told Sam she hadn't found someone else, which deep in her heart she already knew, but she was grasping at straws. "Well, what should I think? You can't just be too busy. You find time for other things, but you never find time for us." Sam struggled with the last words as her throat constricted and she swallowed hard. She wanted to storm off and leave Halie standing there, but her feet remained planted. Instead, she turned and stared out into the yard, her focus a million miles away, her thoughts mixed and confused.

For several painstaking moments, neither of them spoke. It was Halie that broke the silence. The words flowed from her headlong and without interruption. "Did it ever occur to you that maybe I'm a little overwhelmed? I'm the one who's spent months recovering from that accident on Pinebluff Mountain. I'm the one who uprooted the life I knew in Boston to come live with you. I'm the one who left my job to try and start over here, which as you know hasn't been easy. I've begged hotels, motels, restaurant owners, cafés, and art galleries to hang my photographs on consignment to see if they'd be good enough to stand on their own. I'm not overly proud of having begged. I've worked part time doing small handout photography assignments for Grand Teton — and don't think I don't know they were practically gifts from the chief — and crap nothing stories for the local paper. I've been busy building a portfolio of photographs worthy of hanging in a gallery and researching all that it takes to open and run that type of a business successfully. And what have you done? Your routine hasn't changed except that I've been added to your life. You still have your job. You still have your friends. You still live in the same area, even if it's in a new house. That's the only thing that has changed for you."

Sam stared into Halie's wounded brown eyes, and Halie held her gaze. They stood there for several seconds until Halie stepped forward and pulled Sam to her.

"I'm so sorry," Halie said sobbing, her body trembling. "I—I didn't even realize I felt that way."

"You must have had an inkling along the way. Why'd you wait so long to say something? Am I that difficult to open up to?"

"No, you're not. I guess somewhere along the way I became overwhelmed and didn't want to admit it to myself. Maybe part of me blamed you. I don't know."

"It's not like I did nothing though, but maybe if I'd have been around more—"

"It's not your fault. I knew changing my life around wasn't going to be easy. I wanted to be with you. I still do. You've been so great. You've done more for me with helping get the gallery going and supporting my dream than anyone else would have done, even with the added responsibility you have at work. I don't know why I got so mad. I'm sorry. It wasn't fair. You're the one who saved my life by being in it."

Sam's heart softened. She reached her arms around Halie and held her close. "It's okay. You've been through a lot, and I should have been more sensitive to what was going on. I'm glad you let it out. I'd rather know what's bothering you than guess. You don't need to be sorry."

"No, I'm sorry and I should be. I've not been fair to you. Although, I'm actually glad the thoughts came out too. Somehow I feel better."

"Talking's a start. We'll work through this together."

"No matter what, I need you to know that I love you with all my being, Samantha Takoda Tyler. Please don't ever forget that. I'm sorry if I haven't shown you how much. Will you let me make it up to you?"

"I don't know," Sam said in partial jest. "I may need a whole lot of convincing."

"Oh," Halie said in that suggestive tone that had lain dormant for some time. "I think I can find a way to convince you without too much trouble."

"No doubt," Sam replied, knowing Halie owned her heart. Yet in the recesses of her mind she wasn't so certain their problem had been resolved.

Chapter Two

THE NEXT DAY, Sam awoke with renewed energy and decided to tackle the yard work she'd been putting aside. After an hour of nonstop digging, followed by another hour of laying gravel and bricks to encircle a flower bed, she stood and wiped her forehead with the back of her hand. She grabbed the water bottle she'd set near the base of a young maple tree and took several long, satisfying gulps. The cool water trickled down her throat and replenished much of what she'd sweat out. The weather was warmer than forecast for Teton County on this first Saturday in July, but she didn't mind. Without much humidity, the heat remained tolerable.

Sam scanned the panoramic mountain range in the distance. She never tired of taking stock of the majestic snow capped mountain peaks that stretched upward toward the vast, azure, Wyoming sky. Her eyes scanned the rolling hills of lush fields of grass and sagebrush dotted with aspen and pine trees. She inhaled deep. In the past year, regardless of their troubles, she'd thanked her lucky stars many times over for all the events that fell in place for her the prior summer, including those which allowed her to buy the ranch house for her and Halie.

A couple of months after the helicopter crash on Pinebluff Mountain, Halie ended the lease on her apartment in Boston and Sam left the government housing she'd been assigned in the park, and they purchased the house in Kelly. Sam's boss, Chief Thundercloud, waived the requirement for Sam to live in government housing because although the ranch house was built along the boundaries of the park's southern district, the area of her responsibility within the park, part of the property was within park boundaries. As much as she loved the house and property, Sam knew that if Halie hadn't recovered from the crash, she would never have bought it.

As the clouds gathered and the wind increased, Sam surmised the unusual warmth of the past few days wouldn't last much longer. She replaced the cap to her water bottle and set it under the tree. She sped up to finish her work and then rolled the wheelbarrow containing her work gloves, pick axe, shovel, level, and leftover bricks into the shed. Once outside, she closed and locked the barn-like doors and brushed the dried dirt off the bottom of her work jeans. Straightening, she heard Halie's voice call to her from the deck.

Sam's gaze followed Halie's slim frame as she ran toward her. Jake followed in close pursuit. Sam's love for Halie was so great, at times she didn't know how to contain it, and last night she was glad it wasn't necessary. A devilish grin crossed her face. She was surprised either of them possessed the energy needed to do the work they planned to do today, but she'd welcome that kind of tired any day.

Halie gasped for breath before coming to a halt, the phone held out in front of her. "It's Charlie. Coco's missing. Charlie said he wasn't out in the pasture with the other horses when he called them in, and when he went to check on him to see if he was in his stall, he wasn't there either."

Sam's smile quickly vanished. "What? How can that be?"

"I don't know. You'd better talk to him."

Sam took the phone, her eyes focused on Halie. "Hey, Charlie. What's going on?"

"Hi, Sam, I'm so sorry about this, but as soon as I found out, I called," Charlie said.

While Sam listened, Halie stroked her arm. Jake plopped himself on the lawn, rolled over, twisted back and forth, and kicked his hind legs in the air.

"When was the last time someone saw him?" Sam said.

"No one's seen him since lunch time. I interviewed all my workers," Charlie said.

"Was a gate left open?"

"Not that I'm aware of. If someone left it open, they're not admitting to it."

"Okay. Thanks for calling Charlie. I'll be there in a couple of minutes," Sam said. She handed Halie the phone and kissed her warmly on the lips. "I've gotta go. Charlie's not sure how long Coco's been gone. The last time anyone saw him was at lunch time. It's not like him to run off. I'm sorry about this. I know you were planning a special dinner for us. Hopefully he didn't go far and I'll be back in time to enjoy it."

"Just be careful and don't worry about dinner. I love you."

"I love you too. Be back soon," she said. She tried to convince herself that Coco was fine and that she had nothing to worry about. Sam ran toward the house. "Come on Jake. Let's go get your buddy, Coco."

Jake sprung up and let out a bark of excitement before he bounded off after Sam.

Sam reached for her Stetson as she headed through the house and out the garage. She opened the hatch to the Expedition for Jake, shut it once he was safe inside, and got into the driver's seat. Seconds later they sped out of the driveway and on to Tynes Sunshine Ranch.

CHARLIE TYNES' PROPERTY bordered on their own ten acre lot, so the trip only took Sam a couple of minutes. Past Charlie's mailbox, she pulled the wheel from the Expedition sharp left, drove up the dirt drive, and parked in front of the stables. She kicked up a cloud of dust that drifted over the vehicle before she stepped out and let Jake loose. Jake ran toward Charlie.

"Hey, Charlie," Sam said. She attempted a positive tone, trying not to let him sense her anxiety.

Charlie's near toothless and tobacco stained smile was absent from his leathered face as he reached down and petted Jake. "I'm so sorry, Sam," he said as he stood, scratching the side of his elbow. "I honestly don't know what happened. I mean, yeah, I'm still down a man, plus Tim's been on vacation, but I hired a couple of high school kids for the summer to help out, so it's not like no one's watching the place, and they're good kids. I kept my eye on them when I first hired them. They're real responsible. I don't know where he could have run off to with no one noticing. Even though they're not admitting it, someone must have left the lower gate open."

"It's okay, don't worry. Jake and I'll find him," Sam reassured him. "He's a sucker for a Red Delicious." Sam tossed the apple she'd been wiping against her jeans in the air.

A smile cracked through Charlie's harsh appearing exterior. He patted Sam on the shoulder. "So he is. Good idea. Bribe him with food if you have to. You'd better get going then. Take Sugar. I've already saddled her up for you."

Sam met Charlie for the first time nearly five years ago when she'd brought him Coco to board. She took an instant liking to him. He treated her as an equal. Once Sam became his neighbor, they shared several occasions where they helped one another out. She appreciated his forethought of saddling Sugar.

Sam led Jake into Coco's stall and held out Coco's blanket for him to smell before they started out. The tough part, she knew, was deciding where to search first. Coco's scent and that of the other horses was all around the stables and nearby pastures. Jake wouldn't be much help to start them off. After a few minutes of contemplation, sitting on top of Sugar near the edge of the property, Sam headed northeast along the main trail in the direction of the Grand Teton Mountains. She hoped if Coco ran off on his own, or if, God forbid, someone stole him, they'd have stuck to the main trail.

After a few minutes riding, and every five minutes thereafter, Sam whistled and called for Coco. Each time she expected to see him galloping over to meet them, and each time became disappointed when he didn't appear.

Jake pranced next to Sugar, now and again straying to chase a nearby sage grouse, but on every occasion ended up next to Sam's side without her having to utter a word.

The winds continued to strengthen and the skies darkened. The smell of rain hung in the air. "We won't have much longer before this spirals into a nasty storm," she said to Jake. They'd been on the trail for an hour before she second-guessed that perhaps she'd chosen the wrong direction in which to head, but then Jake barked several times in a row. He spun around and stared at Sam as if to say "hey, come on," then darted off into the shrubs.

Sugar's head jerked up, her nostrils flared, and she jerked forward, ears pointed back. "Whoa there little one," Sam said as she pulled back on the reins. Sugar was Halie's horse, small-framed in comparison to Coco, but strong nonetheless. Sam stroked the side of Sugar's neck. "That's just Jake getting excited, and probably all about nothing, okay, so you settle yourself. The last thing I need is another horse running off and leaving me in the dust. That's it—good girl," Sam said. She directed Sugar off the trail.

A pathway of disturbed grasses stretched out before them. Sam's adrenaline quickened. Jake was on to something. She inspected the ground noting two sets of hoof prints in the soft soil, both leading in the same direction. As she continued on, grassland matted with wildflowers and shrubs soon gave way to small pine thickets and eventually a patch of forest alongside the mountain. Tired of ducking under and around branches, Sam stepped off Sugar and led her through the darkening maze. The ground beneath them was now firm, though slick with pine needles. The combination of hardened earth and ground cover hid the tracks. Sam was beyond thankful Jake accompanied her.

Thunder rumbled close by. The deeper they headed, the more worried Sam became that Coco had been stolen. Sam knew he'd never have wandered this deep into the woods on his own. She was also aware that she didn't have her gun with her and hoped she wouldn't need it. "Coco! Coco! Where are you boy?" she called out.

As the last word passed Sam's lips, seemingly out of nowhere Sugar reared up and knocked Sam off her feet onto the rocky ground. She landed full force on her right shoulder and arm. "Dammit Sugar, what the heck's gotten into you!" Sam straightened and sat up, knees bent in front of her. Pain shot up her arm while a high-pitched ringing flooded her ears. For a second, nausea overtook her as she watched Sugar run a hundred yards off in the direction they came. Her vision blurred. She thought she might pass out. Only after the ringing subsided did she realize what spooked Sugar, and she froze in place.

A rattlesnake lay coiled not more than two feet away from Sam, its tail oscillating back and forth, head and upper body raised and pointed in her direction. Piercing black eyes stared at her and sent a chill down her spine. Had she landed a foot closer, she'd probably have been bitten. Sam remained still, facing the snake, knowing that while it continued to rattle its tail, the threat of being bitten remained real. Sam understood she needed to back away, but before she could move, Jake approached from the side.

"No, Jake! Stay!" Sam yelled, afraid he'd attack. "You stay!"

Jake moved slower, head low, stealth-like, but didn't stop.

"Jake! Please! What did I say?"

At Sam's second, insistent command, he did as he was told. He not only stopped moving forward, but also retreated several steps before lying down. His eyes remained locked on the snake.

"Good boy," Sam praised. She breathed deep. The rattler remained motionless except for its tail and its thin, black, forked tongue jutting in and out. With painstaking slowness, Sam placed her left hand behind her strained back as she pushed away from the snake with her feet. The burn in her right shoulder intensified as she moved. After placing a couple of feet between them, the rattling stopped. Sam recognized she was one step closer to safety.

Seconds later, the snake slithered toward a grouping of rocks and disappeared between them. "Come on boy," Sam said to Jake as she managed to get to her feet, still a bit shaken. Sam rubbed Jake's head with her left hand and breathed a sigh of relief. "You are such a good boy, you know that? Such a good boy." As the initial euphoria of having avoided the snake subsided, Sam's mind re-registered the fact she hadn't found Coco yet, and that now she had another problem to tackle—her injured arm. The way her limb hung listless at her side, and the extent of the pain radiating through it, she guessed she dislocated her shoulder. Yet she had no way of making forward progress without her arm swaying when she walked. She wished she'd brought her EMS bag with her. Her mind searched for a solution. Then she said to Jake, "Hey buddy, can you go get Sugar?"

Jake let out a bark. Tail wagging, he ran toward Sugar. Sam watched as he circled behind the now calm horse and herded her back toward Sam like a sheep dog.

"You are definitely one of a kind," she said to Jake. "I'm one lucky person to have found you." She petted him on top of his head. Sam moved next to Sugar and stroked her slow on the side of her neck several times, talking to her in a calming fashion. Then she unclasped the solid brass scissor snap from the bridal bit below the attachment for the cheek pieces. She clasped the scissor snap to the loop at the other end of the rein and held the now circular rein against her shoulder to see how far it draped below her elbow. After adjusting the strap to shorten it with her teeth, she lifted the makeshift sling over her head with her left hand and pushed the strap under her right elbow, wincing as she did so. A slight measure of relief followed, as the sling did its job and took pressure off her damaged shoulder. Satisfied the temporary fix would hold, she addressed Jake. "Let's go get Coco."

Ten minutes later, the first raindrops fell. Sam was afraid the rain might wash away Coco's scent, and along with it, their chances of finding him. The throbbing in her shoulder and arm remained intense, and Sam noticed numbness in her fingers. She opened and closed her fist several times in an effort to regain feeling. Still, she was more worried about Coco than herself. As they marched on, the rain fell more steadily. One loud thunderous rumble or flash of lightning, no matter how far away, and Sam resolved they'd have to call it quits and try again tomorrow.

Although the nightmares of losing her friend Tina on Grand Teton three years ago to a lightning strike hadn't haunted Sam since Halie found her way into her life, the stark reality of Tina's death and the unpredictability of lightning's power hadn't escaped her memory. She'd run into enough trouble for one day. She'd not take a further risk. It wasn't only her life she had to think of now.

Jake shook the rain from his soaked coat and barked as he sprang up and down in place on his front paws.

"What is it boy?" Sam asked. Hopeful anticipation returned as she leaned over and petted Jake with her good arm. Water streamed off the rim of her Stetson as she bent over. Then Sam heard it, the snorting and neighing of her pal Coco. She tied Sugar's remaining rein loose to the branch of a young tree as her heart raced with the anticipation of seeing her friend. She moved as fast toward Coco as her bad shoulder allowed.

Coco stood alone, thirty yards away, with his reins tied into a tight knot around a tree trunk, unable to move his head more than a few inches, and unable to lie down. "Oh, God," escaped Sam's lips. She hoped he hadn't stood like that for long. Coco's eyes were open with fear. Sam touched him. He felt heated. "It's okay boy. It's okay. Mama's here," she reassured him, stroking his side. She scanned their surroundings. Unable to comprehend who would take Coco and mistreat him as they did, Sam struggled with her anger. For a brief moment, her thoughts shifted to doing serious harm to this person before she regained control and refocused on Coco and their current situation.

Certain they were alone, Sam walked Coco to where Sugar was standing. She ran her hand down Coco's legs and across his smooth coat, checking him over, searching for signs of injury. He appeared okay, other than the sweat still covering his coat. The rain would help cool him. For that she was thankful. She grabbed a water bottle from its holder and pulled open the top with her teeth. She took a short swig, then streamed some in Coco's mouth, though most of it fell to the ground. Jake and Sugar were next. Coco nudged her in the chest for more, coming dangerously close to her arm, but she ran out of water. She remembered the apple she'd brought with her and snatched it from Sugar's saddlebag. She held it out to him. Coco stomped his hoof and swooshed his tail before wrapping his lips around the tasty treat.

"Yeah, looks like you'll be okay mister," Sam said, stroking the side of his neck. "But we better get back while the going's halfway decent and get you rehydrated." Coco walked next to Sugar and Jake took the lead, head held high.

Sam shivered in her wet T-shirt, angry she hadn't grabbed her raincoat from the Expedition earlier. Her shoulder ached. The rain brought with it cooler temperatures as afternoon morphed into evening. The air was invigorating for Coco, but did Sam no favors. Still, she knew she'd soon be home and once again in the arms of her lover, and that vision alone helped warm her.

FIVE MINUTES BEFORE seven o'clock in the evening, the phone rang. Halie raced to pick up the receiver. "Hello, Sam?"

"Hi Halie, no, it's Charlie. I wanted to give you a heads up that Sam's at the ranch with me and she found Coco. She'll be on her way home soon," Charlie said.

"Thank God. I was so worried. Are they okay? How's Sam?"

Charlie hesitated. "Coco's fine. She's resting in her stall. And you know Sam. Nothing can stop her when she puts her mind to it. She's relieved to have found him, that I know for sure."

"Yes, Coco's like family. Thanks so much for calling Charlie, and have a good night, what's left of it." Relieved, Halie hung up the phone. She ran upstairs and pulled a large, terry bath towel off the shelf in the linen closet for Sam. Downstairs, she grabbed one of Jake's bath towels off his stack of towels and rags from the closet floor and then anxiously waited for them both.

As soon as Jake bolted in the house through the garage door, Halie stopped him in his tracks. "Oh no you don't. You stay right here mister," she said. She covered him with a towel and rubbed him dry. But before she finished with him, he squirmed from her grasp. First he shook himself, then continued his bolt through the kitchen, around the corner, into the dining room, and out of sight.

"Where's he off to in such a hurry?" Sam said. "Oh, never mind. I see the wet towel on the floor."

"Samantha Takoda Tyler. Look at you. What happened to you, or shouldn't I ask?"

Sam smiled and shrugged with her left shoulder. "I had a little accident—may have dislocated my shoulder—but it's no big deal."

"No big deal! You're kidding, right? Only you would say something like that. On top of it, you're a soaking, filthy mess. I'm taking you to the emergency room as soon as we get you cleaned up," Halie said as she embraced Sam with the bath towel.

"Ouch!" Sam yelled. "Careful with the shoulder."

"Oh, don't be such a baby. I am being careful. What happened anyway?"

"Sugar got spooked by a rattlesnake and knocked me over. Luckily I wasn't on her when she reared or I'd probably have a broken my arm instead of walking away with only a dislocation."

"Oh, God," Halie said, already having loosened her grip. "Why am I not surprised? Trouble seems to have a way of finding you." Halie held Sam close until she stopped shivering. "We'd better get you upstairs and into the shower."

"Sounds like a plan."

Chapter Three

"BUT WHO WOULD do something like that?" Halie asked, after finally hearing the details behind Sam's rescue of Coco. "And why?"

Sam sat across the table from Halie at Molly's bar, her right arm in a sling. The emergency room doctor confirmed Sam's diagnosis of the shoulder dislocation and x-rays revealed no bones were broken. Since much of the evening already escaped them and Sam knew Halie couldn't wait to eat much longer, nor could she, considering the loud growls that emanated from her stomach. She had declined anesthesia before the doctor relocated her shoulder into its normal position. In hindsight, she decided the decision was not one of her better ones, the pain being greater than she'd imagined. Plus, the move didn't save her much time since another x-ray was needed to reassess the bones after relocation. On the bright side though, she suffered no artery, nerve, or other damage, and for that she was thankful. She could handle a few days in a sling to keep her arm immobile.

Sam reached for her glass of wine with her left hand and took a generous sip before answering Halie, the smooth, fruity liquid warming her insides. "I have no idea. I've been wondering the same thing. Whoever tied him up like that though must be one heartless person."

"Or angry."

"Here you go ladies," Molly said. She winked as she brought over two plates of veggie burgers with special house sauce, sweet potato fries, and two side salads.

Molly T. Moose was the owner of The Wandering Moose, a local favorite. The outside of the bar was not nearly as inviting as the inside, a fact which kept away most of the tourists and filled the bar with local clientele instead. Molly was family. She lived with a woman from town, and together they served what Sam thought were some of the best meals in town. Molly was the one who helped bring Sam and Halie get back together when it appeared their relationship was in trouble near the end of Halie's stay last summer. For that, Sam was eternally grateful.

"Anything else I can get my two favorite customers?"

"Nope, we're good Mol, thanks," Sam replied for them both since Halie had already taken her first bite—a large one at that—and was unable to answer.

"What? What's so funny," Halie managed after swallowing.

Sam enjoyed watching the extent to which her partner relished her food. "Nothing," she replied. "Except for I love the fact that some things never change."

"I was thinking the exact same thing this afternoon when you left, but for a different reason."

Before Sam could ask what the reason was, Molly swung around, retracing her steps. "By the way ladies," she said, "I've got a juicy piece of information hot off the gossip chain that I thought you two might have particular interest in."

"Spill it," Sam said.

"I heard Felice Lohan was released from jail two days ago."

"What?" Sam said. "Already? Time flies, doesn't it?" She glanced at Halie who appeared as surprised as she was. "I'm glad you told us. We hadn't heard. What's she been up to? Is she working yet?"

"No idea. Tim Jr. was in for dinner earlier and told me he'd seen her in Jackson yesterday. He used to have a crush on her you know."

For a second Sam thought it a strange coincidence that Felice, who'd shown interest in Halie last summer, wasn't out of jail two days, far as they knew, and Coco went missing. "I know. I'd suspected he took a liking to Felice years ago when she and I'd been dating. Thanks for the info Mol," Sam said.

"No problem, enjoy your dinners."

Once Molly was out of earshot, Halie said, "You don't think Felice took Coco today, do you?"

"You read my mind. It's possible I guess, but somehow I don't think so. I think she's learned her lesson. Plus, in the end, she did cooperate with the Game and Fish Commission and Fish and Wildlife with regard to fingering David Reingold."

"She did, but probably only to cut short her own time behind bars."

"True. I wonder where she'll find work now. I'm sure the park won't rehire her," Sam said before taking a healthy bite from her char-grilled veggie burger.

"I'm sure they won't either. They'd be crazy to. I think no matter what she tries to do she's going to have a hard time, at least around here. Most everyone knows what she did. Maybe she'll move."

"Maybe. A move might be the best for everyone."

"Agreed. I have a feeling that whether she had anything to do with what happened to Coco today or not, she could still be harboring bad feelings toward us—me for rejecting her, and you for uncovering the truth about her involvement in the trading. Do you know who took care of her son while she was in jail?"

"The chief said her sister took him in. I just wish Felice had gone to see the chief earlier with her troubles, before she let herself get roped into the whole fur-trading thing with Reingold. The guy was such a sleaze. He must have smelt the desperation for money on her. If she hadn't crossed the line with him, I'm sure all the rangers at the park would have helped her get back on her feet. We could have held a fundraiser for her. There's no doubt we would have raised enough money to get her on her feet again. None of this had to happen. I don't know why she didn't ask for help."

"Only she knows that. Let's not talk about her anymore though, at least for now. This is our night and our anniversary weekend. Let's celebrate us instead."

"You're right." Sam reached for Halie's hand and held it across the table. "You know, I still remember what you were wearing, the first day I saw you in the chief's office."

"You do?"

"I do. You wore a cognac colored lambskin leather jacket and jeans, a sexy, light tan, cashmere sweater, and sparkling diamond-studded earrings that glistened as brilliant as your eyes did. I, on the other hand, recall walking in with dirt and blood on my uniform. God only knows what you were thinking."

"I remember that too, but I thought you were so handsome. The only things I noticed were the strength you commanded by your stance, how fit you appeared, and those unbelievable emerald green eyes that still melt me today. I don't think I even noticed the blood on your clothes at first. If you hadn't been so against my being there and thrown out that 'having to babysit' me comment after finding out you were supposed to be my guide, you'd have captured my heart from day one."

Sam felt her cheeks warm. "And if I had my life together a little better at that time, you'd have captured mine too. Regardless, I admit I wrestled with not falling for you. I'm thankful every day that you came into my life, and that things worked out like they did. I don't know what I'd have done if I'd lost you in that helicopter crash. Right now, I feel like the luckiest woman on the planet."

"I do too. I love you immensely."

"I've got a surprise for you."

Halie's eyes sparkled as she reached for a fry and bit off the tip. "What is it?"

Sam extracted two tickets from alongside her forearm in the sling. "I was going to give these to you later, but I'm finding I can't wait that long. It's nothing major, but how would you like to go see Andréa and his orchestra at Whitman Hall on Saturday night?" Sam bought the tickets months ago as part of her anniversary present to Halie because she knew how much Halie would enjoy it, though she personally didn't have an ear for fine music. Watching a football game was more her style.

"Oh my god, yes, yes, ten times yes. I don't know how long it's been since I've gone to a concert."

"Good, I'm glad you like the gift. One more thing though." Sam watched as Halie's expression appeared to turn from joy to concern and back to joy again. "Would you do me the favor of wearing this to the concert when we go?" Sam placed a thin long object wrapped in tissue paper on the table in front of Halie. "I had to take it out of its box, or it wouldn't fit in my sling," Sam said with a grin. "Not exactly the way I planned on giving it to you, but the day hasn't worked out like we'd planned either."

"You are something else, you know that? Before I open this, is there anything else stashed in that sling of yours?"

"Nope, that's it. I'm clean," Sam said.

Halie removed the tissue paper and uncovered a diamond tennis bracelet, one that was an exact match to her diamond studded earrings, the same ones Sam said she'd remembered her wearing the first day Sam met her. "It's...it's beautiful Sam. Yes, I'd be honored to wear it."

Moments later, Molly swung by with dessert. "You sure two pieces will do it?" she asked.

"Believe it or not, I'm not actually that hungry for cake anymore," Halie said.

"Not hungry?" Molly replied with a baffled expression.

"Well, not this minute. If Sam's okay with it, I'd like to take the cake to go," Halie said.

Sam leaned in, face flushed. "And what exactly are you proposing?"

HALIE WOKE NEXT to Sam, her head resting on Sam's healthy shoulder. She thought about how lucky she was to have this warm, loving, and kind woman lying next to her, to love for as long as God willed it, which she hoped was a very, very long time. She felt bad that she hadn't realized how much her prior inattention to Sam caused a plethora of unnecessary hurt. She only wanted happiness for them both. She watched Sam's chest rise and fall, and listened to the beating of her heart. She breathed deep, grateful for her good fortune. Then she gently ran her fingers through Sam's long, dark hair.

Sam's eyes opened slowly as she stirred.

Halie propped herself up on her elbow and studied her. Tears of joy welled up inside. "What is it about you that makes me feel like I can't get enough of you?" She asked as she stroked Sam's arm and ran her fingers playfully over her chest.

Sam pulled Halie closer to her side. "I don't know, but I feel the same way about you. I love you more than I can say."

"You don't have to say it. You show me every day, and every time you make love to me," Halie said.

"Oh, yeah? Then I think I'd like to tell you again how much I love you," she teased. Sam kissed the side of Halie's neck and traced her fingers down her side.

Chills coursed through Halie's body as her own center warmed. She slid lower next to Sam and swung her leg between Sam's thighs. "Mmm, please do," Halie managed before Sam's kisses met her lips, and melted away the world around her once more.

A CRASHING NOISE, followed by Jake's barking, startled Sam

awake. She wasn't sure what she heard, but Jake's barking told her something wasn't right.

Halie awoke seconds later. "What's going on? Is everything okay?"

Sam sat up, winced from the pain in her shoulder. "I'm not sure. I thought I heard a noise, and Jake definitely did. I heard him barking downstairs a few seconds ago."

"What time is it?"

Sam glimpsed at the clock. "It's twelve-thirty." Before Sam had a chance to say another word, Jake was at the side of their bed.

"What's up fella? Something spook you?" Sam whispered.

Jake sat with his paws up on the side of the bed. Sam stroked the top of his head, which helped calm him down, but he didn't leave. "I guess I better go see what's up."

"Don't you think you should call the sheriff first?" Halie added in a frightened tone.

"I don't think it's anything to worry about, or I doubt Jake would be up here with us." Sam put on her sweatpants and sweatshirt and then slid into her moccasin slippers. "My guess is an animal wandered too close to the house and he heard or smelled it and got excited. Just in case though, you stay here. If you hear anything unusual, give the sheriff a call. I'll be right back."

"If there's nothing to worry about, why are we whispering?"

Sam said nothing. She merely shifted her gaze at Halie.

"Sam, I love you."

"I love you too. Don't worry, I'll be careful." She reached for the top drawer of the nightstand, opened it, and pulled out the handgun she'd tucked away deep in the back, the one she kept for safety reasons, never expecting to have to use in her own home.

She and Jake headed down the stairs. When they reached the bottom step, Jake ran over to the living room window, barked once, then glanced in Sam's direction. Sam held her gun in her left hand. With her back to the wall, she fumbled for the living room light switch. When she found it, she flicked the lights on. She was surprised by what she saw. One of the tall picture windows revealed a gaping hole. Shattered glass lay strewn across the tile floor. A large rock lay on the floor on top of glass shards. "Jake! Come here and sit," Sam yelled, afraid he'd cut his paws.

Jake did as he was told. "You stay here, okay?" she said, before walking around the rest of the downstairs making sure no doors or windows were broken into. She flicked on the switch for the outdoor floodlights and peered into the yard but saw no one. Jake watched with his head tilted. "Good boy, you stay." Once she determined the house was safe, she yelled upstairs to Halie that it was okay for her to come downstairs.

Sam stood next to Jake in disbelief, trying to comprehend who would have done this to them and for what purpose. Two strange occurrences in one day struck Sam as far too coincidental. They didn't have any enemies, at least none she was aware of.

Halie joined her a few moments later. "I can't believe this. What's going on?"

"I don't know, I was asking myself the same question. Until this point I've felt safe living here, but I'm beginning to wonder how safe the area is. I don't know why anyone would do something like this."

"I'll go get a dust pan and clean this up," Halie said.

"No, leave it for now. I think we should call the sheriff's office first. Let's make sure we keep Jake away from the glass. Why don't you take him in the kitchen and make a pot of coffee and I'll call the sheriff's office. I think we're going to be up for a while."

"Coffee's a good idea," Halie said. She leaned in and kissed Sam on the cheek. Then she hugged her. They held onto each other for a full minute before separating.

Shortly before one o'clock, a deputy sheriff arrived at the house. He didn't need to knock. Sam was waiting at the front door for him and led him into the foyer.

"Evening, ladies," he said, "I'm Deputy Jenkins. I got here as soon as I could."

"We appreciate that, Deputy, and we're sorry we had to call you out here tonight," Sam said.

"It's not a problem. I'm going to have a look around, if you don't mind," he said.

"Of course, whatever you need. As you can see, someone threw a rock through the window," Sam said, pointing to the left wall of the living room. "We haven't touched anything."

The living room was a large open space with high ceilings and pine beams traversing it from one end to the other. The floor was made of large square pieces of Arizona mud red Spanish tile. The tile floor extended beyond the foyer and into the dining room. In the center of the living room wall, between the two large ceiling-to-floor windows, was a fireplace. A southwestern style rug with orange, brown, yellow, red, and turquoise designs lay on the floor in the middle of the room. A rectangular, rustic wooden table stood on the rug, as well as two comfortable leather sofas on opposite sides. Above the fireplace hung a sensual picture of a Native American Indian woman, and colorful Indian pottery and artifacts were set all about the room. On the matching rustic wooden end tables stood lamps made of antlers, and on one end table also sat a pewter framed photograph of Sam and Halie. Much of the living room contained pieces Sam owned when living in the cabin she rented from the park her first five years living as a resident there. Framed photographs Halie captured during their time together which Sam favored, also adorned the walls.

The deputy took a few steps into the living room. As he stepped closer to the damaged window, pieces of glass crunched under his boots. Sam watched as he reached down and lifted up the rock, weighing it with his hand. The tile was cracked underneath where the rock landed. He scanned the remainder of the nearby floor before he made his way over to Halie.

"I made some coffee," Halie said. "Would you like some?"

"No thank you ma'am, but I appreciate the offer. The rock cracked your tile floor."

Sam walked into the dining room and met the deputy before the entrance into the kitchen. "I can fix that. What I can't fix so easily is restoring the sense of security we thought we possessed."

"I understand. I'll need to take down some general information and then document anything you might have heard or seen tonight, or anything you saw or felt was suspicious prior to tonight. I'm guessing nothing was stolen? No one made entry into the house?"

"No, and it's a good thing, because I don't think our dog would have taken too kindly to them," Sam replied. "Nor would I." Over the next several minutes she provided him the remaining information he'd asked for, and told him about Coco's abduction. All the while, she sensed the deputy was withholding information from them. She soon found out her intuition was right.

"Do you have any enemies that you know of, or know of anyone who doesn't like either one of you?" Jenkins asked.

"No to both questions, as far as we're aware of," Sam said. "That is, if you don't count the people I've arrested in Grand Teton over the years, but that's my job. You certainly know how that is."

Jenkins nodded in agreement and jotted down a few more notes. "Have either of you two ladies been outside the house this evening?"

Sam answered. "Not since we got back from dinner, but after I heard the noise, I scanned the yard and didn't see anything. Why? What's going on?"

"I think you should both come with me."

Sam and Halie exchanged worried glances. They grabbed light coats from the front closet and followed the deputy along the brick walkway toward the garage. The night was quiet and otherwise perfect, Sam thought, befuddled by the act of cowardice against them, until it became crystal clear what the deputy withheld from them inside.

The headlights from his vehicle and the flashing red and blue lights on the patrol car highlighted the spray-painted words on their garage door "GO BACK HOME! DYKES NOT WELCOME!"

Sam and Halie stood side by side with their arms around each other's waists. Sam felt like the air had been sucked from her and merely stood in disbelief. Neither one spoke. Halie withdrew her arm from Sam and stole a glance over her shoulder, even though no one was around.

"I'm sorry," Jenkins said. "I know how you both must feel."

Halie shook. "I'm sorry, but I don't think you do."

"You feel violated. It's normal. It'll pass." Jenkins tucked his note pad and pen into his jacket pocket. "I've called for backup so we can inspect the yard and see what evidence we can uncover. Tomorrow, we'll interview your neighbors. I'll have extra guys patrolling for the next few days as well. Do you have somewhere you can stay until this window is fixed?"

"We could stay with friends of ours, but I'd rather not leave," Sam said. "Especially with the dog. Our friends have a cat and I'm not sure they'll get along."

"I don't recommend staying, but if you do, you'll need to secure that window tonight then, from the inside so you don't disturb the grounds."

"I understand. I've got plywood in the garage large enough to nail over the damage, and as fellow law enforcement, I'm equipped to take care of us should there be a need," Sam said.

"Noted. Look, we'll do our best to find out who did this. I promise."

"Thanks," Halie said. "We appreciate your help."

"Again, it's no problem. As I said, we'll put extra patrol in the area and call immediately if you hear anything unusual. You ladies take care."

Chapter Four

SAM AND HALIE ate breakfast early on Sunday. Neither slept much after the incident. "Are you sure you're up to going to the gallery today?" Sam asked.

"I'm sure. There's not much I can do here. Besides, I still have a lot to do to prepare for the opening and hopefully I'll be busy enough to keep my mind off this."

"I'm going to give April a call and see if I might be able to board Coco and Sugar at the ranch where she works, if the owner approves, until all this blows over. I don't trust leaving the horses at Charlie's right now. Whoever took Coco could do something worse the next time around. I'm not giving them that chance." Sam's best friend April managed a private American Quarter Horse ranch. "If not, I'll have to check out a few other places."

"It's a good idea. Charlie won't like it, but I'm sure he'll understand. Plus, it won't be forever. I should go." Halie stopped dead in her tracks and stared out the front windows. "Oh no, I don't believe this. I wonder who called *them*."

Sam followed her line of sight. "Great, just what we needed."

"I think you better handle this, don't you? After all, didn't you tell me you acquired some public relations experience working at the park at least once during your career? This should be a cake walk for you."

"Sure, take off and leave me with the sharks."

"Hey, wait a minute. I used to be one of those sharks if you recall," Halie said.

"I know, I'm kidding around. I realize they're only doing their job. I'm surprised they're out so early on a Sunday though. Are you sure you don't want to stay and help me muddle through this?" Sam said.

"Nope, they're all yours. Besides, maybe it's not such a bad thing if this gets out to the media. Better they put a face and story behind what happened rather than let idle gossip abound. I better go. Love ya. Bye." Halie left after she planted a quick peck on Sam's cheek.

"Okay, bye. Be careful."

"I will," Halie said. Then she closed the door to her Jeep and pulled out of the driveway seconds before the media vans pulled in.

THE MORNING AIR at the start of the new workweek was exceptionally chilly. Walter Pipp slunk up the driveway in a pair of worn, fuzzy slippers, long flannel pajama bottoms, a grey T-shirt with a tear near the top right shoulder, and a cigarette draped from his mouth. Smoking added ten years to his appearance. Covering his nightwear was a blue terry robe that hung open over his skeletal frame. Rays of sunshine made their way through the leaf canopy overhead, illuminating orange lilies, which glowed in sunlight that filtered through. He was too busy catching his breath to pay attention to the flowers as he made his way toward the morning paper. Before bending down to pick the paper up, he temporarily removed his cigarette, then hacked once and spit out a ball of phlegm before reinserting his smoke.

The paper wasn't bundled or wrapped in the thin, cheap plastic it usually came in. Instead, it appeared only to have been rolled up and thrown haphazardly from a car window, having unrolled and scattered when it hit the pavement. Part of one section landed in a puddle. "God damn kids these days," Walter hollered as his cigarette bobbed between his thin lips. "They don't have a clue what they're doing, some of 'em. Take no pride in nothing. No pride in nothing. Not like in the old days."

Taking two deep puffs, he bent over, reassembled the paper, then straightened and headed back to the house. Walter entered the kitchen through the back door. "I'm back Nitro," he said. Nitro was Walter's pet rat. Walter kept him in a crate that occupied over half the kitchen table. He kept Nitro in the kitchen because that's where Walter spent most of his time. The kitchen and bathroom were the only two neat and clean rooms in the entire house. The rest contained year's worth of accumulated junk. Walter wasn't what one would consider a hoarder, but he wasn't far from becoming one either. His one love, besides Nitro, was his business, which he kept impeccably neat, clean, and well organized. It was a complete contrast to most of his home. His business gave him a reason to live, and he ran it well. His "work" was everything to him, and he'd do almost anything to keep it thriving.

After taking a sip from his cup of coffee, Walter let Nitro out of his cage. The pure white rat scrambled across the table, up the arm of Walter's robe, and settled on his shoulder. Nitro fiddled with Walter's ear. Walter craned his neck and gave him a kiss. "You're the best, you know that?" he said. He handed Nitro one of the rat's favorite, homemade, dried fruit treats, then read the paper like he did every morning while Nitro darted off to enjoy his prize. A few pages in, Walter couldn't believe what he read. He leaned back with a satisfied glint in his eyes and grin on his face. "Well I'll be damned," he exclaimed. "Maybe there is light at the end of this tunnel."

HALIE MEANDERED INTO the kitchen. It was Monday morning. Hair tussled, she breathed in the luscious smell of fresh brewing coffee. Sam stood in her pajama shorts and sleeveless nightshirt, putting toast into the toaster oven. Halie allowed her eyes to dance over Sam's hundred and forty pound muscled body for a brief moment. Part of her wanted to run her fingers through Sam's long dark hair and kiss her deeply, but the other part felt like sitting down. The lethargy she felt was not something she was used to. On her way to the chair, she found compromise and kissed Sam on the cheek. "Morning," she said, then sat.

"Morning. What? No hug?"

"I'm sorry. I'm tired I guess. I didn't sleep well the last couple of nights. You should let Jake in though before his barking wakes up the neighborhood," Halie said.

"Not many people to wake up," Sam replied. Only their one neighbor down the street was close enough to be within earshot.

Halie followed Sam over to the sliding glass door to the backyard and gave her a hug. "I'm sorry. Don't mind me. How come you're still here and not at work?"

"I called the chief in the afternoon yesterday and told him what happened. I asked for the day off so I can grout around the new tile I replaced, finish painting the garage door, and call a few window places to see who can fix this window the quickest."

"Good idea. I can still see the writing through the primer you put on the garage door yesterday. It'll be nice when I can't see what's under there anymore, although I'll still know what's been written."

Jake bolted through the door when Sam opened it. "I know, we can't change that, but at least I can make it less visible. That's why I'm staying home."

"I hate to admit this, but yesterday, on my way to the gallery, I couldn't help but think someone was watching me. It's strange. I don't know how to explain it. I feel different though, and not in a good way."

"I understand. It's normal. And like Jenkins said, it'll take some time. Once they catch whoever did this though, things will get back to normal, I promise." Sam handed Jake a cookie on his way back into the kitchen. Then she placed two slices of bread on each of their plates.

"Did you feel uneasy yesterday?" Halie asked.

"No, but I'm trained to deal with difficult situations like these and you're not," Sam replied. "I've been thinking though. We could install security cameras. Having them might make you feel better."

"It might, but then again, you can't cover everything, and they can't follow me everywhere. Plus, why should we have to live like that? I don't know why everything always has to be a struggle. Just when you think things are on track — bam — something else has to happen and set you back."

Sam appeared uncertain what to say and remained silent.

"That's life I guess. I forgot to ask you yesterday — did you check in with the detective to see what they found out after inspecting the yard?" Halie asked.

Sam held the coffee mug to her lips, took a sip, and sat next to Halie. She grabbed a knife. "He didn't indicate they'd found anything substantial, as far as I could tell, or if they did, they didn't tell me. Personally, I don't think they're taking this too seriously since no one was physically hurt," Sam said. She reached for the cream cheese and spread a knife-full onto her toast.

"That may be, but someone could have gotten hurt. And we are talking about significant property damage. What I never could understand is why people can't go about their own business and if they don't like something, they should stay away from it. I'm not asking everyone to love me, just to let me live my life the way I let everyone else live theirs. I don't know. It's so frustrating sometimes. I don't even want to get started," Halie said. She bit hard into the toast. "What about the reporters? How did that go?"

"All right I guess. I'm not big on being in the eye of the media as you know."

"Yeah, I remember the chief telling me that he still hadn't figured out how you and Jake managed to slip inside the ranger station undetected last year, after the helicopter crash, while he got stuck answering all the reporter's questions."

Sam smiled at the memory. "That was pretty funny. Seeing him standing there, with that perplexed expression on his face, knowing he was cursing me out on the inside, gave me the first chance to relax that entire day. Toby and I reveled in a good laugh at his expense," Sam said. She watched Halie devour her last piece of toast. "We have more you know," Sam said, glad the incident hadn't suppressed Halie's eating habits.

Halie closed the top on the jelly jar and butter container and pushed her chair from the table. "Thanks, but no," she said. Her tone mirrored Sam's sarcasm. "I've put away plenty for now. I think I'll take a jog before I shower and go. I need to do something to boost my energy level and shake this humdrum feeling that seems to be hanging on me since yesterday. You want to join me?"

Sam stood and cleared the plates. "On the jog, or in the shower?"

"On the jog," Halie said, as she slapped Sam lightly on the butt.

"Well, a gal can ask, can't she?" Sam replied. "No, I've got a lot to do today. I think I'll do a short work out on the Universal and then shower."

"Okay. I'll take Jake with me then. The exercise will do him some good."

"It will, and he'll love you for it. Besides, I think he's been packing on a few pounds lately."

JAKE PRANCED ALONG at his usual pace. Halie had trouble keeping up with him. Each time he extended his lead by twenty yards or more, she experienced an overwhelming sense of unease and quickly called him back. Her mind whirled with crazy thoughts of Saturday night. She tried to figure out who would have a problem with them. Who found out they were gay? Who didn't already know? She wondered if the trespasser was one person or more than one, and if they'd be left alone now, or if the other night was the beginning of more to come. Had Jake scared them off? What if he hadn't? What if Sam had been away? Worse, what if Sam intervened and got seriously hurt or killed? Maybe security cameras wouldn't be a bad idea. As she tried to shake the negative thoughts taking hold, she checked behind her to make sure no one was following them. Her heart beat faster as the negative thoughts continued. Walking in a half dazed state, she jumped when a squirrel scampered through dry brush. "Damit," she said. "This is crazy."

She rubbed the back of her neck and reprimanded herself for overreacting. She needed to regain control. She breathed several deep breaths and convinced herself that everything would be okay. If she'd tell herself those words often enough, eventually she assumed they'd have to take hold. She became so focused on calming herself that she didn't notice Jake had once again taken a large lead, or the branch dipped low across the road, and nearly walked into it, before even the branch startled her. Her nerves were raw. Wanting nothing more than to retreat to the safety of their home, Halie forced the negative thoughts from her mind, quickened her pace, and soon caught up with Jake again.

HALIE WALKED INTO the gallery with as confident a demeanor as she could muster. She didn't want Susan to notice the insecurity she felt. Susan Weston was her first hire. "Hey Susan, morning."

"Hey," Susan replied.

Halie knew something was wrong by the flat tone of Susan's reply, and the fact she didn't ramble on about the weekend like she normally did on a Monday. "What's the matter?" Halie asked.

"Oh nothing," Susan said. She placed her hands on the counter she stood behind.

"It can't be nothing," Halie replied. She recognized the sigh of defeat in Susan's voice. She herself felt much the same way. "I know you better than that. Did you have a bad date last night? Is your ex pestering you again? Are the kids okay?"

Susan was a divorced mother of two boys who moved from Casper, Wyoming back in with her mom. Her mom's small two story house in Kelly was near the center of town, nestled between two similar type homes.

"You sure cover all the major bases, don't you?" Susan said.

"I'm concerned about you."

"Brian's acting out again. I think he's still mad at me that we had to move. We got into an argument last night and he stormed off out of the house for the second time this week. The thing is, I'm worried because God only knows where he goes. He doesn't tell me, but that's how the kids are these days. He says he hangs out with his friends, and it's not a big deal, and I shouldn't make a big deal out of it, but I can't help it. My mother tells me I should leave him be, but I'm afraid he's going to get hooked on alcohol or drugs or something."

"Like his dad did?"

"Exactly. I don't get it, because other times he's such a great kid. He's respectful and helps in the home, and he's always looking out for Tommy. He loves playing ball and doing other stuff with him. You know, doing things with his brother I'm not that good at. Things his dad should be doing with them both. He's even nice to his grandma." Susan let out another sigh. "I don't know what to do with him."

Susan's oldest son Brian was sixteen, and her second, Tommy, was seven. If Tommy had been an unplanned pregnancy, no one would ever know it. Susan doted on both her boys as if they were the only two people in her life.

"Have you tried sitting down with him when he's not angry and talking with him? Try to get a hint at what's bothering him?"

"Not exactly. I don't know what to say to him that won't get him madder than he already gets. I mean, he's a pretty big guy for his age."

"He wouldn't hit you, would he?" Halie said. She understood that Brian's father had been abusive and worried Brian might follow the same path.

"No, I don't think he'd ever do that, but he does seem to be changing, and not for the better."

"You think he might blame you for your husband leaving?" Halie asked.

"I'm sure that has something to do with it. Tommy was too young when David left, so he doesn't remember anything, but I'm sure Brian remembers us fighting. He just doesn't know the real reason why. I didn't have the heart to tell him his dad was a creep and a looser."

"How about trying therapy? Just for the two of you. It might give you a neutral and controlled space to be able to talk things out," Halie said, placing her right hand on Susan's to comfort her.

"I thought about that too. I've been saving some money, and once I get a little more together, if he agrees, I think we'll do that, before things get out of control."

Before Halie could answer and voice her agreement, the gallery door swung open and in strode a cocky Walter Pipp from the fish and tackle shop he owned next door. Halie had forgotten to lock the door when she entered. Walter's scowling dark eyes and a weathered and wrinkled forehead did nothing to improve his appeal. He dressed neatly enough, but nothing made up for his metallic personality. The smell of stale smoke emanated from his clothing.

"Morning *ladies*," Walter said in a raspy tone. "Not interrupting anything, am I?"

"You wish," Susan quipped.

Halie peered at him with annoyance, removing her hand from Susan's. "What is it we can do for you this morning Walter, or are you just making your monthly rounds to see if we're still planning on opening in a few weeks?"

"My, my, aren't we touchy this morning. Get up on the wrong side of the bed today, did we?" As he spoke, he wrapped the rolled up morning paper against his right leg and grinned. "Can't a neighbor stop by to see how you're all doing? The first year in business is going to be the toughest you know. Most businesses don't make it. I'm concerned is all."

Halie wished she could push him right back out the door, but since she couldn't, she remained still. "Yes, I believe you've mentioned that already, several times, but lucky for us, we're looking forward to the challenge. If I were you, I wouldn't worry about us so much. Time will tell." Halie knew the real reason Walter visited. He'd bid on the empty store next to his, which was now her gallery, at the same time Sam and Halie placed their bid. His plan was to rip down the wall between the stores and expand his shop, but they managed to outbid him, and not by much.

Walter Pipp stood motionless for a moment, lifted up the paper, glanced at it, and returned it to his side. "Well, okay then *ladies*. I'd leave you with 'don't work too hard', but I can see you're already doing that. Take care and if you need anything, you know where I am."

"Yeah, we do," Susan said, "and how lucky we are to have you so close. Thanks, Walter, but I think we can manage fine on our own."

They watched him walk out. His pants, baggy at the butt, swished back and forth. They both cracked up after the door shut behind him. This time Halie locked it once he left. Afterword, they went back to work, Susan no longer appearing upset.

SAM KNOCKED ON the hardwood portion of the glass paned front door to Halie's photo gallery. She held a cardboard tray holding three fresh brewed cups of coffee she'd purchased from The Brew Master a couple of stores down.

Sam recognized earlier that Halie wasn't herself that morning. She'd guessed she wanted Jake with her on her jog more for her own protection than for his health, which was understandable given the circumstances. She wished she could have prevented the incident from happening, but she recognized the event was outside her control. She hoped her visit would express support and help ease Halie's apprehension in a positive way.

When Sam knocked on the door, Susan let her in. Sam loved the ambiance of the gallery. The coloring and choice of lighting was fresh and bright and clean. The hardwood floors were immaculate and the few select photos that already hung from the walls breathed the life

Halie put into them. To Sam, walking into the gallery already felt like walking alongside Halie on a sun filled afternoon. She couldn't wait to see the end product.

"Hi Susan," Sam said. "Thanks for getting the door."

"Sure thing, Sugar."

When Sam met Susan for the first time, she'd guessed her to be about six years older than her, somewhere around thirty-four, or maybe even a tad older. She was straight as straight could be, and a real knockout with a slim, curvy-in-all-the-right-places figure, and a welcoming smile. Sam was glad she was straight, or she knew she'd probably be jealous as hell since she worked with Halie, even though she knew she could trust Halie.

"It's good to see you again," Susan replied. "Don't be such a stranger. Just because you finished all your handy work in here, doesn't mean you can't stop in just to say hello."

"Yeah, I know. I've been kind of busy though," Sam said as she grabbed Susan's coffee. "Here you go, black no sugar, right?"

"You got it. I could use it too—had kind of a rough evening, but things are going better now."

"That's good, seems like rough evenings are going around."

"Yeah, Halie finally told me about your incident at the house. I'm sorry Sam. Some people can be real jerks. Believe me I know."

"Thanks. We're trying to deal with it as best we can. I think I'm more okay with it than Halie is, but at least the last couple of days have been quiet."

"Thank the good Lord for that. I would hope whatever happened was a one-time deal. I read your comments in the paper," Susan said. She walked over to the counter and grabbed the local paper. She opened to the article to which she referred, flipped the pages over and folded them back, so Sam could read it. "Here take it. It's a good article. I like what you said."

"Oh, thanks. I can hardly remember myself. I'll read it in a minute. So where's my honey-pie?"

"She's in the back room. I think she's setting up the books, though I'm not sure how successful she's being. I heard a few curse words coming from in there. I'm so glad I don't have to do that stuff."

"Me too," Sam said. "I'll see you later Susan. Make sure you give those kids of yours a big hug and kiss from me, will ya?"

"Sure thing, Sugar."

Sam went into the back and tapped on Halie's halfway opened office door. "May I come in? Coffee delivery gal at your service."

"Sure, come on in." Halie stood up and stretched her back. The smell of hazelnut coffee filled the space between them.

Halie's office was small, but elegant and modern. Two comfortable red fabric chairs faced her shiny wooden desk, the top clear except for one folder, her computer, keyboard, wide flat-screen monitor, and a picture of her and Sam. Two of her favorite photographs, matted in white and framed with thin black frames, adorned the walls.

Halie's eyes met Sam's. "You must be new, because I would have remembered someone as smoking hot as you. I think my partner back home would get mad at me if she knew what I was thinking right now, but I'll say it anyway. I want to ravage your body right here and now," Halie teased.

"Sounds like that walk did you a lot of good this morning—you seem different."

"I'm trying. That's about all I can say for now."

"That's about all you can do. Hey, are you serious about the ravaging part?"

Halie walked over to Sam and gave her a kiss that would linger with her the remainder of the day. Then she took her coffee and sat behind her desk. "I know I've been a little distant the past couple of days, but I'm sure this will pass."

"I'm sure it will. Besides, you know I'm always here to protect you." Sam stood in front of Halie's desk.

Halie inclined her head. "I know. Thanks for the afternoon coffee. What brings you by? This is a nice surprise."

"I missed you. That and April called me this morning and said I could bring Coco and Sugar by today. The owner has open stalls and said he'd love to help out. I've got them in the trailer, so I can't stay long."

"That's great. I hope they'll be okay at that place, though. They won't know anyone."

"They have each other and they'll make new friends. Plus, we'll still visit and ride them, and the arrangement's only temporary. How's it going with the books?"

"Okay, I guess. I want to make sure I don't lose track of anything. I set up a budget and I'll monitor expenses against it monthly. I can't wait to open and start making some money to help pay for all the expenses I've already accumulated."

"Are you nervous—about the opening?"

"I'm not, really. You and Susan have been a great help, and if anything, I'm ahead of schedule. I have another person to interview tomorrow whose photographs look promising. If his portfolio looks as good as the couple of the photos of his I've seen, we'll be lucky to have him show his work here."

"Your work and the work of the artists you selected so far is amazing. You're going to do fine, I know it."

"Thanks sweetie, that's nice of you to say. But how about you come on over here and give me one of those kisses only you can give."

"I'd rather you come over here," Sam said in a sultry tone.

The corners of Halie's mouth rose as she rounded her desk. "Is that so," she said in a seductive tone. She placed her left hand on Sam's chest and backed her up against the desk as her lips found Sam's. Her kiss was intense and nearly buckled Sam's knees. Sam felt the heat rise within her and wished they were home instead of in Halie's office.

With a knock on the door, the two quickly separated.

Susan stuck her head in the door. "Sorry to bother you, but UPS is here with a delivery that needs your signature."

"Thanks Susan, I'm coming."

Once UPS left, Halie escorted Sam to the front door. As Sam was in the middle of saying her good-byes, she stopped midway, an anxious expression evident on her face.

"What's the matter?" Halie asked.

"Didn't you feel that?" Sam said.

"Feel what?"

"The ground move."

"Shoot. I wish one of my boyfriends would tell me the ground moved when they got near me," Susan said.

"No, I'm serious you two. Tell the truth. Didn't you feel it?"

Susan and Halie both looked at one another and signaled no.

"Are you sure?"

"I'm sure," Halie said, "but while I've still got you here, I want to show you something."

Sam surrendered, certain she'd felt the ground shake. "Okay, but only another minute."

"Great." Halie led Sam by the elbow to the other side of the gallery.

"By the way," Halie said, "Our friend Walter Pipp stopped by again today to see how we're doing."

"How kind of him. It's nice to see he's still so interested in seeing us do well."

"Isn't it though? What's that you're holding?" Halie asked.

"Oh, the local paper. Susan gave it to me. I wanted to read the article in it about us. She said they did a good job with it."

"Great. Don't throw it away. When you're done with it, I'd like to read it too. I've got a funny suspicion that's what Walter was gloating about earlier. He carried a paper rolled up in his hand when he walked in. He strutted in all smug and smiles, but didn't say anything."

"I wouldn't be surprised in the least."

Halie pulled open the drapes that covered a second storage area, which was mostly empty except for a few supplies stacked along the left-hand wall.

"Wow, you did a great job cleaning up in here. What are you going to do with all that extra room now?" Once Sam got the words out and took stock of Halie, she knew she shouldn't have asked the question.

"That's where you come in," Halie said, a smirk-like smile covering her face.

"Is that so? How did I know you were going to say that?"

"Because you know me so well and love me so much," Halie said.

"All true. What have you got planned?"

"I was thinking about putting a frame shop back here."

"You sure you want to take that on right from the get-go?" Sam asked.

"I'm still mulling it over, but I wanted your input."

"I don't know. I think you'd do fine without it, but I'll support you either way," Sam said.

"Susan worked part time in a frame shop. It might work out. It would save us money in the long run. The room needs to be painted though and I thought ceramic tile on the floor would add a nice touch."

"I see. Well, it sounds like you've already made up your mind."

Halie's facial expression gave Sam the answer she needed.

"I should have known. That's fine, but I'm not sure when I'll be able to get to it. Depends how my shoulder feels. It may be after the opening. I better let you get back to work. Plus, I've got horses to relocate." Then, before walking out the door she yelled over her shoulder, "See ya Susan. Behave."

Before the door shut behind her, Sam heard the words "See ya, Sugar — not likely," which made her grin.

Chapter Five

A FEW MINUTES before the end of her workday, April made her rounds through the recently renovated barn to make sure all the stalls were properly cleaned and fresh bedding was put down.

"See ya April."

"Have a good night Jason, and thanks again for helping out earlier when Mr. Peterman arrived," April said as she petted one of the horses already in his stall for the night. She strode through the center concrete aisle. The stable held fourteen horses, seven on a side in twelve foot by twelve foot stalls. She stopped to give extra attention to Coco and Sugar, who hadn't settled in to their temporary housing situation yet, before continuing on. Outside the second to last stall on April's right sat a wheelbarrow facing away from the stall, filled with soiled hay. The sound of a shovel scraping concrete followed. As she got closer April noticed Cali was still cleaning the stall.

Cali Brooks was a mere twenty-three. Her petite, fragile appearance belied her strength. Her brown hair hung in a ponytail out the back of her baseball cap, swaying back and forth as she shoveled hay.

"Hey Cali, what's going on?"

"Oh, hey, April," Cali said. She kept working and would not meet April's gaze. "I'm running a little behind today."

"How come?" April asked. She could tell something was up.

"I found out this morning that my roommate—my best friend and the whole reason I moved out here—decided to toss me from the apartment. Apparently, he wants to live there with his girlfriend, who doesn't like me."

"Seriously?"

"Can you believe that? She thinks I'm a threat or something. Please," she drew out that last word. "So I'm running behind schedule because the grain delivery was late—"

"Don't worry about it. What do you have left to do?"

"I've got this stall to finish mucking out, and the next one over."

April picked up the one end of the wheelbarrow and rolled it toward the manure pile.

"What are you doing?" Cali asked.

"Helping you finish, what's it look like," April said in a warm tone. "Go ahead and start on the next stall. I'll wrap this one up as soon as I get back."

"You don't need to do that, although I appreciate it, but I can handle it on my own."

"I know you can, but I'd like to help."

When April returned, Cali swept out the stall she worked on and

removed the water bucket and feed tub from the adjacent stall. April
placed the wheelbarrow in front of Cali's stall.

Cali decided to use the shovel to clean out the manure and wet
bedding, leaving the pitchfork for April.

"So, how much time did your roommate give you to find another
place?" April said, as she spread the cleaner bedding over the floor.
Since it felt thin, she grabbed a whole bale of straw.

"Not much — a couple of weeks. It's my fault really. I never signed a
formal lease agreement with him. I didn't think I needed to. Goes to
show one never knows. I'll find something though, I'm not that
worried."

April could tell by the sound of Cali's voice that she was worried.
"I'll ask Corrine to keep an eye out for you at the real estate office," she
said as she fluffed up the fresh straw with the pitchfork.

"I appreciate that, April. Thanks."

"No problem." In the recesses of April's mind, the idea of renting
their spare bedroom to Cali emerged, though she said nothing. She'd
have to discuss it with Corrine first. They could use the extra money,
with the real estate market slump not letting up, and they could help
Cali out at the same time. But she also knew renting didn't come
without its own set of problems, and other than Cali's work ethic, she
didn't know much about her on a personal level. "Hey, how are your
other two jobs going? You still working at the animal hospital two
nights a week and teaching those art classes at the elementary school on
Wednesdays?"

"I am, and I love it. It's a shame so many schools are cutting back
on art and music programs though. They're thinking of canning the
program there next year. They tell you the supplies are too costly, that
the kids aren't interested in it anymore — crap like that. I think the kids
are plenty interested, they simply need some motivation."

"If they end the art program, maybe it'll make it easier for you to
decide which career path to follow."

"I don't think so. I'm torn because I love working with animals and
I think I'd make a good vet, but then I love working with the kids too. I
thought I'd have it figured out by now though. That was the whole
point of coming out here — to find myself and find direction."

"Give it some more time. I'm sure you'll make the right decision.
Besides, better to take the time now than to jump headfirst into
something you'll regret later."

THOUGH THE WORK week passed without further incident, Halie
was not herself. She tried not letting the vandalism event get to her, but
she wasn't as successful as she'd hoped. She became quieter and
withdrawn, distant emotionally once again from Sam. She hadn't
expressed an ounce of excitement over going to the concert since the

night Sam gave her the tickets.

Lunch was spent eating sandwiches in silence across from one another. Sam couldn't stand the quiet anymore. "Are you still up to going to the concert tonight?" she asked.

"I don't know. I've been thinking about it all morning," Halie said, closing the lid to the pickle jar. "What about the house? What if something happens again while we're out? Maybe it's too soon."

"Believe me, I wouldn't be heartbroken about not going, but I think it'd be a mistake. I'm upset about what happened too, but I'll be damned if I let this get the better of us. We shouldn't give anyone that kind of power," Sam said as her cheeks turned flush.

Halie hesitated a moment. She read her lover's reassuring eyes. "You're right. We should go. Screw whoever did this. Jake will watch out for the house and extra patrols are still ongoing, so we should be okay." Halie's words came out sounding strong, but inside worry prevailed.

AFTER THE CONCERT, Halie lay in bed next to Sam with her hand on Sam's chest. "That concert was so powerful, suggestive, and beautiful. It felt like he was singing to the two of us. It made me forget about everything else for a while."

"I know what you mean, I felt it too. I had a hard time keeping my hands off you during the performance and making love to you right there."

"I'm sure that would have raised some eyebrows." Halie said. "I wish I felt like I had the energy to reciprocate that thought."

"Maybe the energy will come to you," Sam teased. She nibbled on Halie's ear.

Halie twisted away. "Under other circumstances, I know it would, and you'd be in big trouble, but as soon as we pulled up to the house, I could see that damn writing in my mind on the garage door again. That did it for me. I can't relax. I thought I could by now, but I can't."

Although disappointed her charm wasn't enough to win Halie over, Sam tried comforting her. "It's only been a week. You shouldn't be so hard on yourself. I've got news that might help in that regard anyway. Mom called earlier today when you were in the shower."

"Your mom?"

Sam indicated agreement.

"How's she doing?"

"She's fine. She was sorry to hear about what happened to us, but said we should stay strong. I told her we were."

"Well, we're trying," Halie said.

"She mentioned that my brother Matt was coming to visit her at the end of the month with my two nieces, Jessie and Katelynn, and she asked us to come for that week too. Or, if we couldn't stay the week, then at least a few days. She very much wants to meet you and thinks it would be great for you to meet part of the family too."

"Really? She definitely wants to meet me?"

"Of course she does. She doesn't keep asking for the heck of it. She knows we're busy and all, but she said it'd be nice to get to know you and see, in the flesh, who's stolen her daughter's heart away," Sam said.

Halie gave Sam a soft tap on the chest. "She didn't say that."

Sam kissed Halie on the cheek. "No, she didn't say that last part, but she said to tell you she loves you and hopes we'll consider the visit."

"I'd love to go, but I don't know. What about Jake and the gallery? I'd only have a week after we'd get back before the opening."

"I thought you said you were ahead of schedule?"

"I am, but you never know what might come up."

"I thought about Jake too, and figured I could call April and Corrine and see if they'd consider taking him for a week."

"What about Lula-bell?" Halie asked.

"Jake doesn't pay much attention to cats. I'm not sure why that is, but they don't seem to bother him."

"That's not what you told the deputy."

"I only brought up the cat as another reason to stay in the house. But to play it safe, if April and Corrine agree, I figured I could take him over there for a test-run to see how he does."

"We could use a break. This might work out. And I would love to finally meet your family."

"Great, Mom will be thrilled. The only sticking point now will be to try and convince the chief to let me go. It would have been easier if Matt and the kids were visiting at the end of September, but I guess because of school, they can't."

"Hopefully he'll be okay with it." Halie moved sideways and pulled Sam's arm around her. "You okay with only holding me tonight?"

"Yeah, that's fine." Sam was truthful. Although she would rather have been making love to Halie, she was content. She held her partner close in her arms and felt her breath next to her until they fell asleep.

THE NEXT MORNING turned out to be a beauty. The air was a dry seventy-eight degrees and the sun shone bright. Sam got out of bed before Halie, and made coffee and waffles for their Sunday breakfast, along with a small bowl of fruit salad. A short while later, Halie joined Sam at the kitchen table.

"I'm tired. I don't think I slept very well last night," Halie said.

"Morning to you too."

"I'm sorry. I think I'm still half asleep. Morning." Halie leaned over and gave Sam a kiss on the cheek. "Breakfast looks great. Thanks."

"You're welcome. Not only didn't you sleep well last night, but you tossed and turned like a guppy flailing in a near empty pool of water."

"That bad, huh?"

"Yeah, that bad." Sam sipped her coffee. "You want to tell me about it?"

"There's nothing to tell. I don't remember the dreams, really, although I do remember the sensation of being chased in one of them, but I don't know who I was running from. I don't remember getting caught either though."

"At least that's a plus. Maybe in your dream you should stop running, and when whoever's chasing you catches up to you, you kick the crap out of them."

Halie laughed for a brief second. "Easier said than done."

"Well, it is your dream after all. Or just add me to it and I'll kick their butts," Sam said.

"I'll give it a try next time."

"Good. Have you looked outside yet? It's gorgeous out," Sam said.

"No, I haven't actually."

"I thought maybe we could go for a hike today. The temperature's perfect and Jake would love it too."

"I don't know. I'm kind of tired. I might rest for a while and then head to the gallery. You go with Jake though. He would love it."

Sam felt a twinge of pain in her heart. "If you're tired, why go to the gallery? I thought we could spend some time together. I miss you. We need more us time, like we had last night at the concert. Or at least I know I do."

"What's that supposed to mean?"

"Nothing. You're hard to read sometimes though. I sense you're shutting yourself off again, and I don't want that to happen. And I don't understand why you'd rather go to work than spend time with me," Sam said.

"The gallery's not really work to me and it helps occupy my mind. I know you don't fully understand what I'm feeling, but when I'm in the house, I can't stop thinking about those nasty words etched behind the paint on our garage door and the hate behind them."

"That's why I suggested we get out and go for a hike."

"I don't feel safe enough to do that yet. I jump at every noise, Sam. At least in the gallery I can lock the doors and for a while, get wrapped up in my work."

"I'd hoped you'd feel safe enough with Jake and me by you, but I can't force you to go. I think it would help you though if you changed your thinking around a bit and trusted in me more."

"It's not a matter of trust."

"To some degree I think it is. It's also about thinking outside the small enclosure you seem to be encasing yourself in. I won't push, but I'm here if you need me," Sam said. She finished her fruit salad and went upstairs to take a shower, wondering how long it would take Halie to regain control of her life, and what else she could do for her to make that happen.

THE WORK WEEK passed as Sam predicted, with neither Halie nor Sam having much time to spend together. Halie remained engulfed in preparations for the gallery opening and the Jackson Hole Fall Art Festival, which wasn't due to kick off for a month. And with the increased summer traffic at the park, Sam was beyond busy and often came home later than usual or covered the night shift, neither of which helped matters as far as their relationship was concerned. Sam tried making small conversation during the week, but Halie was distant and not overly responsive. Although there were no more incidents at the house or elsewhere, and Sam was able to re-board Coco and Sugar in Charlie's stables, Halie seemed to be getting worse instead of better. Friday night Halie's restless and jerking motions in bed kept Sam up a good portion of the night. The next morning, Sam resolved she'd talk to Halie again, even if it meant Halie'd be mad at her.

When Halie awoke, Sam stroked her hair. "Morning."

"Morning. How long have you been awake?"

"Most of the night."

"Ugh, me again?" Halie asked.

"Yeah. Look, I know I said I wouldn't push you or anything, but I can't stand seeing you this way, and you walk around like I barely exist."

"This has nothing to do with you."

"It has everything to do with me. I have feelings too. I care about you, but you won't let me help you. Instead, you hide away or get angry with me instead of placing the anger where it should be."

Halie looked into Sam's eyes. "It's hard to fight a ghost. I'm sure I'd feel better if the sheriff's office at least had leads in the case. I'd feel even more wonderful if they arrested someone."

"I know that, but in the meantime, we have to take control of our own lives. You should have gone hiking with me and Jake on Sunday. Nothing happened to us and I think going would have helped you regain some of the confidence I think you may feel you've lost," Sam said.

"I do feel helpless most days," Halie said. She touched the side of Sam's face. "What's the weather supposed to be like this weekend?"

Sam smiled. "Rain this afternoon, but clearing and sunny tomorrow."

Chapter Six

ALTHOUGH THE FACT that additional patrols from earlier in the month ended and Halie still wasn't herself, Sam conceded she had been making some progress. During the week that followed, both remained busy, but Halie didn't appear angry at Sam anymore. Still, Sam looked more and more forward to their vacation in New Jersey as each workday passed, drawing them nearer.

A sunny day marked the last Sunday in July; perfect flying weather for their trip to New Jersey. Sam let Halie sit in the window seat of the airplane. Once Sam got comfortable next to her and fastened her seat belt, she watched the string of passengers, who had not yet found their seats or a space to stow their carry-on luggage, snail their way to the rear of the plane. Very few wore happy expressions. Sam was amazed at the amount of carry-on luggage people brought with them, especially with the continued increase in security and the limited overhead compartment space in most planes. She and Halie had not brought any carry-on luggage, opting to check it instead.

No fan of flying, Sam studied Halie and smiled. Halie's presence provided Sam comfort and reassurance that everything would be okay. In the row opposite and one behind them, Sam noticed the overhead compartment was so packed, that the last passenger to cram his things in couldn't get it closed. The flight attendant wriggled her way past Sam. She held a blanket in her hand. Sam watched the flight attendant stuff the blanket under a large roll-on carry-on bag whose handle was the apparent culprit of the problem. Sam appreciated the fact that if they now encountered turbulence during the flight, the overhead compartment would likely remain closed and no one would be injured. Problem resolved. Now they were that much closer to takeoff. Sam cracked her knuckles and realized Halie was staring at her.

"Are you okay? You seem a little tense?" Halie said.

"I do?" Sam rubbed the back of her neck. She tried to loosen her muscle's tightening grip. "A little I guess. It's been a while since I've flown."

"It'll be fine. I promise."

Sam knew she was right, but couldn't relax. She watched the activity on the tarmac instead. A van with big black dog paws printed all over it zipped past and around to the other side of the plane. A few seconds later, she heard the door to the luggage compartment under the plane latch into place, and the captain welcome them on board.

Moments later, when they were safely in the air, Sam breathed a sigh of relief and loosened her grip on the armrests. "You know it's strange, but from up here looking down, you realize what a small speck each one of us is on this planet. It makes me feel so insignificant."

Halie placed her hand on Sam's thigh and looked deep into her eyes. "Well, in no way are you insignificant to me," she whispered. "You're the most important person in my life."

Sam smiled back at her. The warmth of Halie's hand on her thigh spread throughout her body. She missed Halie's touch so much, at times her body ached. Lately, she hadn't felt like the most important person to Halie and wasn't sure if she still was. Hearing the words reassured her. She leaned over and whispered in Halie's ear, "I love you."

Halie leaned back. "I love you too."

Sam hoped a week away would do them both some much needed good. She couldn't wait to see her mom. She began to relax, closed her eyes, and fell asleep.

A short while later, Sam heard the popping of soda can tops and ice cubes clinking as they fell into plastic cups. Then the aroma of coffee drifted through the cabin. She opened her eyes. "What's this?"

"You were sound asleep when the flight attendants came by, but I got you some coffee. I figured you might like some when you woke up," Halie said.

"Thanks. I am thirsty." Once Sam sipped her coffee and the flight attendants passed by again to collect everyone's garbage, Sam noticed Halie grinning at her somewhat devilishly.

"Now what?" Sam said.

"Nothing."

"Oh no, it's more than nothing. I know that stare."

"It's nothing. It's only that the 'fasten your seat belt' sign went off twenty minutes ago. I guess I was curious why you're still belted in so snug?"

"Are you kidding me? Oh no, I don't take my seat belt off until the plane lands."

"Why not? They wouldn't change the sign if it weren't safe," Halie said.

"Up here, anything can happen. Nope, I stay belted unless there's no way I can get around it." Sam scanned the area to make sure no one was listening. "I'd have to be turning yellow though before I'd get up. I so hate flying."

"Now there's a visual I could have done without. I'm sure you're not the only one on this plane that hates flying. Two thirds of the passengers probably don't like it either," Halie said. "All I can say is I'm glad you're the one who suggested we go. At least the preflight anticipation wasn't a killer. Be glad we were able to get a flight out of Jackson Hole and didn't have to drive two hours to Idaho Falls first."

"Yeah, but I'd be a lot happier if we didn't have to stop in Salt Lake City on this flight and have to go through landing and takeoff all over again. Throwing in those extras is no treat."

"I don't like that part either, but at least we're together. I'm teasing you, anyway. I'm nervous too, but not about the flying part—about meeting your mom."

"You shouldn't be. Mom's super sweet and I'm sure the two of you will get along great. She said she'd pick us up at the airport, but I told her we'd get a rental and meet her at the house. It's too much driving, there and back."

"The offer was nice, though. I am looking forward to meeting her. I'm sure she has lots of stories to share about when you were a kid growing up."

"Yeah," Sam said. "I'm sure she does. Luckily Matt will be there to share in my pain."

HALIE HAD NEVER been to New Jersey. When the plane approached the landing, she focused her attention out the cabin window and was surprised by the amount of industry that blanketed the landscape. She observed numerous large, white, storage tanks, smoke stacks spewing steam and smoke, parking lots filled with rows and rows of trucks, and a maze of train tracks leading in every direction, cargo trains visible on some of the tracks.

After a smooth landing, they taxied to the terminal. On her left, across a highway, from one end of the horizon to the other, she saw cargo ships and large metal cranes painted blue. The cranes stood several stories high. They swung wide, loading and unloading cargo containers.

"It's so industrial and congested here," Halie said. "Who'd ever want to live in New Jersey?"

"That's where you're wrong," Sam said. "What you're looking at is Port Newark, a major shipping port in the area. Jersey has plenty of other areas that are beautiful and varied, ranging from mountains, to open farmland, to sandy beaches. This area's deceiving. You'll see."

"If you say so. It's too bad this is the view people get when arriving in the state."

"Yeah, I guess it kind of is. I don't think anyone who lives here notices though," Sam said.

Halie discovered Sam's words rang true once they were headed down the Garden State Parkway. Buildings and other man-made structures gave way to stretches of roadway with farms on each side, and later transformed into expanses of pine forests. She saw firsthand the reason New Jersey was called The Garden State and now thought the name apropos. The closer they got to the shore, the soil morphed from a rich brown color to a sandy yellow-white and the topography flattened.

The ride from Newark Airport didn't take as long as Halie imagined. The New Jersey Turnpike wasn't busy at all, but the Parkway heading south did have a fair amount of traffic on it, as did the local roads, even at that hour.

AT HALF PAST six in the evening, Sam parked the rental in front of her mom's garage and stretched her back. "Well, we made it," she said. "I don't see Matt's car. I guess they aren't here yet."

"That's good in a way. Then I don't have to meet everyone at once," Halie said.

"I suppose so," Sam said, giving the house a once-over. The shore house Sam spent many summer vacations in appeared much the same as she remembered it, though improved. It brandished a fresh coat of white paint and once faded, salt-sprayed black shudders were now a crisp, dark purple. The driveway was newly paved. The "front lawn" was made almost entirely of river rock and hinted at a professional landscape job with bayberry and elderberry bushes, cactus, scattered tuffs of beach grass and patches of black-eyed susans near the front steps. June Tyler had refused her daughter's offer to have a complete remodel of the home done, but Sam was glad her mom finally used a portion of the money she'd sent to her to do much needed fix ups.

"Sam, this place is so cute," Halie said. "I can see the ocean from here. I knew you said your mom lived by the shore, but I didn't know she was right on it."

"Yeah, it's a small house, but I think she's got one of the best spots, right next to Island Beach State Park."

"I'll say."

"Her house is the last one on this stretch of shoreline before the park. The park has miles of protected beach and wildlife before you reach the actual bathing areas. She's got lots of privacy."

"Privacy. I like the sound of that," Halie said. She swung the car door open. "Wow, it's hot. You don't notice with the air-conditioning on."

"It's not so bad though, you'll see. The ocean breeze cools things down a bit." Sam said.

"I don't care. The air feels nice. Oh, here comes your mom. What a sweet looking woman. I definitely see the resemblance between you two, even better now seeing her in person."

"Oh, uh, thanks," Sam said.

June Tyler wore her wavy brown hair shoulder length and her eyes were as green as Sam's. She stood about five foot three, donned a killer tan, and appeared young for her age.

"Hey, you two," June yelled as she walked swiftly to the car, her arms outstretched. "It's so good to see you both. Come on over here and give me a big hug."

Halie got out of the car, extended her hand and said, "Hello Mrs. Tyler, it's so nice to finally meet you."

"Nonsense with the Mrs. Tyler—you call me Mom, and come on

over here for a hug."

Halie peered over her shoulder at Sam as she stepped from the car.

Sam rested her hands on her lower back. She came out of a backward arching stretch, when she caught Halie's glance. Sam grinned before Halie was engulfed in her mom's arms.

Sam's smile widened as she rounded the front of the car. She was happy her mom was so welcoming to Halie, not that she doubted she wouldn't be. "Okay you two, break it up. Where's my hug?" she said.

June Tyler released Halie and reached for her daughter. She squeezed her hard and gave her a kiss on the cheek. "I missed you, Sammy. It's so good to see you both."

"I missed you too, Mom, and Halie's been looking forward to finally meeting you. I'm so glad we're here."

"Me too, sweetie. You two must be exhausted. I know that trip's no fun. Come on in the house and we'll have some dinner."

"Okay, let me get our bags out of the trunk," Sam said.

"I'll give Halie a quick tour in the meantime," June said. She placed her arm around Halie's back and motioned her toward the front door.

Sam tidied the inside of the car and checked to make sure they didn't leave anything valuable behind before hauling the suitcases from the trunk. She plodded up to the front door, and once inside smelled her mom's cooking. Memories of savory dishes eaten during her youth and fresh baked cakes brought comfort, it also caused her stomach to growl. Sam carried the bags upstairs. Her mom and Halie were in the spare bedroom to the right.

The center of the attic style room allowed enough space to stand up straight and was quaint. Two twin sized beds with light oak headboards rested against the rear wall. In the center, a large window with white ruffled curtains overlooked the ocean, a half dresser underneath. The floors were made of hardwood and were covered with an oversized teal, orange, brown, and purple colored throw rug in the center.

"This is where the kids will stay. You guys can take the other room across the hall," June said. "Matt can sleep on the pull-out sofa downstairs."

"You don't think he'll mind?" Sam said.

"No, he's done it before," June said.

Sam turned left at the top of the stairs and set their luggage on the floor next to the bed. Their room was similar to the other bedroom, except it held a queen-sized bed, a full-length dresser, and a wooden desk with a chair. In addition to a window overlooking the front yard, the corner bedroom contained a second window overlooking the side property as well. On top of the dresser stood a cream colored ceramic lamp with a stained glass shade and a basket with assorted flowers. The house was equipped with central air, a feature it didn't have when the Tyler family visited on their summer vacations when the kids were young.

"So that's about it," June said to Halie. "It's small, but it's plenty for me. Oh, and the bathroom up here is over there between the two rooms."

"You're home is lovely, Mrs. Tyler, and the location is fabulous," Halie said. "I love that this room is so bright and friendly."

"I'm glad you like it, and please, call me Mom, remember? That or June, whichever you prefer, but Mrs. Tyler makes me feel old."

"Oh, sorry...Mom," Halie said.

"Apology accepted, now let's all head downstairs for dinner. I prepared one of Sam's favorites, pecan burgers with mashed potatoes and gravy, and asparagus. I also baked a strawberry cheesecake for dessert. Sam told me you'd enjoy that, Halie."

Halie's eyes opened wide and her smile broadened. "I know linking the word 'love' with a food item is a bit extreme, but I *love* strawberry cheesecake. Thanks so much for thinking about me, but you shouldn't have gone to so much trouble."

"Nonsense, I've been looking forward to this visit for weeks, so why not feed you something you like."

"I like most foods, and tonight I think I could eat a horse I'm so hungry, though I'm leaving ample room for desert. We didn't have enough time during our stopover in Utah to grab anything decent at the airport, and they don't give you much worth eating on the planes these days," Halie said.

"Good, because I made plenty and I'm not crazy about leftovers. Matt won't be here until the morning with the kids. It's just the three of us tonight."

"I don't think you have to worry about leftovers," Sam said as she gazed at her partner. "For a petite woman, this one can pack it away."

"As can you, if I recall correctly," June said.

The kitchen was a decent size, plenty of cabinet and counter space and ample room to move freely around the wooden table and four chairs surrounding it. The table was already set. The stove was full of pots and a few dishes soaked in the sink.

"Sit, girls, relax. I'll be done in a minute."

"Do you need any help, Mom?" Sam asked, though she already knew the answer.

"No, it's all done, I simply have to warm up the gravy."

"So Matt's not coming until tomorrow? I thought they'd be here today," Sam said. She sat at the table next to Halie, leaving the spot at the head of the table for her mom.

"The kids had a birthday party to go to at one of their friend's houses. You know how kids are, so Matt figured he'd drive up tomorrow morning instead. He said the girls get up early anyway and that they should be here in time for breakfast."

"Oh, good. We wanted to take you all out for breakfast one day anyway, so we'll do it tomorrow. That'll give you a break too," Sam said.

"Well, okay sweetie, but you don't have to. I don't mind cooking."

"I know, Mom, but we want to," Sam said.

JUNE SERVED THEIR food in record time, for which Halie was glad. The meal looked and smelled so delicious she couldn't wait to dig in. And once she took her first forkful, her taste buds did a happy dance.

"This meal is fabulous. The burgers are melting like butter in my mouth and these garlic mashed potatoes are wonderful," Halie said. She savored every flavor. "Now I know where Sam gets her knack for cooking."

"Thank you. Though I hate to admit it, I think it comes from years of experience. That and lot's of love, of course. As far as Sam's concerned, I don't know how she learned to cook, because God knows I could never get her to do it when she lived at home."

"I wasn't that bad," Sam said.

"Oh yes, you were," June said. "She hated cooking. She always opted for the outdoors and getting dirty."

"Some things don't change," Halie said. She envisioned Sam's most recent run in with dirt when she walked through the door soaking wet and dirty the night Coco was taken.

"Yup. She roughhoused with her brothers and friends, hung out in the woods and in their tree fort playing cowboys and Indians."

"Please, Mom, I'm sure Halie's not interested in-"

"Nonsense, now hush, of course she is," June said.

Halie laughed, picturing Sam squirming to get away from the womanly duties of the house, though she didn't recall seeing any woods when they pulled in, only a few scraggly trees and pines scattered across a mostly flat and open landscape. "Where was that? This wasn't the house Sam grew up in?" Halie asked.

"I'm sorry," June said. She set her fork on her plate and took a sip of water. "I skipped ahead a bit. When Sam was little, and right up until the kids all moved out of the house, we lived in the northern part of the state—in the mountains. After Sam's father died, part of me wanted to move away and start fresh, but the other part didn't. The kids all had their friends from school there. Plus, they went through a rough enough time dealing with their dad not being around, that I didn't want to uproot them entirely. I didn't have the heart to move. We created a lot of good memories in that house."

Halie kept her eyes on June Tyler as she spoke, feeling the love she embraced for her family come through her words and expressions. On occasion, she nodded in understanding, but remained silent.

"But then after my brother passed away three years ago and willed me this house, I decided the time was right to move. I always loved his house. We made lots of nice memories here with the kids too. We used to come down here all the time in the summer, for long weekends and vacations."

"Sam's uncle didn't have any other family who wanted the house?" Halie asked, surprised.

"No. My brother never married. He was a bit of a loner I guess. He liked to fish and hang out with his buddies at the local watering hole. He was a good man though, kind and easy mannered, and he loved the kids, especially Sam. He used to take her out in the ocean on his shoulders, like her father did when he was alive, and dunk her in and out of the water until she'd scream 'mercy.' She loved it, always wanting to go back in."

"It sounds like you did have lots of fun here," Halie said.

"I see you fixed the place up quite a bit too," Sam said. "Thank goodness for central air."

"You can say that again. We usually get a nice breeze, being right on the water and all, but it can get awfully hot down here and the humidity is what'll kill you further inland. Central air was one of the first things I did to upgrade the house. Then I had the master bedroom downstairs redone. I combined it with what was once your uncle's study, and built a deck off it. It's like a sanctuary out there for me."

"You're not afraid of living so close to the water?" Halie asked.

"No, and as far as I'm aware, the house has never taken on water. We don't usually get huge waves unless there's a storm, and even then the water hasn't gotten anywhere near the house. The ocean looks closer to us than it is."

"Mom's a trouper," Sam said in jest. "It'll take more than a little storm to rattle her."

"That's true," June said. "Now why don't you give me a hand with these dishes Sammy and then we can sit in the living room and I can show Halie some baby pictures of you."

"Oh, great! Like you haven't embarrassed me enough today already," Sam said.

"Oh, knock it off already, you. I'm your mom and that's what mom's do."

"Yeah, yeah. Seriously though, why don't you sit with Halie and I'll do the dishes. You did enough tonight. Dinner was wonderful," Sam said.

"Thanks sweetie. That sounds good. I'll put on the coffee, so we can have that dessert later, that is, if you both still want it."

"Oh, yes we do," Halie jumped in. She didn't give Sam a chance to say no.

Sam stood by the sink shaking her head.

"What?" Halie said.

Sam held her hands in the air, palms out.

After dessert, conversation continued effortlessly late into the evening. Halie was glad she had some time to spend with Sam's mom before Matt and the kids got there. She found June easy to get along with and a pleasure to be around. She noted many of the qualities Sam inherited from her mother.

HALIE LAY IN bed waiting for Sam to finish up in the bathroom. The time was almost midnight, and she was exhausted, but not too exhausted to get in a little dig she was waiting to give Sam all evening.

Sam walked into the room and sat on the bed. "I'm glad you got a chance to get to know Mom today. I think she enjoyed your company a lot."

"I'm glad I got to know her too. Your mom's such a great lady. I think she and my mom would get along pretty well."

"I'm sure they would. I'm glad we came. I missed Mom a lot. It's nice seeing her again. Thanks for coming."

"I'm the one who's thankful to have been invited. It's nice getting to know her better and learn more about you at the same time."

"Oh, yeah?"

"Yeah," Halie said.

"I'm so proud of everything she's done with the house. It looks great." Sam tucked her legs under the covers. "I don't know about you, but I'm beat. Is it okay if I shut off the light?"

"Please."

Sam leaned over and gave Halie a long, soft, kiss. "Good night, honey. I love you."

"Good night, Sammy. I love you too."

Sam grunted. "What? Oh, very funny. You were waiting for that, weren't you?"

"Who, me?"

"Guess I stepped right into that one. Wait until we go to see your parents. You know what they say about payback—"

"Yeah, yeah. I say bring it on."

Chapter Seven

MATT AND THE kids arrived early the next morning as promised. Bear hugs were enjoyed by all. During breakfast at the local diner, Halie got acquainted with Matt, Jessie, and Katelynn. Sam thought it would be fun afterward if they all went over to Pirate's Cove and played mini golf and let the kids ride the water slides. The temperature hit eighty-five degrees at ten in the morning and was forecast to rise into the nineties. Sam was glad that their trip appeared to be relaxing Halie and bringing her back to her old self.

"You kids go ahead," June said. "If you don't mind Matt, I'll drive your car home and you guys can go with Sam and Halie. That way, when you get back later, I'll have lunch ready."

"You sure you don't want to go, Ma?" Matt said.

"Yeah, Grandma, are you sure?" Jessie asked.

"I'm sure. Grandma needs to rest. After lunch we can go swimming, okay, and Grandma will go in the water with you."

"Okay," the kids shouted.

Matt gave June his car keys and clambered into the back of the rental with his two kids. "God, Pirates Cove. I haven't been there in years. Do you think it's still open?"

"I hope so," Sam said. "That was one of the neatest mini golf places around. I'm sure the kids will love it."

"The kids, huh?" Halie said.

On their way to mini-golf, Sam stopped at the liquor store and picked up a couple of bottles of wine for later. When she got back in the car, her ears were assaulted by the kid's yells that they wanted to play a name game in the car.

"I get to start," Katelynn said. "I see an object from the car and yell it out. Then we go around the car in a circle, Halie, Auntie Sam, Jess, and then Dad, and back to me, with each person coming up with a word that starts with the same letter of the word I yelled out."

"Yeah, and it has to be an object, it can't be a person's name or anything," Jess yelled.

"The person who can't think of another word, before we get to the mini-golf course, loses," Katelynn said. "And you can't take too long. You have to be quick, say three seconds, or you're out."

"Okay," Sam said, "I'm in." She was amused by their enthusiasm, thinking back on the games she played as a kid. With all the technology of today, she didn't think kids played these simple games anymore.

"You're in trouble," Matt added. "They've got a ton of these games up their sleeves, and they're good at all of them."

Sam pulled out of the liquor store parking lot and Katelynn

shouted, "Okay we're starting now...billboard."

Halie was next, and added "bucket." Around in the car came "baseball," "baby," "barn," "basketball," and "bounce."

Katelynn yelled at Halie, "You lose! 'bounce' isn't an object. Okay, now you're out and Auntie Sam picks the next word."

Sam scanned the horizon and shouted "seagull," and the game started up again.

WHEN THEY RETURNED to the house, Sam noticed her mom standing outside between her house and the neighbors' house to their left. Her mom, almost as if transfixed, watched a tall, blonde woman walk away from her. Sam turned first to Halie and then to Matt and the kids, who didn't seem to notice anything. When Sam glanced back, June Tyler swung around and jogged toward the back porch.

"Okay, ride's over, everyone out," Sam said. "Last one to the house is a rotten egg."

"Grandma, Grandma, we're back," Jessie and Katelynn yelled.

"So I see," June said. Then she swept them both into her arms in the kitchen. "Did you kids have a good time at mini-golf?"

"We did," Jessie spouted. "Auntie Sam was really good. She beat Halie and Daddy, but she couldn't beat us!" she said.

"That's because you and your sister are lower to the ground and have a better angle on the ball," Sam protested.

"Oh, Auntie Sam! You're funny," Katelynn said. She and Jessie both started giggling.

"I'm glad to see you all had a good time, now let's eat lunch and then we can go swimming later." June said, wiping her brow. "I'm hotter than a cat on a hot tin roof."

"You're not the only one," Matt said. "I can't wait to take a swim."

After they ate, Sam and Halie stayed on the porch and shared a cold beer. Sam was more than happy to relax and watch everyone else down by the water. She wasn't used to the kid's high energy and savored the silence.

"What do you think that was all about with Mom and the neighbor?" Sam asked.

"What do you mean?"

"I mean the way they appeared to be looking at each other," Sam said.

"I don't know. Do you think something was wrong?"

"Not exactly. I got the sense Mom didn't want us to know she'd been talking to her. When I glanced over, she ran off and then pretended she'd been in the kitchen the whole time making lunch."

"True, I did notice that. I don't know. It's interesting though."

"Maybe we can ask Mom to introduce us, the next time we see her neighbor outside," Sam said.

"What are you thinking? You have that devilish likeness to you."

"I do? No, I don't think so. I'd call it more like daughter's intuition."

THAT NIGHT AFTER dinner, they all played a game called Sorry that the kids brought with them and were, of course, exceptionally good at. Everyone talked during the game and all were clearly enjoying their time with the family. After Jessie and Katelynn both won two games each, they wanted to play poker.

"Poker? Who taught you two to play poker?" Sam said.

"Daddy did," Jessie answered.

"Daddy, huh?" Sam said. She fixed her glare on Matt.

"Well, not exactly. They taught themselves," Matt said. He shot a quick glance at June as he fidgeted in his seat. "Every Thursday night, a couple of the guys come over and we play cards. We get started kind of early, so we don't end up playing too late with work and all the next day. The kids stay up for like an hour or so and watch. They're smart beyond a doubt and picked up the game on their own."

They both agreed in simultaneous fashion. "Yup, we did."

Sam smiled. "You did, huh? Well, why don't we deal those cards and see how good you two really are? What do you say? Who's in?"

Everyone yelled that they wanted to play.

"What kind of poker do you girls play?" Sam asked.

"Five-card stud with joker's wild," Katelynn said. "Does everyone know how to play?"

Halie answered first. "Sort of, but I haven't played poker in quite some time. Maybe you can give me a little refresher."

"Sure!" Katelynn said. A twinkle lit in her eye. "Everyone gets dealt one card at a time until someone gets a jack. That's the person who'll be the first dealer and after that, the dealing goes to the person on the dealer's left. The dealer puts a card face down to the player on his left and goes around the table dealing a card down in that direction." She motioned clockwise. "Then the dealer does the same thing, but gives a face-up card to everyone, and then you make your first bet."

"Who bets first?" Halie said.

"Whoever has the highest card. The dealer tells everyone who that is. After that, three more rounds of face up cards are dealt and we bet. Who ever thinks they have a bad hand can drop out when they're up."

"Do they get to pull back their bet then?" June said.

"No," Katelynn said. She drew out the 'No'. "But you don't lose more by staying in. Jokers are wild, so they can be any card you want. Since we're playing with jokers being wild, five of a kind is the highest hand. Then comes a royal flush, then a straight flush, four of a kind, a full house, a flush, a straight, three of a kind, two pairs, one pair and then no pair where the highest card would win."

Then Jessie went on to explain what cards made up the different kinds of hands.

"Whoa, whoa, oh, my goodness," Halie said. "How do you girls remember all that?"

"We just do. Jess and I play together a lot, so it kind of sinks in. I can make you a cheat sheet if you want."

"I think that would be great, it would help me a lot," Halie admitted.

June laughed. "Your Grandma could use one too," she said. "Come on in the kitchen. I'll get you girls some paper to write with and in the meantime, I'll get us all something to drink and snack on."

"What will we use for betting chips, Grandma?" Jess asked.

"Well, how about pretzel sticks?"

"That's a great idea, Grandma," Jess said.

"Yeah, then we can eat our winnings if we get hungry," Katelynn added.

Matt's face lit up as he watched and listened to his daughters. "I'm blessed with these two, that's for sure."

"That you are, brother," Sam said. "That you are."

They played for a couple of hours. The girls cleaned up on the majority of pretzels. June was the first one out of the game, followed by Sam and Matt. Halie hung in the longest, but then lost her last pretzel when Jessie got a full house against her pair of kings and eights. Jessie and Katelynn battled until the end when Jessie finally won.

"All right now kids, off to bed with you," Grandma June said. "It's getting late and I think your dad wants to take you girls to the boardwalk tomorrow, so you better get some sleep."

The kids yelled "good night" and ran around the table giving everyone a good night kiss on the cheek, including Halie.

Halie glimpsed at Sam.

When the kids were gone, June said, "So, what do you ladies have planned for tomorrow? You might want to take advantage of the forecast, because I think on Wednesday a storm's supposed to move in."

"What about you, Mom?" Sam said. "What are your plans?"

"Oh, don't worry about me. A little quiet will do me some good. I did want to take you ladies over to meet my PFLAG group while you were here. We meet once a month on Tuesday nights."

Halie turned to Sam who responded with an inconspicuous nod of approval. "We'd love to go with you," Halie said.

"Good, I'd like that."

"Maybe I'll take Halie jet skiing tomorrow morning in the bay. I haven't done that in years," Sam said.

"Oh, that sounds like a lot of fun," Halie said. "I've always wanted to do that. Do you Jet Ski, Matt?"

"No, our sister was always the crazy one who liked to do stuff like that. I stuck to basketball and safer land sports. I'd watch it out there with her if I were you. I've seen her on one of those things, and she loves the speed."

"I had no idea. We have another thing in common then. I used to ride a motorcycle back in Boston, mainly because I liked the speed and freedom of it, so I think I'll be fine."

"Really, you did?" Sam said. Her voice raised an octave. "You never mentioned that."

"I guess it never came up in conversation."

"Too bad I didn't know you then. I would have loved to have ridden with you," Sam said.

Matt shook his head realizing even more so how those two were meant for each other.

"Well, that's settled." Sam stood up off the chair. She rubbed her backside. "I think we better hit the hay then. Tomorrow's going to be a busy day for all of us."

THE TRAFFIC AT the Jersey shore picked up measurably as the week progressed. As soon as kids were out of school, the shore towns were alive with business. Not until after Labor Day do many of the restaurants close their doors for the season, creating an almost ghost town like feel.

Once they maneuvered through the traffic, Sam and Halie spent the morning jet skiing on Barnegat Bay. Every time a boat sliced through the water anywhere near them, Sam sped toward the boat's wake and rode the Jet Ski over it, lifting them off the water for a second or two before slamming down again. Then she'd slice through the water in the other direction and attack the wave from the opposite side as salt water sprayed them, keeping them cool. Each time Sam neared a wave, Halie grabbed her waist tighter. Sam enjoyed having Halie so close to her it almost hurt.

After lunch with the family, Sam and Halie took a beach blanket, one of the bottles of wine they bought, along with two glasses, and headed off for a leisurely barefoot stroll down the beach. A few stragglers wandered that end of the beach, so they couldn't hold hands walking, though Sam wanted to. The warm breeze off the ocean glided against them, caressing their bodies. Other than a few seagulls squawking above, and the rush of the ocean breaking against the shore, their surroundings were quiet.

Halie stroked Sam's arm with her free hand. "God, Sam, this is so wonderful and relaxing. I love being able to walk along the beach like this with you."

"I know. I'm enjoying our walk too." Sam felt the desire for Halie rise within her. She could still feel Halie wrapped around her body, pressed close, from earlier on the Jet Ski. That vision, coupled with the sight of her in her cut off jean shorts and tank top added to her growing wish to be close.

As they walked, Sam enjoyed the unencumbered lightness of the moment; the respite from responsibility and reality. She noticed a change in Halie over the past couple of days, which lifted Sam's spirits. Halie was smiling more and joking with her again, a familiar reminder of the life they shared early in their relationship. Being away from the house and the unease that hung around it appeared to relax Halie. Sam was glad to see her unwind and hoped the freeness would last.

"Let's set the blanket over here," Halie said. "It's a somewhat secluded spot."

Sam spread out the blanket. She waited until Halie sat. "How about a glass of wine?"

"Sure," Halie said. "Do you know what I was thinking about while we were walking?"

Sam uncorked the bottle and poured a generous portion into each of their glasses. "No, but I'm all ears if you'd like to share."

"I would. Even though you always seem to forgive me, I wanted you to know I still feel bad at times about how I shut you out and blame you for a lot of the things I have trouble dealing with on my own."

"I don't want you to feel bad. I want things to return to normal between us," Sam said.

"I know, but it's important for me to know that in your heart, you understand that I don't take the way I treat you lightly, and that I care about you more than you can imagine," Halie said.

Sam set the wine bottle into the sand and re-corked it. "I appreciate you sharing. Deep inside I know you care, but sometimes my head over analyzes the past, which leads to conflicting thoughts and worries. I work on not over thinking things, but sometimes it's difficult for me not to."

"I'm hoping in time, I'll be able to put your mind at rest. In the meantime, do you know what else I was thinking?" Halie's tone became more devilish.

"No, but I think I want to."

"I was thinking about how much I wanted to kiss your lips, run my hands all over your body, and make love to you right here, Samantha Takoda Tyler. What do you say to that?"

Sam glanced around, but saw no one. "I'd say our thoughts intertwined a few minutes ago, only you may have taken them a little farther."

"Is that so?" Halie set their glasses into the sand. Then she pulled Sam toward her and kissed her on the mouth, slowly at first, then with increased hunger and passion.

Sam's cheeks flushed in an instant. The pounding of her heart quickened. Intense warmth radiated through her body. A tingling sensation shot through her core. As she pulled away and regained her breath, she said, "Why do you have such control over me?"

"Because I love you more than anything in this world, even if I don't show it as often as I should."

The warmth from the sand radiated through the blanket. "I love you as much and more, if that's even possible."

Halie stared into Sam's eyes as waves crashed onto the shore. Little black and white birds flitted about above the water. Halie touched Sam on the thigh and caressed her gently. "Knowing the extent of my love for you, I don't think that's possible, but I'll let you claim equal if you'd like."

"Equal it is then," Sam said as she leaned in for another smoldering kiss.

Chapter Eight

THURSDAY CAUGHT UP to Sam and Halie before Sam knew it. On Friday morning Matt would take the kids home. He scheduled a work meeting for Friday afternoon. The storm blew through the day before and now the sky was clearing, but the water remained too rough to swim in.

Sam stood near the kitchen sink and dried the breakfast dishes while the family tossed ideas around on how to spend their day. During a break in the conversation, Sam said, "How about we head over to the nature center on Island Beach and take a nature tour?"

"Yeah!" Jessie said. Her yell was followed by a similar one from her sister.

"I'm in," Matt said. "If the kids are happy, I'm happy."

"Sounds good to me," June said.

All eyes were focused on Halie. "Me too, let's go."

"Let me finish the dishes and then I'll call and find out what time the tours are."

Halie took the dishtowel from Sam's hand. "I relieve you of your duty. You make the call—I'll finish here."

The next tour was scheduled for eleven o'clock. Sam drove to the nature center, which was located a few miles in from the main gate on the one lane road that ran down the center of Island Beach. At the southern most end of the island sat Barnagat Inlet, but they didn't travel that far. When they passed the Governor's Mansion, set back behind the dunes, they made a left into the nature center's parking lot. Once inside the building, they huddled near the entrance.

A slim park ranger in her early twenties with large brown eyes approached, her strides long. "Hey there, my name's Ranger Bartlett. Are you here for the eleven o'clock tour?"

"Yes, we are," Jessie yelled. She jumped up and down. "We're not late, are we?"

"Oh, no. You're right on time."

"My Auntie Sam is a park ranger too, aren't you Auntie Sam?" Jessie said.

"Uh, yes, that's true, I am," Sam said. She wasn't sure why Ranger Bartlett appeared to stare at her with piercing intensity.

"That's interesting. Where do you work?" Ranger Bartlett asked.

Sam cast a brief look at Halie with an innocent expression.

"Grand Teton National Park. That's in Wyoming," Jessie said. She spoke before Sam could answer. "It's lots of hours away by plane."

"That's very cool. And aren't you kids the cutest thing," the ranger said. "How old are they?"

"Jess is seven and Katelynn's eight," Matt said. He ran his fingers through his hair and along the nape of his neck. "They were very excited to come on this nature trip."

"That's good. We're going to learn lots of interesting things today, and everyone will leave here knowing more than they did when they walked in the door, I promise. Follow me," Ranger Barlett said.

They walked through the building and out the back door onto a wooden walkway. Sam let Matt and the kids go first, and then her mom. She fell to the rear next to Halie.

"That woman could have burnt a whole through you, the way she was gawking," Halie said.

Sam recognized Halie's seemingly mild annoyance. "I know. I don't usually pick up on that stuff as you know, but she wasn't exactly being discrete. It made me uncomfortable, especially with the kids there and all."

"I don't think the kids noticed. Your mom probably did, but they didn't, and your brother certainly didn't. I think he's a bit smitten with our tour guide."

"You think so? She's a little young for him. I'm staying back here with you where it's safe."

"Oh, you think so, do you? I wouldn't be so sure of that," Halie said. She slapped Sam light on the rear.

Sam turned in Halie's direction as Halie grinned and shook her head.

From up ahead, Ranger Bartlett's powerful voice trailed back to Sam and Halie. "We'll start out on this trail that runs through the dunes," she said. "Island Beach is an island nine miles long. The Atlantic Ocean meets land on one side and Barnegat Bay on the other side. Because it lies between these two bodies of water, it's subject to wind, rain, and beach erosion."

"What's erosion?" Jessie said.

"That's when the side effects of the weather eat away at the beach until less and less of it exits."

"That's not good," Jessie said.

"No, that's not good," Ranger Bartlett replied. "What we have here then, is the island's first line of defense from damaging winds and waves— the grasses. These taller ones are American Beach Grass and the lower ones are Japanese Sedge."

Katelynn called to her grandma, "Is the American Beach Grass what you have in your yard, Grandma?"

"I think so sweetie," June said.

"The secondary lines of defense," Ranger Bartlett continued, "are plants such as these: Poison Ivy, Seaside Goldenrod, Common Bayberry, and Prickly Pear Cactus."

"Grandma has those prickly pear plants too," Jessie said.

The ranger chuckled and peeked over at Matt, who shyly looked away.

"Maybe she's bisexual," Halie whispered into Sam's ear.

"Maybe," Sam said. "That'd be good for Matt."

They followed the trail farther inland. The sun beat strong on Sam's back. Ranger Bartlett informed them of the plants and animals in the thicket community, the transitional community near the roadway, and the mature forest community. The forest community consisted of trees such as the American Holly, Atlantic White Cedar, various oaks, and Pitch Pine. She also explained the importance of why people should not disturb any of the insects, reptiles, birds, mammals, or plants that lived in those communities or remove them from the island.

"Island Beach is home to over one hundred different bird species including hawks, owls, sparrows, herons, egrets, ducks, gulls, sandpipers, pelicans, starlings, loons, and other more common birds as well," the ranger added. "They all rely on the thick brush for protection and food." Ranger Bartlett paused for a moment, as if gauging whether or not she was losing the girls' interest. Then she led everyone closer to the water. "I have a secret to tell you girls, but you have to promise not to tell anyone, because most people don't know this," the ranger said. She winked at Matt.

"We promise! We promise!" they yelled in unison. "Tell us, please!"

"Okay. Way back, around the sixteen hundreds to early eighteen hundreds, this island was home to pirates and smugglers," Ranger Bartlett explained. "In fact, it's thought that storms have wrecked and sunk over one hundred and twenty five ships around the eighteen thirties between Point Pleasant and the Barnegat Inlet. The risk of wrecking a ship became so bad, they used to call this area the Graveyard of the Atlantic."

The girl's eyes widened, and at first all they could say was "Oooh." Then Jessie said, "That means there could be treasure in the water or maybe even washed up on shore, doesn't it?"

"That's right. But most of the treasure has already been found, and in order to protect the island today, no treasure hunting is allowed. If some of the treasure happened to wash up on the beach though, well, that's another story," she said.

"Oh, boy! Did you hear that Dad? There might be treasure. Can we hunt for gold later, Dad? Please, huh, please? Maybe with that storm yesterday, some trinkets might have washed on shore."

"Some trinkets, huh? You'll have to talk to your grandma about that."

"Is that metal detector we used to use when we were little still around, Mom?" Sam asked.

"You mean the one I bought because *you* wouldn't leave me alone about hunting for coins and gold, when *you* were their age?"

Halie chucked as Sam's face flushed. "Yeah, that's the one. Well anyway, maybe we can put new batteries in and see if it still works. Halie and I could take the kids up and down the beach after lunch, if it's okay with Matt."

The girl's stares traversed from Sam to their dad.

"That's fine with me," Matt said. "Knock yourselves out. Only don't forget about me when you find a treasure chest of gold."

AFTER POLISHING OFF sandwiches at the house, Sam and Halie took the girls on their treasure hunt along the beach as promised. Halie brought her camera. Not one cloud dotted the sky. The waves were strong and several feet tall, and a few surfers were out landing larger than usual waves. Jet skiers were also present. The sun glistened off the waves. The mild breeze cooled Sam.

"You girls take turns holding the metal detector. Katelynn goes first because she's the oldest. I'll time it. We rotate every fifteen minutes, okay?" Sam said.

"Okay," they said.

The kids walked up ahead, with Sam and Halie not far behind. Halie glanced over at Sam and gave her a quick kiss on the cheek at the same time Jessie veered around.

Jessie slowed her pace until Sam and Halie caught up to her. "You guys are in love, aren't you? Like Dad and Mom used to be?"

The question broke Sam's heart, but at the same time was so cute and innocent. "That's right sweetie, the same way."

"Do you think it will be forever?"

"I hope so Jess, we feel like it will," Sam said.

"I hope so too. I wish Mom and Dad would have lasted forever."

"I'm sure they did too, but you know, that doesn't change the fact they love both of you girls more than anything. Nothing can change that special bond. You'll always have it."

A huge smile crossed Jessie's face. "We will? Are you sure?"

"Yes, I'm sure," Sam said.

Jessie was quiet for maybe half a minute and then she added, "So if you have kids, then they'd have two mommies? That's what Dad said."

Sam was impressed. "Yup, they would, and we'd love them as much as your mom and dad love you. For now though, we have Jake to take care of."

Jessie laughed. "Oh, yeah. I wish you could have brought Jake. Dad won't let us have a dog. At least he hasn't so far. I think we're wearing him out about getting one though." Then she skipped along the beach next to her sister.

"I'm glad I got to meet your brother and the kids," Halie said. "The kids are so precious."

"Yeah, they're something else. They have so much energy." Sam squinted at her watch and then yelled over to Katelynn. "Okay girls, time to switch."

After a couple of minutes, Katelynn slowed and walked in between

Sam and Halie. "Auntie Sam, are there sharks in this ocean?"

"Sure, but most don't swim this close to the shoreline."

"Do you think they ate pirates years ago when their ships got wrecked?"

"I don't know sweetie, I hope not. I think they had enough other fish to eat. I understand sharks don't particularly like the way people taste anyway," Sam said.

"Oh, well that's good," Katelynn said. Then she redirected her line of sight at the sand and their footprints. "How come when the water rolls over our feet and then when you can see the sand again, so many air bubbles pop up?"

Sam didn't answer right away, so Halie interjected. "That's because of air pockets trapped under the sand and also because hundreds and thousands of little crabs burrow into the sand for protection from the birds, and they have to breathe."

"Crabs? What kinds?"

"Oh, I don't know. All kinds. You've got big horseshoe crabs and little hermit crabs, mole crabs, ghost crabs, lady crabs, green crabs, rock crabs, and even clams and mussels," Halie said.

"Wow! You know a lot about that stuff. How come?"

"Well, back where I grew up in Scituate, Massachusetts, we lived near the ocean too and people went crabbing and clamming a lot, so you pick up on that stuff."

"Was it like this ocean?"

"The water's a lot colder there and the shoreline is rockier, but it's the same ocean and it has lots of the same animals in it," Halie said.

"Like sharks?"

The corners of Halie's mouth turned upward. "Yes, like sharks, but also bluefish, lobster, shrimp, and lots of other fish."

Jessie yelled from up ahead. "It's beeping, it's beeping! I found something."

Sam and Halie gathered around the spot Jessie already started to dig. A second later, Jessie held up a coin. She wiped it clean before she handed it to Sam. "What is it Auntie Sam? It has an Indian head on it."

Sam felt the coin between her fingers and flipped it over. "This is a Buffalo Nickel from 1913. You don't see many of these around. This is a great find, kids. It's not a gold coin, but it could be worth a lot of money. You should hold on to it. Make sure you don't spend it."

"Wow, wait until we show Dad what we found," Jessie said.

"Do you girls want to search a little longer or head back?" Sam asked.

"I'd like to stay a little longer if that's okay," Katelynn said.

"Sure, I don't mind, I could be out here all day," Sam said. She smiled at Halie.

Halie smiled back, then turned toward one of the jet skiers. She lifted her camera and took a few pictures of the man "cutting it up" on the waves.

The jet skier angled into a wave and did a complete flip.

Sam never saw anyone circle around in the air like that before. "Wow, did you see that?" Sam said.

"Not only did I see it, but I got it on film. If this comes out good, I'm going to hang it in the gallery. This should be a great shot," Halie said.

"That guy is something else," Sam said. "I wish I could ride like that."

"Oh, no you don't, Ms. Tyler. I want you around for a good long time. Don't even think about it."

Sam smirked at Halie. "Come on, we better catch up to the girls, they're getting too far ahead of us."

Halie ran off first and yelled back, "I'll race you."

When they got near the kids, the jet skier made his way near them, close to the shore. He waved them over. Sam told the kids to stay where they were and she and Halie went to see what he wanted.

He bobbed back and forth in the water on his Jet Ski. "Hey," he yelled. "My name's Colin Mitchell. I'm a semi-professional jet skier, among other things. I saw you on the shore with your camera and I was wondering if you happened to get a picture of the flip I did back there."

"I did, it was great. You're very good. I'm a photographer, so I know a good shot when I see it," Halie said.

"Thanks. If the photograph's any good, I'd like to buy it from you. I'd pay up to a thousand dollars, depending on how well you captured me."

"Are you kidding?"

"No, I'm dead serious. If I give you my address, do you think you'll remember it?"

Halie glanced at Sam. Sam indicated that she'd remember. "Go ahead," Halie said.

Sam made a mental note of his address, repeating it over and over in her head until it stuck. Then they both waved good-bye and trudged through the sand toward the kids.

"What did he want Auntie Sam?" Jessie asked.

"He wants to buy one of the pictures Halie took of him in the ocean, for quite a nice penny too."

"I hope you're getting more than a penny," Jessie said.

Sam tussled Jessie's hair. "Yeah, we'll get way more than a penny. That was just an expression. I think we better get back to the house now, how about it you two?"

"Yeah, then we can tell Grandma and Dad the good news about our nickel and Auntie Halie's picture," Jessie said.

Sam and Halie looked at each other. Sam sensed they shared the warmth and glee at the words Auntie Halie.

When they returned to the house, June and Matt were sitting on the porch; June in a wicker rocker, and Matt in a lawn chair. Both sipped on a drink. Not even up the last step, the kids started in with the coin they found and kept right on talking. Sam went inside and poured herself and Halie a glass of spiked punch her mom had made for herself and Matt. She poured the kids fruit juice, and then joined them on the porch for some chatter and relaxation.

The afternoon passed quickly. Later that evening, the kids suckered them into another name game, but this one was harder and a lot more fun than the one they played in the car. The game included clapping, and it required hand-brain coordination, which messed up the adults after the couple of drinks they'd had, making the game all the more funny.

Everyone sat in a circle with legs crossed. Jess started out as the leader. She set the rhythm, which was a mix of a slap on the thighs, a clap of the hands together, and snaps of the fingers.

Jess's first rhythm went like this: slap, slap, clap — then on snap, snap she said, "Names of animals."

Going around the circle clockwise, next to Jessie, Katelynn did the same thing, slap, slap, clap, snap, snap, and said "goat." The game would continue until someone either messed up the beat or ran out of an animal's name. The person who messed up sat out until only the winner was left. The end result was that Sam sat a lot, but they all laughed equally as much.

THE NEXT MORNING was a difficult one. Matt and the kids were packed and hugs were given and taken. The girls cried in unison while Grandma assured them she'd come visit them soon and Sam and Halie said they'd see them again too and that they'd send them pictures of Jake and pictures they took during the week. When the heaviest of sobs abated, Matt pulled out of the driveway.

"It's so quiet with the kids gone," Halie said. "It feels odd in a way."

"It does," June said. "I love it when they come, but it's so hard to see them go."

"Hey, Mom," Sam said. "Why don't you invite your neighbor over for dinner tonight? We'd love to meet her."

June was surprised that Sam would want to meet her neighbor and wondered why she asked. Containing her nervous energy she said, "Who, you mean Maggie Seymore?"

"If that's the neighbor you were talking to the other day when we came back from playing mini-golf with the kids, then yes."

"Oh, uh, yeah, that was Maggie. Sure, I don't see why we couldn't, although I can't guarantee she'll come, but she'd probably like to. I'll ask her. I think that would be nice, actually."

"Good, it's settled. Is she married? She should bring her husband, if she is."

June smiled at her daughter, a suspicious yet affectionate smile. "No, she's not."

"That's fine. I'll cook, and you can have the evening to relax," Sam said. "Seven o'clock okay?"

"I have a better idea," Halie interjected. "I'll cook and you guys can catch up with each other. How does that sound?"

Sam started to voice objection, but Halie put her hand up. She winked at Sam, which halted any attempt Sam might have made in protest.

"Sounds good you two, I'll let you know." June said.

"HEY BABY," COLIN said. He placed an arm around his wife's waist and kissed her on the side of the cheek. "Will you keep an eye on Cody? I wanted to take the four-wheeler out for a spin."

Colin Mitchell was a young man in his early twenties who married his high school sweetheart soon after graduation since he'd gotten her pregnant with their son.

"Do I have a choice?"

Colin smirked as he walked out the back door. "Thanks," he called back. He skipped the porch steps as he headed for the truck. "Keep practicing, buddy!" he yelled to Cody, who was playing on his battery operated four-wheeler. "Show Daddy how good you're getting when I come home okay?"

Cody nodded, then drove into a small bush. The four-wheeler churned, but didn't go anywhere.

Colin jumped from the truck and ran to his son. "I told you, you've got to keep your eyes focused on where you're going, right?"

"Right. Where ya going? Can I come?"

Colin kissed his son on the head, and pulled his toy truck free from the shrubbery. "Not today. Dad's got some things to take care of, okay? I'll see you later though," he said before making his way back to the truck.

Eileen Mitchell watched her husband from the kitchen window and shook her head.

Twenty minutes later, Colin stood in front of a familiar townhouse door and rang the bell.

A tall, short haired blonde with full lips and mascara laden eyes, dressed in a tight white sun dress and white sandals with silver pearls, wearing large silver bangles on her arms, opened the door. "What are you doing here today?"

"I missed you, Sugar," Colin said. He handed her a bouquet of two dozen red roses.

"Yeah, right," she said. "Me or the sex?"

"Same thing, no?"

"Whatever. Come on in," she said. She grabbed him roughly behind the neck and pulled him inside before closing the door.

HALIE STOOD IN the kitchen slicing up eggplant. She placed the even slices on a cookie sheet. At seven o'clock sharp, a succession of rapid knocks landed on the back door.

Halie heard June yell from the living room, "I'll get it, it's probably Maggie." Before Halie was able to rinse her hands off and wipe them dry, June was at the door and let her neighbor in.

"Hi," Maggie said to June. Then she leaned in and gave her a hug. "I brought a bottle of wine for dinner. It's red. I hope that's okay."

"Hi. I'm glad you could come. That's great, the kids love red wine," June said. She took the bottle from Maggie and picked at the seal over the cork.

"The wine will go perfect with dinner," Halie interjected. She sensed tension in the air. "We're having linguini with eggplant and mozzarella in red sauce."

"Sounds fantastic..." Maggie said.

"Oh, I'm sorry," June said. "This is my daughter's partner, Halie Walker."

Maggie extended her hand. "It's a pleasure to finally meet you Halie. June talks about you and her daughter often." Maggie Seymore was an exceptionally pretty middle aged woman. She was tall and slender with large hazel eyes and wavy brunette hair. She wore a white button down blouse, snug fitting jeans, and brown leather sandals. The only jewelry she wore was a silver ring on her index finger and small silver earrings with turquoise hearts embedded in them. Maggie's handshake was firm, yet gentle.

"It's nice to meet you too," Halie said. At the same time, Sam walked into the room.

Maggie faced Sam as June introduced them to one another. After the usual pleasantries were exchanged, they all stood awkwardly staring at one other, until June offered wine, which everyone gladly accepted.

The kitchen smelled of garlic sautéed in olive oil. Maggie sipped her wine. "Mmm, it smells great in here. It's making me hungry," she said.

"Believe me, it's making me hungry too," Halie said.

"No surprise there," Sam added. "I don't think there's a time when you're not hungry. At least I haven't seen it yet."

"Very funny. Now why don't you be a sweetie and hand me my glass of wine, and then let me finish up here in the kitchen, okay?"

"Whatever you say, Honey-pie." Sam did as she was asked, then threw in a peck on the cheek for good measure.

"Thanks, now scoot."

While Halie cooked the pasta, June motioned everyone else into the living room. After they sat, Maggie said to Sam, "Your mother has told me so much about you and Halie. I can't believe how you two met, and then how close you came to losing her so soon thereafter. You must feel even more blessed now."

"Yes, thanks. I do. I can't even begin to tell you what that day on the mountain felt like for me. I didn't know if she was hurt or not, or if I'd be able to find her and the others before it got dark and cold. If it wasn't for my dog Jake, I don't know if I'd have found them in time."

"Thank God it all worked out in the end. Your mom showed me the article Halie wrote on Grand Teton and the proposed park shutdown last summer. The story was excellent and obviously succeeded with its intended impact, since I hear the park remains open," Maggie said.

"Yes, thankfully. I'm sure the pictures and interviews and the overall story was a major factor in that decision. Halie's very talented."

"She appears to be, from what I've read. Was that the last article she wrote?"

"It was. After recovering from the crash, she came to live with Jake and me." Sam paused for a second and then continued. "You know, I'm glad my mom filled you in on our lives, but I wish I could say the same about yours. It seems that for some reason she's decided to keep you all to herself."

"Yes," Maggie said. Her tone was stern, but it did not appear directed at Sam. "That is unfortunate, isn't it?" Her gaze was focused on June.

Halie walked into the living room. "What's unfortunate?"

"I was merely telling Maggie that it's unfortunate Mom kept all her information about her to herself and hasn't told us anything about her, and Maggie agreed with me." Sam crossed her left leg over her right leg, resting her ankle on her knee as she glared at her mom.

"Yes, well, you know, sometimes it's better that way," June said. Her tone was sheepish and immediately after speaking she drank deep from her wineglass.

"I don't think it's ever better that way, Mom. In fact, aren't you the one who always told your kids to live their lives the way they want, as long as they make sure they're good to other people along the way?" Sam asked.

"Sounds like solid advice," Maggie said.

"Okay, you two smarty-pants," June said. "Since the two of you seem to be on the same page and my hold out appears futile at this point, I'm sorry. I'm sorry I haven't been honest and I'm sorry I've been in the closet."

Halie couldn't believe what she'd heard.

June continued. "Yes, Maggie and I are lovers. We have been for several years now." Her words were spoken crisp and matter of fact at first, but soon her speech slowed and her tone became filled with affection. "I didn't know how to tell you both, especially you Sam, with your father and all."

"I knew it!" Sam said. She jumped up and gave her mom a hug. "I knew it the minute I saw the two of you the other day. I'm glad you told me. Look, Mom. Dad died a long time ago, and I know you'll always love him in a special way, but that doesn't mean you can't live the rest of your life and be happy. And nothing changes how I feel about you or Dad. I have to say though, I was surprised that you — well, you know —"

"Fell in love with a woman?"

"Yes."

"Believe me. No one was more surprised than I was. And then after it happened, I kept thinking to myself, well, maybe the gene does run in the family. You certainly got it."

"Yes I did, and I'm grateful," Sam said. She moved closer to Halie, grabbed her hand, and gave a squeeze. "What I don't understand is why all the secrecy. I mean I think it would have been easier for you, especially knowing about us. Are you in the closet with everyone around here?"

"She is," Maggie answered for her. "No one knows, and she's asked me to keep it that way."

"Yes, well that's because — well, I don't know, I feel a bit odd about it I guess. Not about our relationship," June said, placing her hand on Maggie's thigh, "but about the situation. I mean, I accepted you, Sam, for who you were, once you told me you were gay. In fact, I was proud of you for having the courage to be yourself and still am, but at the same time I wanted to protect you and fight for your rights. That's why I joined PFLAG and stayed with them for so many years. I think that when family members speak out on behalf of their gay kids or siblings, it has a much greater impact on the public's perception of gays in a positive light, than if someone gay speaks out. I was afraid to lose that and I didn't want people to think I joined the group because I ended up being gay. I joined it for you and I fought for your rights and those of other people like you."

"You never told me that," Maggie said to June. "I had no idea that's why you stayed closeted." She stood. "Come here." Maggie put her arms around June and held her in a long embrace. Sam and Halie joined them, and soon all four women were locked in one tight huddle.

"All right now, all of you," June said. "Enough of this mushy stuff. I'm hungry. Is dinner ready yet?"

"I thought you'd never ask," Halie said. Her stomach growled like that of a baby tiger.

The conversation at the dinner table, now with the veil of secrecy lifted, was lively and entertaining. The time sped past much too quick. During dessert, Halie told June and Maggie about her photo gallery, and all the work she and Sam had put into it.

"Did you know your mom has artistic abilities herself?" Maggie said.

"She does?" Sam replied. She never saw her mom exhibit any interest in the arts.

"She certainly does. She paints some wonderful pictures, but keeps them hidden in her bedroom closet," Maggie said, after which she flashed what appeared to Halie as a bragging smile June's way.

"Oh, nonsense," June Tyler spurted. "They're nothing. I simply paint for fun and it relaxes me. In fact, I only recently started it up in the last couple of months."

"I'd love to see a couple of them, Mom," Halie said. She paused for a moment, having gotten no response, and added, "Please."

"Yeah, Mom, please," Sam said.

"Oh, okay. If you're all going to gang up on me, what choice do I have?" June got up and walked into the master bedroom. She returned carrying two paintings, each several feet high and several feet wide. She set them with care on the floor, and let them rest against the wall. She moved to the side.

Sam and Halie exchanged silent glances.

"I remember when your Mom painted these," Maggie said. "I couldn't believe her talent and she'd poo-poo'd the paintings as if they were nothing."

Both paintings were of the shore. One was of a little wooden seafood restaurant on the bay, its outdoor deck filled with customers sitting next to the docks, the pier bustling with commotion. Small fishing boats and sailboats dotted the water. The detail was exquisite as if the scene remained in motion. The other was of a sunset on the beach. Striking hues of orange, yellow, and red touched the ocean. In the distance dark silhouettes of two lovers held hands as they basked in the remaining sunlight and serenity of the moment. The silhouettes were cleverly depicted so the person viewing the painting could imagine the figures however they wanted — as a man and a woman, two women, or two men.

"These paintings are magnificent," Halie said. "They should be hanging in an art gallery."

"Halie's right, Mom, these are fabulous. I had no idea. Are you sure Halie's not your birth daughter, because I don't have an artistic bone in my body."

Everyone laughed.

"You know, Mom," Halie said, "I've been thinking about putting a corner in my photo gallery for local artwork. For drawings and paintings and stuff, maybe even something for kids, but I'm not sure about how to go about it yet. I'd love to start the artwork corner with one of your paintings though."

"Are you serious?" June said. She lifted her hand to her chest.

"Of course I am. I can have it packaged tomorrow and shipped to the store."

June shifted her attention to Maggie, her eyes appearing to ask for her approval. "Well, I guess so if you think it's good enough. Take whichever one you like."

"Thanks," Halie said. She stood and gave June a hug. "This is so perfect. I'm not sure which one I should take though." She paused and looked both paintings over again. "I think Maggie should decide."

Maggie smiled at Halie. "Thank you, that's very thoughtful. For what are now obvious reasons, I'm partial to the painting of the lovers walking along the beach, and if June would allow me to, I'd like to have that one framed for my house. I think the other would be great for the gallery."

Halie noticed June's acquiescence to Maggie's response was made with a sparkle in her eye, their connection so close, no speech was necessary. The intensity between them almost made Halie blush. "Good, the little seafood shack wins," Halie said. She lifted her glass with a toast and took a healthy sip along with everyone else.

Chapter Nine

SWEAT TRICKLED DOWN the side of Ronni Summers's rounded face and between her ample breasts as she wiped the tailpipe of her motorcycle with a dampened T-shirt dabbed in chrome cleaner. The smell of the rust-orange cream-like liquid, interfused with the smell of the wax she'd moments before rubbed onto her gas tank, was as welcome a fragrance to Ronni as was engine oil and grease. In this arena, life made sense and calm existed.

Ronni's habit, when she was upset or frustrated, was to either clean her bike or work with her dad on one of the antique cars he was restoring. Since she wanted to be alone today, the bike won out. Gliding her hand along the chrome, she felt the tiny pieces of rust pitting on the pipe through the cotton fabric of the shirt. She rubbed each bump with vigor until only smoothness remained. After completing one side and buffing off the dried chrome cleaner until the bike shone like glass, she started on the other side. Her knees strained during the task, but she'd not let up until every inch of the motorcycle that could shine sparkled at her. Satisfied, she stood aside in her worn out blue jeans, white T-shirt, and scuffed up brown Danner work boots and admired her work.

As the sun edged its way up the driveway, Ronni pulled out a cigarette and lit it, enjoying the first long drag. She watched lazily as the reflection of clouds careened across the bike's deep purple gas tank. Each side of the tank was painted with the head of a female black panther. Ronni connected with the primal power the sight of the panther evoked. She cherished her bike more than almost anything, aside from her mom and dad. No matter how messed up her mom became or how badly her mom treated her in the past, Ronni loved her all the same.

Content with her day's work, she stepped on her expired cigarette butt, kicked up the stand on her bike, and rolled the motorcycle into the garage. One week to Sturgis. She and her bike were ready.

SATURDAY NIGHT'S OPENING of the photo gallery came upon them quickly, but Halie was prepared. The flyers and personal invitations were mailed on time, the caterer was early, and the champagne was properly chilled and waiting to be poured into fluted glasses. Halie bought the glasses especially for the occasion. The gallery was in pristine condition. Soft, slow, instrumental music played in the background.

As Halie straightened her white silk blouse she'd tucked into her black dress slacks, she worried about the turnout. She knew April and

Corrine would come with a guest. Susan would be there, but she was more of a helper than a guest.

"Don't worry. You look great, the place looks great, the weather's perfect. You'll have a nice night, I promise. And if for some unlikely reason you don't, I'll make it up to you later," Sam said.

"Sounds like a plan," Halie said. She admired how exquisite Sam looked in her dark grey slacks and deep purple cotton shirt worn loose under a dark grey vest, the sleeves rolled to three quarters length. The shirt was unbuttoned far enough to show cleavage. Sam wore black leather dress shoes. "Thanks for the vote of confidence. The way you're dressed tonight, I can't imagine my not taking you up on that offer if things don't work out."

Sam's tone deepened. "I sincerely hope you do, and so as not to sabotage your event, the offer stands if it's a great night as well."

"Good to know," Halie replied. "Do you think a lot of people will show up? What if no one shows?"

"Stop worrying. People will come. With free snacks and alcohol, relaxing music, gorgeous photographs, and a blindingly radiant host. Good luck keeping them away."

Halie's cheeks flushed. "You do know how to crank up the charm, don't you?"

"I try."

"You do better than try. Geez, I wish the caterer would hurry up prepping the snacks already. I wanted to sample them before anyone arrived, to make sure they were up to par."

Sam chuckled. "Oh, of course, you definitely want to make sure of that."

Halie shot Sam a fierce glance, but unable to maintain the facade, broke her expression into a warm, loving smile. Although the visit to New Jersey sped by, as did the few days before the opening, Halie was glad to be home. Unfortunately, the worries she left behind during that week away latched onto her after her return. The freeness she experienced in New Jersey washed away the moment they landed in Jackson Hole. She felt badly about it, especially since she knew her moods also affected Sam, regardless how much Sam tried to hide it. Determined not to be the downer tonight, Halie pushed the negative thoughts from her mind and refocused instead on the night ahead.

As the guests and visitors filtered in and out and the evening wore on, Sam had been right. The opening was a huge success. Halie was happy her few close friends were around her. Their presence gave her the confidence she needed to shine. Several expensive photographs sold as well, which Halie hadn't planned on. She basked in the moment, but the moment didn't last. When Walter Pipp showed up, the atmosphere and success of the evening spun one hundred and eighty degrees around and out of control.

Walter entered the gallery dressed in a pressed and cleaned sport coat and khaki pants. His hair was neatly combed, and with the exception of Nitro on his shoulder, he would have blended in well and gone relatively unnoticed. In fact, he'd already eaten several hors d'oeuvres and polished off half a glass of champagne before a woman saw Nitro, screamed, and sent the rat into a panic.

"Now what?" Halie said. She turned, following the direction of the stares. She ambled through the crowd in the direction of the commotion. "What the heck?"

There stood Walter Pipp, clearly attempting to calm the frantic women. He tried explaining that the rat was his pet and that yelling would only agitate him, but before he could complete his sentence, Nitro crawled down his pant leg to the floor. As he reached over, Walter spilled his champagne on a guest. People scattered. "A rat, a rat," they yelled. They exited the gallery twice as fast as they'd come in. When the exodus ended, a half dozen people remained. And there stood Walter, holding Nitro.

SEVERAL DAYS PASSED before Halie recovered from Walter's destruction of the gallery opening. Walter since apologized and explained why he came with Nitro, but only the humorous article of a local reporter, who happened to be in the midst of the evening's events and one of the last people to leave, rectified the near disaster. The article actually resulted in bringing in business from people who read about what happened and wanted to hear the story first hand. Susan was more than happy to tell the story, only each time she added a few more embellishments.

By the end of the week, the commotion died down to an acceptable level as the story circulated and interest fizzled. Now Halie got a better idea of what a normal workday was like. Before packing it in for the day, she carried a pile of folded boxes out the back door and lifted them into the recycle bin. She paused to appreciate the warm, dry weather and absently glanced across the parking lot.

Near where she'd parked, she noticed Walter Pipp standing by himself, cigarette dangling out of his mouth and hands perched on his hips. His gaze appeared focused out beyond her car. Halie watched him walk around it, then return to the rear of the store. She heard him mumble under his breath, but couldn't discern what he was saying.

Back inside, Halie searched for Susan. She saw her with a customer and waited until she finished. "That was strange," she said.

"What was strange?" Susan asked. "And why are you whispering?"

"I went out back a minute ago to throw out empty boxes and saw Walter standing in the parking lot, near our cars, having a smoke. He usually smokes by the back door of his place. What do think he was doing out there?"

"I don't know, maybe he was getting something from his truck, or maybe he wanted to catch a few rays of sun. Though somehow I don't think sunning is his thing. Why don't you ask him?" Susan said.

"Because when he saw me, he turned and walked away, like I caught him doing something he shouldn't be doing. I think he was up to no good."

"In what way?"

"I don't know. I've got a bad feeling though. I'm going out there and make sure everything's okay."

Before Halie was able to take more than a couple of steps, Walter trudged through the front door. "Ladies," he said is his usual abrupt tone. "I wanted to let you know I saw a group of kids hanging out by your cars. They slit your front tire," he said to Halie. "I called the cops."

Halie squinted at Susan before she addressed Walter. "Are you kidding? Only *my* car?"

"Yes, why? Were you hoping they slashed everyone elses?"

"That's not what I meant," Halie said.

"Then you should say what you mean."

"Fine, I will. I was just outside, and the only person I saw around our cars was you."

"That's because the bastards ran off after they saw me heading over there. What do you think, I slit your tire?"

Walter waited, but Halie didn't respond.

"Shit, if I were that mean or stupid, I'd have done it weeks ago. What is it with you anyway? You're lucky I saw them when I did or you might have four flats instead of one. I was going to offer to change that tire for you, but since you're being so accusative, you can take care of it yourself," he said. He stormed out the door and slammed it behind him.

Susan eyed Halie with a recriminating glare.

"What? He did this," Halie said with a scowl. "I know he did."

"Personally, I don't like the guy either," Susan said, "but I don't know why you'd think he'd do something like that. He came forward and told you he called the police. Why would he call the police if he was guilty?"

"Because he knew I saw him and he was trapped. Because ever since we got this space and he didn't, he's been against us."

"I'll admit he's been an ass at times," Susan said, "but maybe he didn't see you and was trying to be a decent guy for a change."

"Like he was being last weekend at the opening, bringing his buddy Nitro with him? What was he thinking? Who knows what else he's doing, or has already done. He may be trying to be a decent guy, but I doubt it. Sabotage appears more up his alley."

AFTER SHOVING THE last chunk of toast in her mouth, Sam tucked her ironed gray shirt into her pleated dark green pants. She washed the toast down with one remaining swig from her coffee. She was hoping for some quiet time this Wednesday morning in her office. Time she wanted to use to straighten out accumulated paperwork. At twenty minutes to seven, Sam tied the last knot on her brown leather boots, grabbed her ranger hat, and headed for the door that led from the house into the garage. "I'm going, Honey," she yelled to Halie. She wasn't sure if Halie heard her, but that became the extent of their interactions in the past few days since the tire slashing. The slashing reaffirmed to Halie that whatever happened last month wasn't over. Although the love they held for each other remained deep, the rollercoaster ride they were on strained their relationship. Before she shut the door behind her, she said to Jake, "You be a good boy."

As soon as Sam started up the Expedition and backed out of the garage, a call came in.

"Four-two-zero, Teton Dispatch," Toby's voice crackled.

"Teton Dispatch, four-two-zero, go ahead," Sam replied.

"We got a call about two women spotted on Rendezvous Mountain's Eagle Ridge Trail and confirmation of a mountain lion in their vicinity."

"Roger that. I'm on my way." Sam jumped from the driver's seat, and ran inside for Jake, who was still sitting by the door. "Got a job for you today after all," she said as Jake bolted to the vehicle, tail wagging. Sam scratched a quick note for Halie that she'd taken Jake, and left in a whirl.

Sam had found Jake in Grand Teton National Park three years prior while she was on foot patrol on one of the hiking trails. He'd appeared scared, was nearly starved, and had been left tied to a tree several hundred feet from the main path. She'd taken him to the vet, and when he recovered, adopted him. He helped her through some rough times before she met Halie, and although Sam was the one who saved Jake, she'd always felt more like he was the one who'd saved her. He was a comfort to her now as well, and one of the few things in her life that was remaining steady. Jake could help her locate the hiker's more quickly, an asset she knew he was happy to have her take advantage of.

FROM THE CORNER of her eye, Susan watched as Halie stood with a large framed painting in her hand in front of one of the angled display walls. A chime sounded when a woman walked through the door.

"May I help you?" Susan asked.

"I hope so. I heard this gallery was owned by Halie Walker," the woman said, her right hand tucked in her back pocket. "Is that correct?"

"Sure is. And you are?"

"Felice Lohan—a friend."

Susan immediately recognized the name, and then was able to put the face with it. She remembered seeing her picture in the paper when news of the illegal trapping at the park made headlines after her arrest, and therefore she wasn't happy about seeing her in the gallery. Susan also never recalled Sam or Halie referring to her as "a friend". "So what can we do for you today, Ms. Lohan?" Susan asked. Now her tone was taut.

"Is she in?"

At first Susan didn't respond, uncertain whether or not she should be truthful, but then she knew if Felice walked much farther, she'd see Halie anyway. Susan inclined her head in Halie's direction, then spun around and walked behind the counter. "What time did Jeff's mom say she'd pick you up?" Susan whispered to her son Brian.

"She should be here any minute, why? Don't like having me around?" Brian asked.

"Don't be ridiculous. You know that's not true. It's just that I'm being paid to work, and it's a little difficult when you're here, that's all. I like spending time with you. I wish I had more of it, but unfortunately I don't."

"Yeah, well, so do I." Then in a more quiet tone, with brows furrowed, he asked, "Hey, Mom, who is that woman anyway?"

"Felice Lohan. She's a local. She used to work as a park ranger in Grand Teton with Halie's partner Sam, but she was caught in an illegal fur trading operation in the park. She captured some animals on the endangered species list. Some type of ferret, I think. She spent nearly a year in jail."

"Probably black-footed ferrets. We learned about those in biology last year."

"Sounds about right. Why'd you ask?"

"She looks familiar. Do you think the police are still searching for the person who took Sam's horse last month?"

"I'm sure they are, especially since Sam's in law enforcement, even if she does work for the park. Plus, she knows the sheriff quite well. Why?"

Brian didn't answer right away. "I might've seen her at Charlie's Ranch that morning when Sam's horse was taken."

Susan's eyes widened. "What? Are you sure?"

"I don't know, but I think so." In the next breath he said, "Oh, I gotta go. Jeff's here." He leaned toward his mom, kissed her on the cheek, and bolted out the door.

"Okay, be careful. We'll talk more about this later," she said, but her son was already out the door. Susan couldn't wait to tell Halie what Brian revealed. She wished she could hear Felice's conversation with her boss, but they weren't close enough. She'd have to wait.

"HALIE," FELICE SAID as she rounded the corner. "So it is true. Congratulations on your new place."

Halie tried concealing her unease. "Hi, Felice. Thanks. This is a surprise, what are you doing here?"

"It's good to see you too."

"I'm sorry," Halie said. She set June's framed painting on the floor, and leaned it against the wall. "I didn't mean for that to come across the way it did. How are you?"

"All things considered I'm doing okay." Felice glanced around the gallery. "You seem to be doing well. I'm guessing you're living here now in Jackson Hole. You and Sam are still together?"

"Yeah, we are. I couldn't be happier." Halie's answer was only partly true, recent acts against them made her heavy-hearted, but she wasn't about to go into it with Felice. "Sam had told me about your son. I'm sorry. How's he doing?"

"Thanks for asking. His cancer's in remission."

"That's great," Halie said. "Sam will be glad to hear that."

Felice didn't respond. Halie sensed Felice still harbored bad feelings about the arrest, as she suspected she might. Filling an awkward void, she added, "So what brings you here?"

"I'm not completely sure, to be honest. I was in the area, so I thought I'd say hello."

"You were in the area?"

"Well, I landed a job teaching at Ryerson Central College, at their Jackson campus starting next month. I've got three classes this semester, Bio I, Range Ecosystems and Plants, and Natural History of Regional Ecosystems. I'm teaching a class for the summer semester too, and one of my students told me about this place."

"I'm glad for you," Halie said. She meant it too, yet her feelings regarding Felice remained mixed. She was uncertain how to interpret her visit. While trying to decipher Felice's true intent, Halie heard the faint revving of a Harley engine, its unmistakable sound reminding her of some fun times on her bike in Boston. She reveled in the reminder. An unknown piece of her still missed the thrill of the ride.

"Yeah. This year is the first time they offered those classes in their Jackson campus, so that's going to work out great for me. It's been tough, you know, after what happened and all, finding a job—holding on to friends."

"I'm sure it was."

"This job is a real blessing. Because of it, I'll probably be seeing you around more, now that we work so close to each other. Maybe we could get together—"

At once the gallery door opened and a woman yelled, "Halie Walker? Where are you, gal?"

Halie wasn't sure what to think. Out of the frying pan and into the fire? How much was she expected to take before losing it? She hoped Susan would have already released her from the awkward position she found herself in with Felice, and would have called her over to answer a fake phone call or something equally believable, but no such luck. Now she had potentially another fire to extinguish. "Excuse me, Felice, I think I'd better get that."

Halie walked out from behind the display wall, eyes squinting at the five-foot-seven, hundred-sixty-pound leather clad biker, trying to place the surprisingly gentle and familiar face. Moments later, as the face registered in her memory banks, she yelled, "Ronni!"

"There you are, you little scoundrel," Ronni said. She ran to Halie and picked her up by the waist. She spun her around as though she weighed nothing. "It's so good to see you!"

"I can't believe it," Halie said once her feet hit the floor. "My heart be still. It's so good to see you too, you crazy nut. How long's it been?"

"Too long—way too long."

"You're right. We should never have lost touch. My God, you're so grown up," Halie said. She stepped back a foot or two and got a better view.

"Heck, so are you," Ronni said. Her line of sight scanned up and down Halie's slender frame. "You're even more of a knockout now than you were then."

In the background Halie heard Susan say, "What is it today, a full moon?"

Ronni Summers grew up with Halie in Massachusetts. They were best friends from kindergarten through middle school, before Ronni's parents moved to Kentucky. The pair wrote each other often during their first year apart, and sent each other pictures, but as time progressed, the letters dwindled until they stopped altogether. Halie couldn't remember who had stopped writing first, and now that she saw Ronni again, it didn't matter. All that mattered was her best friend was standing before her in the flesh at a time when she needed the support.

While the two old friends got re-acquainted, Felice repositioned herself within a few feet of Halie and cleared her throat.

Halie completely forgot Felice was in the room. She shifted sideways, "Oh, I'm so sorry, Felice. Felice, this is Ronni, an old friend of mine. Ronni, this is Felice Lohan. Felice is an acquaintance who stopped by to say hello and congratulate me on the gallery."

Felice extended her hand. "Nice to meet you," she said, her tone flat.

"Same here," Ronni said with equal hesitation. "Speaking of which...congratulations from me too. I love the name. Nature's Vision. Clever."

"Thank you."

"You're welcome. But then you always were the smarter of the two of us."

"Oh, I wouldn't say that. You did okay in class, but you always did better working with your hands. Remember what you made in wood shop?"

"I should get going," Felice said. "I enjoyed seeing you again Halie.

I'll stop by some other time when you're less busy."

"Okay, yes, it was good seeing you Felice," Halie managed. Before Felice walked out the door, and feeling a twinge of guilt for cutting their conversation short, Halie added, "and good luck with your classes."

Felice raised her hand level with her shoulder and produced a weak wave before exiting.

Once Felice was gone, Halie returned her attention to Ronni. "You don't know how glad I am to see you right now, and now that you're here, how much I realize I've missed you."

"I felt the same way as soon as I laid eyes on you again. It almost felt like we've never been apart and yet at the same time I sensed that tug on my heart that told me I had missed you a great deal." After a brief silence, Ronni said, "By the way, what was this woman Felice's story? I mean I'm sorry I wasn't overly nice to her, but I didn't get the impression you wanted her around. Are you in trouble? If you are, say the word and I'll take care of her."

Halie smiled. She wasn't sure if Felice was trouble or not, but she was happy she'd left. "Take care of her? Like you did when we were kids and someone was picking on me?"

"Yeah, that's right," Ronni said.

"Thanks," Halie said. She brushed Ronni's arm gently, "but I think I'm okay. A rather long story revolves around Felice. I think she may be a little lost right now and looking for a friend, but I'm not sure I'm ready or want to be that friend."

"Well, if she gives you any trouble, you let me know, okay?"

"I will. We have so much to catch up on. Do you live around here now?" Halie's heart hoped to hear that her friend lived close, at least close enough to visit once in a while. She didn't want to lose touch again.

"No, I'm still in Kentucky, though it's only me and my dad right now. My parents divorced. Mom's back in Massachusetts."

"I'm sorry."

"That's okay, it was a long time ago."

"You're here on vacation then?" Halie's expression revealed her disappointment. She would have loved to have her best friend back in her life.

"Yeah, but now that I saw you, I was thinking about hanging around for a little while."

"That would be fantastic."

"I came with my biker group. I left them at the watering hole down the street. Ray's I think the place is called. I didn't want all of them parking in front of the gallery. It has an upscale appeal—I didn't want us scaring away any potential customers."

"Good thinking on your part, though having you parked out front wouldn't have bothered me at all. It's so great seeing you. I can't believe you're actually here. I have so much to tell you and I want to hear about what's been happening with you."

WHEN SAM ARRIVED on scene, the sun was beginning to rise. She called dispatch to let them know she'd arrived. The parking lot was empty but for one vehicle. She stepped from the Expedition, placed her hat on her head, and let Jake out. She hoisted her EMS bag and marched up the trail.

Sam moved at a brisk pace, with Jake in the lead. Her body warmed posthaste in the cool, morning air. A few trees showed hints of changing color in shades of reds and yellows. Sam was extra cautious, a result of the mountain lion sighting, since they are rarely seen. Mountain lions are reclusive, solitary animals by nature that normally avoid humans unless startled, provoked, or starving.

Half way up the trail, a blood-curdling scream ripped through the silence. Sam ran full speed toward the sound. She now heard another voice, a woman yelling, "I won't let you go! I promise I won't let you go!"

At the edge of the woods, blood covered the branches and leaves of surrounding brush, and small plants lay yanked out, roots visible. As Sam approached, she saw the body of a woman being dragged away from the trail, the jaws of a mountain lion dug firm into her neck near her collarbone. A few more inches, and the animal's teeth would have punctured her jugular, causing her to bleed out. Another woman dragged behind as well, barely clinging to the captured woman's legs. Seconds later, the woman lost her grip and screamed, "No!"

Sam reached for her .45 caliber Sig-Sauer and removed it from its holster. She aimed, but got no clear shot at the mountain lion. Sam yelled as loud as she could and flailed her arms in the air to scare him off, but the animal held fast to its prey.

"Help us, please! Please, help us! I couldn't stop him. He won't let her go! Please! Hurry!" the woman who'd lost her grip yelled to Sam. She was left lying on her stomach.

Jake barked over and over, then lunged at the lion and bit hard into his side before swiftly backing away. The lion let loose of its victim and swiped its claws in Jake's direction. The lion stood growling and defiant, blood covering its jaws.

Sam didn't hesitate. A shot rang out, then another. The bullets found the heart and lungs of their intended target as the lion slumped dead to the ground.

The second woman ran to her partner's side and fell to her knees. "Oh my God, it's okay now, you're safe Baby, you're safe." The woman's voice shook in concert with her trembling body. "You're going to be okay. You're going to be okay."

Sam moved toward the bleeding woman and zipped open her bag. "My name's Ranger Tyler," she said, holding back the nauseous feeling overcoming her as she saw not only the gashes in the victim's neck, but also her scalp partly torn away from her skull from above the eye. "I'm going to take care of you."

The woman let out a grunt.

Sam slipped on latex gloves, folded back the layers of torn skin, applied dressing, and quickly wrapped the wounds. Then she reached for her shoulder mic and called for medical backup and a helicopter before attending to the lesser lacerations on the woman's face and hands.

While they waited for help to arrive, Sam managed to calm the victim's partner down enough to get some basic information from her such as her name and the name of her partner, and what they were doing in the woods at that early, dangerous hour. The woman's name was Melanie Gibbs. Her partner, who the lion grabbed, was named Hillary Coleman. Melanie told Sam she kept having this feeling they were being followed. She'd heard rustling in the brush, but every time she'd stop to check what was there, she saw and heard nothing. When Hillary bent down and grabbed the untied laces on her hiking boots, the mountain lion struck. When he pulled her away, she dove after her partner and managed to grab hold of her leg, but she couldn't stop him from taking her. He was too strong. After that, Melanie couldn't say much more.

Sam was aware now that the mountain lion didn't happen upon them. He was stalking them as prey. When Sam first saw him, her initial reaction was one of shock. She couldn't believe how emaciated he appeared. She estimated he was forty to fifty pounds underweight, and had he not been, he'd probably have weighed in at one hundred to one hundred and fifty pounds. She walked over to the carcass and examined it more closely, her original assessment confirmed. The animal had definitely been starving. Sam noticed a band around the lion's neck and a tag attached to it. She cut the band with her pocketknife, then removed the tag and wiped it clean. On the one side were engraved the words Titan, and on the other a marking that resembled a symbol from ancient times. She said nothing. She placed the tag in her pocket and waited until the rescue helicopter arrived.

WHEN HALIE GOT home from the gallery, later than usual, Sam was already making dinner. She stirred mixed vegetables in a saucepan with fresh garlic from the garden and olive oil. A pot of pasta sat boiling on the stove. Sam already fed Jake and set the table. A white linen cloth covered the table, and in the center, a honeycomb candle burned, spreading warm light on the vase of flowers sitting next to it.

"Mmm, that smells good," Halie said, as she walked into the kitchen, Jake prancing by her side. Then she noticed the table setting. "What's going on? Did I miss something? What's the special occasion?"

she said. She walked over to Sam, put her arms around her waist and, kissed her on the back of her neck.

Sam cracked a smile. She reached for Halie and held her close. "No special occasion. I wanted to surprise you. I love you."

"I love you too. My mouth is watering. What did you make?"

"A vegetable pasta dish with zucchini, sweet baby peas, cherry tomatoes, corn, and peppers, sautéed in garlic, olive oil, and vegetable broth, and seasoned with a touch of chili pepper. And also I grated a little fresh Pecorino-Romano to sprinkle on top."

"That sounds fantastic. When can we eat?"

"It's ready when you are. I'll pour us some wine."

"Wine, too?" Halie asked. They didn't normally drink wine with dinner during the week. Alcohol was reserved for the weekends and special occasions, like birthdays and holidays.

"I thought it might be nice, that's all. Plus, it goes well with the meal."

"I'm fine with it. I'll cut the bread. How was work today? I saw your note this morning that you took Jake with you. Did someone get lost?"

"Not exactly."

"Tell me about it over dinner, and then I've got news to tell you too." Halie sat at the dinner table, sipped her wine, and waited for Sam to serve the pasta.

With her back to Halie, Sam picked the pot up off the stove and removed the lid. "Jake was in his glory today. You should have seen how proud he was of himself, and rightly so," she said. She set the lid in the sink.

"So you found your missing person?" Halie asked.

"Yes and no. We found her, but she wasn't missing." Sam paused while she transferred a heaping sized serving of pasta onto Halie's plate. "She was hiking with a friend, before dawn, on one of the trails leading up Rendezvous Mountain. She was attacked by a mountain lion and dragged off into the woods."

"Are you serious?"

"Very. The bizarre thing is, something like that happening is so rare. Mountain lions are reclusive. If attacks do happen, it's usually in zoos or wildlife sanctuaries, where the animals are caged and frustrated, not out in the wild. In the wild it might only happen when they get startled or spooked, but I don't think that happened here." Sam set the pan on the stove top and sat to eat.

"What do you think caused it to attack then?" Halie asked. She twirled the steaming, vegetable laden pasta onto her fork.

"I'm not sure. The woman's friend said she was walking in the lead and didn't realize her friend stopped to bend down and tie her laces, and when she turned, she saw the animal pounce and drag her away, all in a matter of seconds."

"I can't even imagine that. Is she going to be okay?" Halie asked, unable to discern the answer from the expression on Sam's face.

"She should be, thank God, but as of now she's in critical condition. She lost a lot of blood. She suffered multiple puncture wounds to her neck, face and skull. Part of her scalp was torn back. She'd clearly put up a struggle when I found her, which probably saved her life."

Halie cringed at the horror as Sam provided details. "I'm so sorry, Sam. That must have been hard to witness." Halie set her fork on the edge of her plate and placed her hand on Sam's to comfort her.

"It was. I can't get the images of her out of my head."

"I think it'll take time, but eventually they'll fade. What were they doing on the mountain that early?"

"I asked myself that same question. The woman's partner, Melanie Gibbs, told me they wanted to watch the sun rise together from the mountaintop. She said they'd done the very same thing twenty years ago on that same mountain, and they wanted to recreate the moment."

"They were partners? That's so romantic," Halie said, having gained insight as to why the candle and flowers were on the table.

"Yeah," Sam said. "I can't imagine being Melanie Gibbs right now, with all the waiting, and not knowing. Last year, when I thought I might lose you, I felt like my whole world was slipping away and I had no control over stopping it. The helplessness was beyond frightening."

Halie stroked the back of Sam's hand with her thumb, her eyes searching out Sam's. "It'll be okay. There's nothing you can do at this point to help them. She's in good hands at the hospital. The doctors and nurses are great. You've given her a second chance and I'm sure she'll fight hard to keep it."

"I think so too." Sam sopped up some of the sauce on her plate with a slice of multi-grain bread. "Anyway, enough about my day, how was yours? You seemed anxious to tell me something earlier."

"You sure? I don't mind talking more about what happed with you today, if it'll help."

"No, I'd rather focus on something else."

"Okay, in that case, I had a couple of weird things happen today. One was not so good, but the other was good. Which do you want to hear first?"

"I'll take the 'not so good' one first," Sam said.

"Felice Lohan stopped by the gallery today."

"What? What did she want?"

"She said she stopped by to say hello and congratulate me on the gallery, but I didn't get a good feeling about the visit. And after she left, Susan said Brian asked about Felice. He was hanging out in the gallery this morning waiting for his friend to pick him up, when Felice came in. He told Susan he thought he'd seen her that morning at Charlie's, the day Coco was taken."

"At Charlie's? What was Brian doing at Charlie's?"

"That's what I asked her. She said he's been working there a few days a week since the start of summer vacation. She thought she'd told me that already, but she hadn't."

"Well that doesn't sound good at all. If this is Felice's way of cleaning up her act, she's got a warped idea about how to go about doing it. Why would she cause trouble after what she's been through? You'd think she'd want to make up for the time she lost with her son. I mean, who knows how much longer he has," Sam said, her tone laced with concern.

"Felice told me her son's cancer is in remission. I didn't get a bad vibe from her though, and her explanation of why she stopped by seemed feasible. She's teaching a summer class at Ryerson and has a few courses scheduled for the fall. One of her students told her about my gallery. I'm glad the word's getting out about the place," Halie said.

"I told you it would. You're work's fantastic, that's why."

"Thanks for saying so, but I think you're a tad biased—for a good reason though. It might be wise if we kept an eye on Felice. Today's visit doesn't change much in my mind, other than the fact of her being at Charlie's the day Coco was taken. It's not like she did anything to me or threatened us in any way today. In fact, she seemed like she needed a friend, which brings me to my other bit of news." The expression on Halie's face changed from concerned to that of elated.

"Is it okay if I clean up while you tell me about it?" Sam asked.

"Sure, I'll help you," Halie said. She picked up their plates and carried them to the sink. "I saw my oldest and dearest best friend, Ronni Summers, today. She came into the gallery while Felice was there. I couldn't believe it."

Sam took the plates from Halie and began washing them in the sink. "Wow, what a crazy day for you. How long has it been since you've seen her?"

"Let's see, it must be ten or twelve years now. And so you know, Ronni was the first girl I ever kissed."

"Great, just what I needed to hear," Sam said. "You could have kept that piece of information to yourself."

"Oh, stop it. We were innocent kids. It meant nothing. I'm telling you because I don't want any secrets between us. We were both experimenting at the time. I know she cared about me though, because neither one of us ratted the other out. And she easily could have. You know how kids can be at that age. More wine?"

"No, I'm fine. Thanks. So what's she doing here? Does she live here?" Sam asked.

"She's on vacation—rode in with some biker friends. She says she's still living in Kentucky, which is the last place I knew she moved to. I didn't get to talk to her for too long, but she also told me she'd lost her job a couple months ago and hasn't been able to find anything since."

"What did she do for a living before she got laid off?" Sam asked.

"She's an auto mechanic."

"Too bad she doesn't live around here then. Last week when I brought the car in for an oil change, Jimmy said he'd just lost a good mechanic. The guy moved to New Orleans where his wife's family lives. She couldn't stand the cold winters."

"Having survived one winter here myself, I can empathize with her," Halie said, "and I'm used to cold weather. On the other hand, winter is beautiful in other ways too."

"I agree. Jimmy said he's having a hard time finding a descent replacement, which is too bad. Is she planning on staying in the area for a while?"

"I don't know. I only know she said she'd be here for at least a week. I'd like to invite her for dinner one night, if it's okay with you," Halie said.

"Of course it's okay with me. She probably has a few hidden stories she can spill about the two of you growing up. That payback to your Sammy comment and all the stories mom told you about me might be coming sooner than I thought."

"Oh, knock it off," Halie said. "I can assure you, you won't dig up anything juicy on me."

"I'm not so sure about that," Sam said. "The innocent appearing ones are the ones to watch out for." Sam dried her hands on the kitchen towel. "Why don't you see if she can come over on Saturday?"

"Saturday would be perfect. I didn't realize how much I missed having my friends around until I saw her again. We were so close. It's a shame. How many special people do you meet in a lifetime?"

"Not many."

"No, I'd think not. I wish she lived closer. After visiting with Mom and Matt and the kids, it made me miss my family too. I wish they lived closer as well."

"I know. I love it here, but the hardest thing is being away from family. Thank God we have April and Corrine though."

"Yes," Halie said in a pensive manner, "although, no matter how nice they are to me and how much I like them, they still feel more to me like your friends than mine. Oh, well," she said, "that may change in time. It would be nice to have an old friend close that I could reminisce with though, over times when we were little."

"Why don't you try and convince Ronni to stay then? She doesn't have a job binding her at this point. I don't know about her living arrangements or other ties, but you could always ask."

"I could, couldn't I?" Halie said. The furrows above her brow disappeared.

"I think I'll draw a hot bath tonight? Do you want to join me?" Sam said.

"I don't know — maybe — okay, yeah, though I am kind of beat." Halie added the last comment so Sam wouldn't misinterpret her intentions and lead to more than she was willing to give that evening.

"It's only a bath," Sam said. She lowered her head and meandered out of the kitchen.

Chapter Ten

SAM WAITED SEVERAL minutes in the police station before she was allowed into Sheriff John Hastings office. She was too anxious to sit, so she paced in an oval pattern in the lobby until she was escorted in.

Sheriff Hastings stood when Sam entered his office and extended his hand. "Ranger Tyler, it's good to see you again. It's been a while." Hastings was a tall man at six-foot-three and weighed a lean hundred and seventy-five pounds. He was nearing retirement, but projected the energy of a recruit.

Sam shook his hand. "Thanks for seeing me without an appointment."

Hastings motioned Sam to sit, then settled behind his desk. "Anytime, you know that. Luckily it's been a slow week so far. Are you here to get an update on our progress concerning your home vandal and the tire slashing?"

"No, but if you have any information on that front, I'd gladly listen."

"Unfortunately, I don't. We've had a couple of break-ins since then, which are a bit puzzling and unusual. You've probably read about them in the paper."

"I have," Sam said. "The thieves are going in through the roofs and stealing money and jewelry. It doesn't appear there's any connection with what happened to us."

"I agree. They're in and out. They don't leave any notes. In your case, we haven't uncovered any clues of significant value other than the statement Mr. Pipp provided regarding your partner's tire slashing incident, and from the information given, it's likely the vandalism to your home and the tire slashing were two separate incidents."

"Do you find his statement credible?"

"We do. There's no evidence to suggest otherwise. The problem is, unless we're lucky enough to catch these people in the act, or find witnesses who can provide enough information with which to identify them, or they become careless, we may never know who did this."

"I understand, but I was hoping that wouldn't be the case, because whoever's doing this to us has done a number on Halie's emotions. Her whole demeanor's changed. I know you've got plenty of other things on your plate, but if your guys wouldn't mind keeping an extra eye out once in a while, I'd appreciate it," Sam said.

"Don't worry, we definitely will. We haven't let this go yet."

"Great, thanks." Sam wasn't happy he ended his sentence with 'yet', but under the circumstances, she was glad the police force remained engaged. Redirecting the conversation she said, "The main reason I stopped by is that yesterday a woman was attacked by a mountain lion on Rendezvous Mountain. I had to shoot the animal. He was severely emaciated, and when I went over to inspect him, I noticed he wore a thin collar and this tag." She handed the small metal tag to Hastings. "The tag indicates this was someone's pet, or possession, but there's no address. Any idea what the symbol on the one side might represent?"

Sheriff Hastings studied the object in his hands. "I'll be damned. It couldn't be."

"Couldn't be what?"

"There's a guy who owns Diamond Hilt Antique Dealers on Shunkerton Rd. This same symbol is on the sign at the end of his driveway. The place has a fancy name, but it's a beat up old farmhouse and barn with tons of junk inside and out. The reason I know about him is I have the misfortune of being married to a woman who loves antiques. And I've been there too, but I've never seen any wild animals on the property, so I doubt he would have been able to hide one there without my noticing it."

"Doesn't mean he couldn't hide one though, does it?"

The sheriff paused. "No, it doesn't. The more I think about it, I wouldn't put it past him either. The guy's been in trouble before. We held him here a couple of nights, on separate instances, for drunken disorderliness and he's been in for fighting and other misdemeanors. I'm surprised the business makes him enough money to survive on, to be quite honest, or that he even has customers—he's got a crappy attitude if you ask me. But then again, my wife still shops there and drags me along, so who knows."

"Maybe the business doesn't make enough money for him to live off of," Sam suggested. "I imagine owning an animal that size would be quite an expense. Maybe he let the mountain lion go because he couldn't afford to keep it."

"Maybe." The sheriff paused again, pushed aside a few papers on his desk, and stood. "All right, you win. Why don't we take a ride over there and see what Mr. Hilt has to say."

HALF AN HOUR later, Sam and Sheriff Hastings were headed down the narrow, bumpy dirt road that led to Diamond Hilt Antique Dealers. With no other cars around, they parked closest to the entrance.

Sam thought Hastings gave a fairly good description of the property, though she couldn't imagine why anyone would buy anything there. Diamond Hilt Antiques struck her as nothing more than a junk yard of rusted and unwanted things. She never saw such a mix of odd items: old bicycles, metal signs, gas pumps, tools, fans, bathtubs, piping, fishing poles, anything and everything. Blue tarps covered several more items and structures farther into the backyard.

They walked up three stairs and onto the wraparound porch before they entered the store. The inside of the store was well kept and items were arranged without appearing overcrowded. The lighting was dim, but a pleasant musk and potpourri of varied spices filled the air.

Joseph Hilt brandished what Sam interpreted as a glint of worry when he initially approached them and then it appeared to her as if he relaxed. His black hair was gray on the edges, but remained darker than his beard. He stood about six-foot, thin build and had small eyes. Sam couldn't make out their color in the dim light. He was dressed neatly, wearing jeans and a gray flannel shirt. He reached out his hand to Hastings. "Sheriff Hastings. I almost didn't recognize you in uniform. Where's the misses, and who's your friend?"

"I'm here on official business, Joe. This is Park Ranger Samantha Tyler. We'd like to ask you a few questions specifically concerning this tag." Hastings held his hand open with the tag visible, and flipped it over. "This belongs to you?"

Joseph Hilt remained quiet at first, as if deciding what to say. "It looks like the tag from my old boxer, Titan. Where'd you find it?"

"Ranger Tyler found it. You say it belonged to your boxer?" Hastings didn't hide the skepticism in his voice.

Again Joseph Hilt paused, this time a few seconds longer, eyeing Hastings and Sam as if looking for clues. "That's right. I'd lost Titan about a year ago. Assumed he was dead. He ran off and didn't come back. Did you find him?"

"This tag was found around the neck of a sixty pound mountain lion in Grand Teton National Park Mr. Hilt," Sam said, no longer able to remain silent. "That mountain lion attacked a woman and nearly killed her. I don't suppose you were aware of that?"

"No, I wasn't. How could I be? I don't appreciate your insinuations. I don't know anything about a mountain lion."

Hastings calmed the situation. "Sorry about that Joe, but I'm sure you can understand the ranger's concern. Mind if we check around outside?"

"I do mind. Do you have a warrant?"

"I don't, but then I didn't think I needed one. Do I need one? Because if I do, I can come back in an hour or so with one, but then I'll have a few of my deputies with me."

Joseph Hilt huffed. "No, go ahead. Your ranger friend rubbed me the wrong way is all."

"I understand. We'll be quick." Hastings placed the tag in his pocket. He and Sam walked through the yard toward the shed in the back.

"Sorry about that," Sam said, "but I know this guy is lying."

"Don't worry about it. Seems to me he is too. Let's keep looking before he changes his mind."

Sam lifted several of the blue tarps, only to discover more garbage underneath. After finding nothing in the shed, Sam was beginning to think they'd hit a dead end until she saw a small foot path behind the shed leading into the woods. She nodded in Hasting's direction.

Fifty yards in they came upon several small rectangular cages with green tarps over top and nothing beneath them but dirt and mounds of trodden down feces. Two of the cages held mountain goats, one was empty, its gate swung open, and the last held a famished looking female mountain lion. Sam bent over and almost threw up. The smell was atrocious. When her dry gagging stopped, she moved closer to the cages. The female lion growled, her large incisors visible, and swiped her paw in Sam's direction.

"I don't blame you girl," Sam said. "We're going to get you out of here, I promise." She inspected the empty cage and found a broken, rusted lock clinging to the gate. She addressed Hastings. "Can you arrest him for violation of the Wyoming exotic animal law?"

"I can and I will. Title 23, Chapter 1, Article 1 prohibits the ownership of big or trophy game. On top of that, he'll be charged with a felony of cruelty to animals, which would carry an additional fine up to $5,000 and or imprisonment up to two years. If he can't pay the money, which might be a good bet, he'll be looking at more time, and that's his best scenario. If the woman you rescued ends up – "

"Please, don't say it. I'm relieved something positive will come out of this whole ordeal. Let's not jinx it." Sam couldn't feel much relief after finding the animals and knowing their owner would likely end up in jail. Her only solace was the knowledge these wild animals would now get relocated and be given the chance to live better lives from this point forward. Once the realization set in, the need to visit Hillary Coleman seized her.

FRIDAY ON HER way home from work, Sam headed to St. John's Medical Center. The last time she'd been in the hospital was a little over a year ago, praying Halie would regain consciousness after the helicopter crash on Pinebluff Mountain. Goosebumps ran along Sam's spine and over her arms as she recalled those frightful days. She never wanted to come that close to losing someone close to her again. Although she knew Hillary Coleman would likely be in no condition to talk to her yet, she was certain her partner would be by her side, and she very much wanted to speak with her.

Sam walked down the sterile hallway past a transport worker rolling an empty bed. When she reached Hillary's room, she peered inside and saw Melanie near the side of her partner. She looked exhausted. Her partner's eyes were shut and her face was bruised, her scalp and neck heavily bandaged. Sam backed away. Uncertain what to do, she headed to the cafeteria, returning with two hot cups of coffee in her hand. Sam tapped the bottom of the door frame lightly with her boot. Melanie lifted her head and waved Sam into the room.

"Ranger Tyler, it's good to see you again," she whispered.

Sam handed Melanie a coffee. "It's good to see you too."

"Thanks, I could use this."

Standing next to the hospital bed, Sam noted Hillary Coleman's hands were bandaged too and several IV drips hung off a rack near her bed that fed into her arm. Monitors beeped from behind her. Sam pried the flap back on her cup and took a sip. "How's she doing?"

Melanie glanced at Hillary. "She's doing quite well, all things considered. As soon as we got here on Wednesday, they rushed her into surgery to fix her scalp and neck injuries. She was in critical condition until the following day when they upgraded her to serious. This morning they said her condition's fair."

"That's fantastic," Sam said. "I'd never have thought she'd have recovered this fast after what I saw the other day."

Hillary stirred and wiggled her feet, then opened her eyes, focusing intently on Sam. "You both don't need to whisper. I'm awake," she said, a smile etching its way across her face. Then to Sam she said, "You're Ranger Tyler?"

"I am," Sam said. She peeked at Melanie with a confused expression.

"Amazing, isn't it?" Melanie said. "I thank the good Lord every day for saving her life and for sending you to us that day."

"I did nothing, the two of you are the amazing ones," Sam said. She faced Hillary. "I don't remember when I've seen such fearless bravery."

"I saw you the other day, before I passed out, but my vision was blurred. Thanks for what you did," Hillary managed, as her eyes welled up. She wiped them with the back of one of her bandaged hands. "It's unbelievable to me the power that animal possessed. I grabbed onto anything I could when he dragged me away, but nothing stopped him. I even managed to whack him on the side of the head with a rock several times, feeling the jolt and pain of him tear into my own neck at the same time, but nothing. Seconds before I saw you I remember thinking to myself, I'm going to die."

"But you didn't die," Sam said.

"No, I didn't."

"I believe it's your tenacity that kept you alive. That and your partner's extraordinary effort to slow the lion down."

Hillary concurred. Eyes remaining intent on Sam, she said, "Yes, she's something else my Melanie. I hit the lottery when I met her I did." After a few moments of silence, Hillary added, "This may be a long shot, but by any chance, is your mother June Tyler?"

Sam donned a puzzled expression. "Yes, her name's June Tyler — do you know her?"

"I think I might. You look like her and she's told me she has a daughter who's a park ranger out west, so I thought it might be you. She lives in South Jersey, along the shore?"

"She does. I don't believe it. It really is a small world. How do you know her?"

"I'm her oncologist. Your mom's a sweet and strong woman. How's she been doing? I think she's scheduled for a follow-up soon. I hope I'll be better by then."

Sam tried to hide the shock she felt as a thousand questions, coupled with fear, ripped through her brain and constricted her breathing. Why didn't she know any of this? Her oncologist? Her mom has cancer? What type of cancer? How bad is it? How could she have not known? Sam needed to pull it together, and quick, if she wanted to find out more. She forced words from her mouth. "She's doing well. I was just there visiting and you'd never know anything was wrong with her unless she told you."

"That's fantastic. Your mom is one brave and lucky lady. As I'm sure you know, medically, she's fine now. Her breast cancer appears to be in full remission." Hillary paused again, as if to muster more strength. "We found the tumor early enough and she handled the radiation well. One or two more visits and we'll be certain her worries are over. I'm more concerned about how she's handling this mentally."

Relief filled every pore of Sam's being when she heard the cancer was in remission. "No need to worry, she's fine — honest. Talking with her, you wouldn't know anything was amiss at all." Sam realized her statement was no lie. "She's quite amazing," she added. Suddenly feeling spent, and wanting only to go home, Sam pulled Titan's animal tag from her pocket and handed it to Melanie. "There's something I wanted you to see."

"What's this?" Melanie flipped the small object over in her hand.

"One of the reasons I stopped by today was to let you know that the attack Hillary suffered was extremely rare, and that this particular animal suffered a great deal at the hands of a heartless owner, until it escaped. It was starving and likely mistook you're partner for a small animal when she bent over. This man obtained and kept the mountain lion illegally. I want you to know he'll almost certainly see jail time. At least two years."

Melanie handed the tag back to Sam. "I don't understand. Why would anyone want to keep a wild animal like that? They've got to be crazy."

"Money was the probable reason. It often is. He also owned a female mountain lion. She was emaciated as well. He said he planned to breed them and sell the pups, but apparently the female wasn't having any of it. If you saw the conditions they were living in, you'd understand why she'd not mated. She'll be taken away and protected now though."

"I'm glad," Hillary said. "Thank you for telling us this. It makes a big difference in the way we're going to feel toward that animal and others like it. Thank God the worst is over for everyone."

Sam nodded in agreement. Her only thought now was to go home, tell Halie about her mom, and hear her mom's voice.

THE PHONE RANG three times before being answered. Sam paced until she heard her mom's voice. "Hi, Mom, it's me," Sam said.

"Hi, honey, this is a nice surprise," June said. "What's up?"

"Not much. I'm calling for two reasons. Well, three actually. One was to tell you that we miss you a lot, the second was to ask you about what you forgot to tell us, and the third is that I wanted to hear your voice." Sam petted Jake on the head. Her pacing roused him from his place of near slumber and brought him to her side, where he sat and leaned into her leg.

"That's sweet, honey. I miss you both a whole lot sweetie, and I'm thrilled you called, but I don't know what you mean about 'what I forgot to tell you.'"

"I know you're seeing Hillary Coleman."

A couple of seconds of silence followed Sam's statement before her mom replied, "How did you know?"

"It's a long story," Sam said, and after relaying it to her mom she ended with, "Why didn't you tell me you were diagnosed with breast cancer? Don't you think that's something I would have wanted to know?"

"You have enough on your mind. I didn't want to burden you with my problems too."

"But that's the whole point. I could've been there for you. Talking about it might have made it easier on you. I can't imagine how you must have felt. I always want to know what's going on with you, Mom, good or bad. You'd want to know if I was sick or hurt, wouldn't you?"

"Well of course I would, but I'm your mom. That's different."

"No, it's not different. I'm your daughter. Please promise me you won't hide anything from me again. I don't want to have to wonder about how you really are. That's more worry than not knowing."

Silence once again followed for several seconds before June spoke. "I never thought of it that way. I didn't want to burden you with my troubles, but you're right. I should have told you. I will from now on, I promise."

Sam exhaled a sigh of relief. "Thanks, Mom."

"Sometimes I forget you're all grown up. I experienced a rough few months—the radiation treatments were no picnic—but I made it through, thanks in large part to Maggie, God bless her caring sole. My illness brought us a lot closer and it's made me value every day so much more. In a strange way, the cancer was a blessing as well as a curse. Thankfully I'm fine now and I feel great. I have a follow-up visit with

Doctor Coleman next month, assuming she's well enough to see me, and as soon as I get back from it I promise I'll call you and fill you in."

"Sounds good."

"How are you guys doing otherwise? How's Halie managing with the gallery on top of all the other nonsense that's been going on?"

"She's doing fine with the gallery, but otherwise not great. Not knowing who our harasser is, is taking its toll on her. I wish I could make her uneasiness go away. I don't like feeling helpless."

"No one does. The police haven't come up with any leads yet?"

"No, nothing." Since Jake fell asleep near her feet, Sam moved away from him and began pacing once again. "I stopped by the sheriff's office yesterday and they don't know more now than they did the day Coco was taken and our house was vandalized. He promised to stay vigilant, so I'm thankful for that. But I'm at a loss on how to lessen the worry for Halie. I wish I could take it from her, but I can't. It kills me to see her hurting, and I miss the old her."

"I think she probably needs reassurance that you're there for her. Time will take care of the rest, unless of course they catch the nut or nuts that are harassing you guys first. Try to stay upbeat though. Eventually they'll either tire of what they're doing, or they'll be caught, of that I'm certain."

"Thanks Mom, I know you're right, I just wish the whole ordeal was over with already. Anyway, I'm sending you a big hug over the phone and one from Halie too. Please say 'hi' to Maggie for us. I love you Mom."

"I love you too honey, and I'm so glad I have you."

Sam choked up on the phone. "I'm glad I've got you too Mom."

RONNI ARRIVED ON time Saturday evening. She stood in the foyer of Sam and Halie's house wearing the same black leather jacket, blue jeans, and the black leather Harley Davidson boots Halie saw her wear at the gallery a few days prior. Only the T-shirt she wore changed. The black Sturgis bike rally shirt with white lettering was replaced by an olive green Yellowstone National Park T-shirt.

"Hey you nut," Halie said as she gave Ronni a baby sized bear hug.

"Hey yourself," Ronni replied, enveloping her friend with her strong arms.

"I can't wait for you to meet Sam. I keep chewing her ear off about you."

"That can't be good. You don't want her getting the wrong impression of me before she's had a chance to meet me." Ronni was about to hand Halie a bottle of red wine just as Jake came bounding toward her through the living room.

"Slow down, Jake," Sam yelled from behind, trying to catch him.

"Whoa," Ronni said, setting the bottle of red wine on the foyer table, with seconds to spare before Jake was on her. He pushed himself in front of Halie, nearly knocking her over, and rammed into Ronni's legs, causing her to retreat a few steps. "Well here's a friendly fella," Ronni added as she reached down and let him sniff her hand.

"Jake!" Sam reprimanded.

"It's okay, he's fine," Ronni said. She pet him brusquely behind his ears.

"Oh, he'll love you forever, if you keep that up," Halie said.

"You be a good boy, Jake, and sit nice," Sam commanded.

Jake sat, thumping his tail, eyes glued to Ronni.

"Impressive," Ronni said.

"He's a catch," Sam said. "You must be Ronni." Sam extended her hand. "It's a pleasure to meet you."

"Same here," Ronni said.

"Any trouble finding us?"

"No, not at all, and the ride was wonderful. I took the highway to Gros Verde River Road like Halie said. The scenery was fantastic. The river on the one side and the wide open grass plains on the other, with the mountain backdrop — it's stunning around here. You're both very lucky."

"We are," Sam said. "Looks like Jake took an immediate liking to you."

"When I saw him charge in here, I wasn't sure at first, but since his tail was wagging, I figured he was okay," Ronni said. "When I was a kid I grew up with a St. Bernard —"

"Oh yeah, I remember him," Halie exclaimed. "What was his name...Chauncey, right?"

Ronni smiled. "Yup. Tough monster too. I used to ride him like a horse. He loved it though."

"Sounds like fun. Let me take your jacket," Sam said.

After handing Sam her jacket, Ronni reached for the wine bottle and gave it to Halie. "For you guys."

"Thanks, but you didn't have to bring anything," Halie said. She waited until Sam hung up Ronni's jacket, then handed her the wine. "How about a quick tour?" she said to Ronni.

"Sure, I'd love it." Ronni petted Jake as he made his way toward her side again. This time he approached in a much calmer manner.

Halie ended the house tour in the kitchen at the same time Sam pulled the vegetable lasagna out of the oven.

"This house is amazing," Ronni said. "I love the way the layout flows and how you guys decorated. It's big, but yet feels so quaint and cozy."

Sam placed the dinner dishes on the kitchen table. "Thanks. I'm glad you think so. We both did a lot of work on it, though most of the decorating is Halie's doing."

"I do what I can. I thought we could eat in the dining room today,"

Halie said.

Before Sam could answer, Ronni interjected, "There's no need. I'm fine with eating in the kitchen. In fact, I prefer it. Look at me. I'm hardly dining room material."

"You're being silly," Halie said, "There's nothing wrong with the way you look. But if you prefer the kitchen, then the kitchen's where we'll stay. We like it better in here too, truthfully."

"Absolutely," Ronni reassured them.

Sam was glad to be eating in the kitchen. She gave the salad bowl to Ronni to start with, then plated the lasagna. "Halie told me you're living in Kentucky. Do you like it there?"

"It's okay. My dad's there, but Massachusetts still feels more like home to me," Ronni said. She handed the salad bowl to Halie.

Sam continued her questioning. "Why'd your parents move? Halie said she was devastated when your family left."

"Believe me, so was I. My dad worked for a large auto parts manufacturer. They wanted him to manage their facility in Bowling Green. The job meant more money, so we followed the money trail. My mom worked in retail at the time. She was able to get a comparable job at the local Westmart. I don't think my dad ever asked her if she wanted to move though. I think he decided we were moving, and that was that. In hindsight, that was probably not such a good thing."

Halie broke off a piece of the lasagna with her fork. She noticed Ronni's expression turn solemn and sensed her friend was hiding something. "I'm sure it wasn't easy for her either."

Ronni bit into the lasagna. "Did you make this Sam? It's fantastic. I'm a meat and potatoes kind of gal myself, but this beats any meat lasagna I've ever made or eaten."

Halie caught the change in subject, which confirmed the topic of Ronni's mom was sensitive to her, only she didn't know why. She wasn't going to pry either. If Ronni wanted to tell her, she'd do so in her own time.

"Thanks," Sam said. "That's quite a compliment. Halie helped me tweak the recipe, but yeah, I made it."

"I gotta know," Halie said, "How the heck did you ever find me?"

"By chance."

"By chance?" Halie said. "How do you find someone halfway on the other side of the country by chance?"

"You're going to find this hard to believe, because I can hardly believe it myself, but it's true. About a year ago, a few of my biker friends from a local women's motorcycling group and I decided to plan a road trip to Sturgis, South Dakota, for the annual biker rally in August. None of us had ever been, though we'd wanted to go for years, but we always found one excuse or another, mostly work related and not being able to get the time off, or having squandered the time off on something else. Once we committed to going, the wait was exciting. We planned our route there and all the stuff we wanted to make sure we'd do when we got there. We found this website from a group that advertised Sturgis bike rally tours. One of the tours took bikers through Yellowstone and Grand Teton before the rally, which we thought would be great, but we wanted to go after the rally. The rally was our main reason for going. The Yellowstone-Grand Teton tour we thought would be a nice side attraction for the ride home. So we went on our own, after the rally ended, using almost the same route they'd mapped out."

"That was smart," Sam said.

"Thanks, I thought so. Anyway, we headed into Wyoming toward Yellowstone. At one of the diners we stopped in, I saw an article about the Jackson Hole Fall Arts Festival. The article displayed a photo of you, Halie, and underneath were a few lines about your photo gallery's grand opening in Jackson. I couldn't believe it. Naturally, I had to stop by. The route we'd originally planned took us through Jackson anyway. We rode in from West Yellowstone through Ashton, Idaho and the Targhee National Forest. Then it was merely a matter of stopping by and hoping you were here. It had to be fate that brought us together."

"I'm a strong believer in fate," Sam said. "Meeting Halie when I did was definitely fate, and the two of us being together today has everything to do with fate. We'll have to tell you more about that later, if you're interested."

"Anything to do with catching up on what's been going on with this one," she signaled with her thumb pointed in Halie's direction, "I'm interested in for sure."

"Then we'll tackle that after dessert. So your trip sounded incredible. How many miles was it from where you live to Sturgis?" Sam asked.

"The trip *was* amazing, more than I'd hoped for. From Bowling Green to Sturgis was close to thirteen hundred miles. We covered a few hundred miles a day, which was tiring, but there's nothing like seeing the country on the open road, and feeling the wind push against you. Scraping the bugs off you is something else, but who cares at that point, right?"

"That's true," Halie said. "I owned a motorcycle for a few years too, when I lived in Boston, but I haven't ridden in a while. I'd love to ride again."

"I could take you after dinner if you like," Ronni said. She snuck a look in Sam's direction.

"Fine with me," Sam said, "as long as you've got another helmet."

"I always carry a back-up," Ronni said, then winked. "You never know when you might need one."

"Honestly," Halie huffed. "So finish telling us about the ride, before you get too sidetracked."

Ronni chuckled. "The timing of the trip panned out perfect for me. I don't know if Halie told you or not, Sam, but I lost my job a couple of months ago."

"Yeah, Halie mentioned that. I'm sorry."

"It's the economy. Worst part is, I lost my apartment because the landlord didn't want to renew the lease. Not because I couldn't pay, but because he *thought* I was too high of a payment risk without a job. Nice guy, huh?" Ronni finished her last piece of bread and washed it down with a sip of water.

"No. Not very. We didn't know about the apartment. What are your plans now?" Sam asked.

"Tuesday I was planning on heading back with my group. I'll be living with my dad for a while until I can get back on my feet. It's a shock to the system to have to go backwards like that and rely on your parents again. They should be the one's knowing they can rely on me now, if they needed to."

"I know this is totally out of the blue," Halie said, "but would you ever consider moving around here? I know I'd be thrilled. Sam said the guy at our local garage is looking for an auto mechanic."

"I don't know," Ronni said. "I mean it would be great having a job again and being close to you guys, but so much would be up in the air."

"He's a great guy, and very open minded. I could take you over there on Monday and introduce you to him, if you're any good and if you're interested," Sam said.

"My dad says I'm one of the best, but I'm sure he's biased. The offer sounds tempting, but if it did work out, where would I live? I'm staying at a cheap motel in Jackson for this trip—splitting it three ways—two rooms with three of us to a room, but after Tuesday, it'll just be me. I'd be okay for a while, but not too long on my own."

"We can ask our friend Corrine if she knows of anything decent and reasonable. She's a realtor in the area. And if not, I'm sure we could work something out until you found a place of your own," Sam said as she cleared the dishes off the kitchen table.

"I don't know," Ronni said. "That's nice of you, but I'm not sure if it's a good idea. It would be a big move I'm not sure I'm ready to make."

"Well, think about it. Maybe Tommy's already filled the position anyway and all this talk's for nothing. Either way, call us sometime tomorrow or latest by six-thirty Monday morning before I head into work, so I know if I should call him or not."

BY THE TIME Ronni left Sam and Halie's home in Kelly, rain was falling. Sam offered to drive Ronni to the motel and pick her up the next day to get her bike, but Ronni declined. She said she'd ridden plenty of times in the rain, but appreciated the offer. Then she slipped on her rain gear and headed out. She thought to herself that she'd have to ask Halie for the vegetable lasagna recipe the next time they spoke, as she was certain it contained a secret ingredient.

Ronni slowed her speed when she noticed the faint hue of orange blinking lights in the distance. As she neared a car, her headlight illuminated a young woman wearing a waist length raincoat over her head and waving a flashlight. She was standing by the front end of her car. Ronni wanted nothing more at that point than to crawl into her warm motel room bed and rest her tired head for the evening, but her conscience couldn't leave the woman alone. It wasn't safe for either of them to be out there together, but certainly less safe for one woman alone. Ronni pulled up behind the woman's car, leaving her bike running for light, and put on her flashers.

She strode to the front of the car. A slender woman stood shivering in the rain, her eyes squinting to look at Ronni.

"Hi. What happened here?" Ronni asked.

"I don't know. I hit a pot hole and the car died on me. I tried starting it, but it won't turn over," the woman said, moving closer to Ronni. She stood barely chest height to Ronni.

Ronni found the woman's voice tender and pleasing. "You didn't run out of gas, did you?"

The woman shot her a glare that clearly indicated a lack of gas was not the issue. "Sorry. I had to ask. Go ahead back in the car and pop the hood for me, but don't do anything else until I say so, okay?"

Ronni lifted the hood and secured it in place before she searched underneath. She checked all the electrical connections and hoses. Everything felt tight and secure. She peeked out from behind the hood and looked into the car. The interior light illuminated the woman's face enough for Ronni to see her pale, but angelic natural complexion and high cheekbones. Sensing internal warmth taking her over, she quickly popped her head back behind the hood, surprised by the reaction she felt. Seconds later, she checked the terminals on the battery, and found the negative terminal loose. She headed to the open car door. Passing by, she first noticed the large, brown, somewhat puffed and reddened puppy dog eyes of the woman, as if she'd been crying.

"Are you okay?" Ronni asked. Her heart raced, but she wasn't certain why. She didn't even know this woman, yet she felt some sort of closeness to her.

"I'm tired, but I'll be okay. Thanks for asking though."

"If there's anything I can do—"

"I appreciate it, I do, but there's nothing—other than the car."

"Sure," Ronni said, refocusing on the task at hand. "Do you have a tool box in the trunk?"

"I do, but I'm not sure what's in it," the woman said. She pushed the trunk release. "It seems like everything always goes wrong at the same time. It might be better if it came in smaller chunks."

Ronni realized the woman was trying to make her feel better by not making it seem as though she were blowing her off. "I hear you," Ronni said. "Unfortunately, that's the way life is sometimes, believe me, I know." Ronni headed to the rear of the car and opened the trunk. She pulled out a pack of cigarettes from under her rain slicker and from the front pocket of her leather jacket. She placed the end of the cigarette in her mouth, flicked on the lighter, and drew a deep breath. Several puffs later, she lifted the toolbox out of the trunk. When she neared the driver side of the car, she took the cigarette from her mouth and dropped it on the road. When she reached the front of the car and turned, she saw the woman lean out of the car and pick up her cigarette butt. Ronni thought the action strange. She took out a wrench and tightened the loose connection. "Okay. Try the key now," she yelled.

The car started up instantly. Ronni closed the hood. "That should do it," she said. She wiped the water from her face and eyes. "You had a loose connection on the battery, but I think this battery's on its way out. If I were you, I'd get a new one the first chance you get."

"Thanks so much for stopping and fixing the car. My name's Cali Brooks, by the way," she said, extending her hand.

Ronni took her hand and shook it. "I'm Ronni—Ronni Summers, and you're very welcome." For some strange reason, Ronni didn't feel like letting Cali's hand go. After an awkward silence, she finally released the tender, soft hand from her hold. When she realized she was still holding the toolbox in her other hand, her face flushed. "I'll go ahead and pop this in your trunk. Take care," she said. Ronni strode away and heaved the box into its resting place. She shut the trunk, then wiped the seat of her motorcycle dry and rode off. Take care? What kind of an exit is take care? You're losing it Ronni.

That night, Ronni lay awake listening to the raindrops fall on the motel roof. As tired as she was, she thought about Sam's offer to get her a job, about possibly restarting her life again, about leaving her dad and being farther away from her mom, and about Cali. She didn't want to move farther from her parents, but she grinned as she recalled Cali picking up her cigarette butt. Ronni figured she must either be a neat freak or one of those environmental types. No one had ever picked up a cigarette butt off the ground from her before. Then she thought, well, she probably shouldn't have thrown it there to begin with. Then she remembered Cali's captivating brown eyes and wondered why they looked so sad. She recalled the heated sensation and electrical charge that coursed through her body when their hands met, and she was certain her heart sped up from the encounter. She had trouble disengaging her eyes from Cali's and remembered not understanding why the draw to her was so intense. The remainder of the night Ronni tossed and turned in her sleep, visions of the charming Cali Brooks floating in and out of her dreams.

HALIE CALLED SAM at the office on Monday afternoon. "How'd

it go today with Ronni? Did you hear anything yet? I couldn't wait until tonight to find out."

"Tommy said he loved her. Do you have a minute?" Sam asked.

"Sure, go ahead."

"I jotted down some notes, because I knew you'd ask and want details. Tommy said he gave her a late model suburban to work on that didn't start most of the time and when it did, it didn't have any power and wouldn't stay running for very long. He said she checked under the hood first, then tried starting it. It sputtered a few times but wouldn't start. She put a fuel pressure gauge on the fuel rail, which he said is what he would have done. He's guessing she saw the pressure was too low, because she immediately put it on the lift, dropped the fuel tank, replaced the fuel pump assembly, and installed a new fuel filter. Three hours later, when she lowered the vehicle and flipped the key, it fired up like brand-new. He was impressed and excited. Not only did he pay her for the three hours she worked in cash, he offered her the job right there."

"Are you kidding? That's so great," Halie exclaimed. She fidgeted with the phone cord on her desk. "Did she take it?"

"She did and he wants her to start tomorrow."

"That's fantastic! I'll call her tonight and congratulate her," Halie said. "That would be wonderful if she stays. I know we have April and Corrine, and I love those guys, but they're more your friends than mine, or at least they were your friends first. Now I'll have my best friend here too. If she does end up staying, she better think about getting herself a car soon, with winter not far around the corner."

"I know. I mentioned that to her too. She said she'll start looking as soon as she finds a place and settles in."

APRIL STOOD IN front of the stable doors, arms crossed, a bridle hanging over her shoulder, and leather gloves clasped in her hand. "What's been going on with you lately?" she asked Cali. "This is the third time you've been late in almost as many days. Keep it up and I'll be forced to hire someone more reliable to replace you. The least you could do is call. I hope you've got a darn good explanation," April continued on without taking a breath, before she realized Cali was crying.

"I'm sorry," Cali said between sobs. "I haven't been sleeping well. I've been spending a lot of time at the hospital. My mom was attacked last week by a mountain lion. She's getting better, but she still looks awful."

"Jesus. Hillary Coleman is your mom?" April asked. "Her story's been all over the papers. I didn't realize—her last name—"

"Coleman's her maiden name. She took it back after her and my dad broke up."

"I'm sorry I barked at you."

"I deserved it. It's my own fault. I should have called and told you what happened. It's not only that though. Everything seems to be falling apart in front of me. I don't know what to do. Soon I won't have anywhere to live. I haven't even had time to search for a place after what happened with my mom. I'm tired. I can't think straight."

"Take it easy," April said. "You have to tackle one thing at a time. I won't let you end up on the street. If it comes to that, you can stay with Corrine and me. We've got an extra room."

"I couldn't do that. I won't impose like that."

"It wouldn't be an imposition. In fact, you'd be helping us out. We could use the extra cash. You could rent it out cheap and stay however long you wanted. I'll even help you move your stuff. It doesn't have to be forever, but long enough until things settle down. In the meantime, you've got some time off coming to you. Why don't you take a few more days and spend it with your mom?"

"My moms, actually," Cali said with a wink. "My mom's partner's here, too. We're taking turns staying with her, but they're going to have to go home soon – their work – they were visiting..."

"I understand. Go on home, get some rest, and think about what I said."

"I will. Thanks."

Chapter Eleven

HALIE STOOD NEAR the register and watched April and Corrine stroll into the gallery. It was the week before the Fall Arts Festival. She was deciding which photographs to display at the festival and which to leave in the gallery. She'd given Susan the day off to spend with her sons, since they'd soon be more than busy with the store once the festival kicked off. Susan was still having a difficult time with Brian, and she mentioned to Halie that she thought a day at the car show and auction in Teton Village would help cheer her son up and alleviate some of the anger he was carrying around inside. Halie agreed.

"Hey there you two," Halie said to April and Corrine as they approached. "It's good to see you guys." She walked around the counter and gave them each a big welcoming hug. "What brings you by today?"

"We wanted to stop by and say hello and also search for a new picture to hang in our living room. I'm tired of the one that's been in there forever. I never liked it that much anyway," Corrine said.

"Yeah, we're finally off this week and plan on spending some quality time together, some of which entails shopping." April rolled her eyes before glancing at her partner.

"Sounds like you love shopping as much as Sam does," Halie said. "I'm glad you stopped by. I've got quite a few newly framed photographs you might like. Did you want to say hello to Sam first?"

"Is Sam here too?" April asked.

"She is. She took the day off to tile the floor for an area I want to use as a frame shop. Then it'll be like one stop shopping here."

"She's a trouper, that one," Corrine said.

Halie walked with April and Corrine to what was once a secondary storage area.

Sam had already laid out the chalk lines and set in the first grouping of tiles at the cross section of the "T" and was working her way toward the back wall. She laid mortar for a four-tile section at a time.

"Hey busy bee, what's cooking?" April asked.

Sam spun around and smiled. "Hey you two! This is a pleasant surprise." She wiped the mortar off the trowel against the inside top of the bucket and placed the tool on the floor, on its side. She stood up slowly, stretched her legs and back. She hugged her friends, careful not to get any of the mortar left on her gloves on their clothes. "I'm glad you're both here. I was looking for a reason to take a break."

"The floor looks great so far. I love the tile you guys picked out," April said.

Sam grinned. "Halie gets the credit for that. I, on the other hand, get the pleasure of putting them in."

"That's right," Halie said, "and loving every minute of it."

"Halie's been pestering me to get this floor in. She's already got an interview lined up for a woman to run the frame shop part time. I think she set it up on purpose to rush me."

"I would do no such thing," Halie said. "I had to nab the opportunity when I could though. This woman sounds like she'd be a perfect fit. She used to work in a frame shop before the owner retired, plus, she paints, which means she's got an appreciation for the arts."

"She does sound perfect," Corrine agreed.

"I honestly didn't want to hire anyone at this point. I know Susan could handle the framing—she's had some experience in that area too, and she could use the money, but her kids are giving her a hard enough time with the hours she's working now."

"Good luck with that. Finding a balance that works for everyone can't be easy, that's for sure. We don't want to hold you up Sam. We're looking for a new picture to hang in our living room. You doing okay, otherwise?"

"Yeah, we're doing okay," Sam said. "Keeping busy."

"I can see that," April said. "You need any help?"

"Judging from Corrine's demeanor after that question, I'd have to say, no, I'm fine. I'm kidding of course. I don't need the help, but thanks for asking. So what's the matter with the picture you've got in the living room? Is Corrine tired of staring into the black eyes of that big old bison?"

Corrine answered for April. "You could say that. But mainly it's because it scares the cats."

"Cats, plural?" Sam asked.

"Yeah, plural," April began. "Well, a cat and a kitten. Corrine swerved out of the way of a stray kitten on our street last week. That move got her a flat tire and a busted rim. She ran the car off the road and onto a neighbor's junk pile. He threw metal drawers out there and all kinds of other stuff from his garage."

"Oh my," Halie said, half in jest and half in a serious tone. "I guess you were okay though, right?"

April chuckled and before Corrine could answer she said, "Oh yeah, she was fine. I wasn't too happy, but she was okay. Now we have another member added to the family, a playmate for Lula-bell. Actually, Lula-bell isn't much appreciating the active little youngster."

"That's so cute," Halie said. She drew out the word cute. "What did you guys name her?"

"Little Miss Trouble," April said. "No, I'm kidding. I named her Jinx."

"Very cute," Halie said.

"Yeah, and appropriate," April replied. "Corrine objected at first, but the name stuck. It fits her to a T. She's always getting into trouble and knocking stuff over. Have you had any more trouble at the house?"

"No, thank God," Halie said, "although my tire got slashed behind the store about a week after the gallery opening."

"Are you kidding?" April said.

"I wish I were. I feel like we're on borrowed time waiting for something else to happen."

"I can understand that," Corrine said. "I'd feel the same way. Let's hope that whoever has or had a problem with you guys has gotten over it. It's got to be difficult dealing with this. I don't know what we'd have done if it happened to us."

"The problem is, there's not much you can do unless you know who you're dealing with," Sam said. "Well, anyway, let's hope this is over. On another note, I know we still have a way to go yet, but would you guys like to come over for Thanksgiving dinner this year?"

"That sounds great," April said. "We never get together with Corrine's parents since they disapprove of our relationship, and my parents are flying out to visit my brother in Washington, DC this year, so I'm thinking we're all yours," she said.

"And happy to be it," Corrine added.

"Great. Jake will love the company," Sam said.

"Well, we better let you get back to work Sam, and we need to take a look around and see if we can find a picture we like," Corrine said.

While April and Corrine scanned the gallery, the mailman came in with a bundle of mail and handed it to Halie. Halie fingered through the stack quickly, pulling out an envelope from a Colin Mitchell, Bridgewater, New Jersey.

SAM LAY ON her back in bed with Halie, Halie's head resting on her shoulder. She stroked Halie's hair and said, "I miss Mom and Matt and the kids."

"I miss them too. I wish we lived closer. Maybe one day we will."

"Maybe. Next up will be a visit to your parents."

"If we can ever catch them at home," Halie said in a joking tone.

"If they know your coming, I'm sure they'll be home. I can't believe that semi-pro jet skier we met by Mom's was serious and actually sent you the money for that photograph."

"I know. I'd almost forgotten about him. He must have really liked it. Either that, or money is no object to him. Whoever heard of a thousand dollars for an unframed photo? That's crazy. There might be a niche here that needs filling. Maybe I can expand my business by offering action photographs similar to that one, but instead on taking pictures on the water, maybe I can take them for extreme snow skiing. You know, like the amusement parks do on their rides, when they set up those stationary cameras."

"But you just started taking lessons with April last year. Do you think you'd be good enough?"

"April said I have a feel for the sport, that I'm a born natural."

"Yeah, I remember you saying that, but extreme backcountry skiing is much different than skiing the slopes," Sam said with concern, adding "and even that can be dangerous. And then mixing in taking photographs while skiing—"

"It's only an idea. Maybe I can start out on the slopes and if I like it and it works out, I can move to backcountry. It's all talk at this point. I'm not sure I'd do it anyway, or even have the time to do it. Susan would probably kill me if I did."

"That would be a guarantee, and if she didn't I might be in line right behind her. I hardly see you as is, so seeing you less wouldn't thrill me. Speaking of which, I forgot to mention something to you about work. The chief put me in for a law enforcement refresher training course. It's at the end of next month."

"Where? Around here?"

"No. They're holding it the agency's training center in Georgia."

"Do you have to go?"

"Yeah, it's mandatory. It's only for three days. I'll leave Sunday afternoon on the thirtieth and I'd be back home on Wednesday the second around five or six o'clock in the evening."

"That's not too bad, but you'll miss Halloween."

"I know. I don't have a choice though. The government doesn't view Halloween as a holiday, so I have to go. You'll have Jake though. You can dress him up to answer the door with you when you give out goodies."

"I was planning on dressing him up this year," Halie said. "I just haven't decided on a costume for him yet."

Jake let out what sounded like a disapproving grunt.

"Make sure you take a picture of him for me, if you ever do manage to get him into an outfit. I've never subjected him to that, so I can't tell you how he's going to react."

"He loves me. He'll do it. And don't worry, I'll take plenty of pictures. What I'm not sure about yet is if I'll be giving out candy though, not without you home."

"It might be a good idea if you didn't, though based on last year's trick-or-treaters, or the lack thereof, it won't be many anyhow. Maybe you could ask Ronni to stay with you while I'm gone. Having someone else around might make you feel better."

"It's a possibility, but you're the one I want around."

THE JACKSON HOLE Fall Art's Festival was a huge success, much greater than Halie had expected. She worked the festival most days while Susan manned the gallery. Halie set up easels on the lawn with many of the wildlife and landscape photos she'd taken in the area, along with the work of others from her gallery. So many people milled about, that Halie's biggest concern wasn't whether she'd sell anything, it was whether she could keep kids and other equally less attentive people from bumping into her work. Ten days filled with paintings, poetry, drawings, music, food, and fun. She'd sold over a dozen photographs, half of which she'd gotten orders to have framed, and sent numerous people to the gallery as well to check out the additional available artwork. And in the evenings, she'd swing by the gallery and go over the day's events with Susan, review orders, and respond to missed phone calls.

The weather on the last day of the festival was picture perfect. The sun shone between a few puffy clouds and filtered its way through the tree branches and leaves to the festival's attendees below. A light jacket or sweater was all that was needed to stay comfortable. Halie spotted a petite young woman standing at around five-foot-two with long brown hair, whom she guessed was in her early twenties, wearing a stylish, light purple v-neck sweater over a white cotton blouse, and tan cargo pants. She stood before one of her photos of a herd of wild mustangs racing through an open field. After several minutes, Halie made her way over.

"Hi, can I help you?" Halie asked in a warm, relaxed manner.

The woman spun around and met Halie's eyes. "I'm drawn to this photograph, though I don't know why. Do you know who the photographer is?"

Halie smiled. "That would be me, Halie Walker." She extended her hand. "I'm the owner of Nature's Vision Photo Gallery in town.

The woman shook Halie's hand. "It's a pleasure to meet you. My name's Cali Brooks. I read about the opening and I've wanted to get over there, but haven't found the time. Your work is amazing. You capture not only the moment, but your photos also display energy and emotion."

"Thank you. That's kind of you to say."

"It's true. I know. I've studied art. It's what I try to teach my kids to capture in their paintings. Some of them are really good, too. It's a shame the school will probably cut the art program next year."

"You're an art teacher?"

"Yeah, part time at the Wilshire Elementary School, among other things. I know schools have funding issues, but I don't think doing away with band and arts programs is the way to go. If you don't open the kids up to the opportunities when they're young, chances are the interest will be lost. I've tried to get the school to hold fund raisers, but they don't think they'll raise enough money."

Halie remained quiet for a moment as numerous thoughts congealed in her mind. "I've always wanted to get more people interested in art, especially kids. I've actually been thinking about holding monthly contests where the prize could be displaying the winning child's artwork in my gallery. I didn't know who to approach about it, or if my idea was even viable." Halie watched as Cali's eyes widened. "I thought that if the photograph, drawing, or painting sold, it would be a huge confidence builder in the child, and the family would keep half the money generated, and the other half would go to charity."

"But what about your cost?"

"I'd only use a small area in the store and I'd be happy to do it. You think it's a good idea?"

"Are you kidding? I think it's a great idea. In fact, I'd be more than appreciative if you'd consider our school as your test school to try out your idea. I'd have to pass it by the principle first, of course, but we might be able to save the art program for even one more year while we give it a go."

Halie's excitement was evident and she wasn't shy to express it. "Great! I love it! Take my card and when you find out whether or not they'll agree, give me a call. I feel good about this. Things happen for a reason, and I think we were supposed to meet today."

"I agree. I'll call either way, I promise. As for the photograph, I'd love to take it home, but I'm kind of in transition with my living arrangements. I'd hate to see someone buy it though, because I love everything about it, including the frame."

"I'll tell you what," Halie said. "Why don't you give me twenty dollars and I'll put a hold on it for you for as long as you need. I'd like someone to own the photo who I know will appreciate it as much as you do."

"Sounds more than generous. I can't tell you how great it's been meeting you today."

"The feeling's mutual."

Two weeks later, Cali Brooks called Halie as promised with the good news that the school accepted the offer, and she let her know the kids were busy working on their first month's creations, excited beyond words. The women mutually agreed Cali would bring the first grouping of artwork by the gallery the first week in November, and from there, Halie would select the winning work of art to hang in the gallery's front window for sale.

HALLOWEEN SNUCK UP on them faster than desired. Sam was gone for less than a day and Halie missed her already. The afternoon before, she'd hugged Sam goodbye and wished her a safe trip. She knew she'd only be gone three days for the law enforcement refresher course in Georgia, but the thought of being alone in the house over Halloween frightened her.

Several nights before, Halie's slumber proved restless and she dreamed strange dreams. In one of her dreams she was surrounded by people, heard the roaring noise of a train, then saw a flash of white, and the next vision was that of her standing alone. The people around her had disappeared. No incidents had occurred since the tire slashing in the parking lot, but that fact didn't make her feel any more secure, especially since the sheriff's office remained in the dark about who committed these crimes against them.

Halie occupied a good portion of the afternoon on the phone talking to her family and friends. Jake lay by her side. After her second call to Ronni, Ronni offered — rather, insisted — to stay with her overnight. Relieved, Halie redirected her nervous attention to cooking a meal for them both.

Jake greeted Ronni when she walked through the door. "I'm ready for you this time," Ronni said. She scratched his back and handed him a bully stick that he immediately took into the living room.

"I'm so glad to see you," Halie said. "Let's sit in the living room and catch up. I made us a few snacks before dinner."

"Sounds good. Where should I leave my bag?" Ronni said.

"You can take it upstairs to the first bedroom on the right. I put fresh sheets on the bed after I got off the phone with you. I laid out some towels too. Your bathroom's right across the hall."

"You didn't need to go through all that trouble. I could have slept on the sofa."

"There's no need for that. We've got plenty of room," Halie said. "You want a beer, or something else to drink?"

"Beer sounds good."

When Ronni returned, Jake had already eaten half his treat and was vigorously devouring the remainder. Ronni sat near him and petted his side. She let out a sigh.

"So what's been going on with you?" Halie asked. "You've been so busy, I've hardly seen you."

"I know. I'm trying to take in a little overtime while it's available. That, and settling in to my place, plus fixing up this Wrangler I bought, hopefully before the winter weather kicks in, eats up most of my free time." Ronni took a long drag on her beer. She scooped up a handful of chips and settled into the soft, brown leather sofa. "I asked Dad to UPS over some of my clothes and a few miscellaneous items, which he did, so at least I have a lot of what I need now. Oh, and he said to say 'hello' to you too."

"That was sweet of him. Tell him I said 'hi' back when you talk to him. How's his health?"

"He's great. He eats well and exercises. He's always got a classic car he's restoring, so that keeps him happy."

"How's your mom doing?" After Halie asked the question, she could see Ronni's expression change ever so slightly, and her body tense. Had she not known her as well as she did, she wouldn't have noticed, but she sensed asking about her mom opened up a sore spot. She noticed it during their last dinner, too.

"She's surviving. She's got her better days and her worse ones."

Halie waited for Ronni to elaborate, but when she didn't, she let it go and decided to change the topic, rather than make her friend uncomfortable. Halie grabbed a few grapes and a chunk of cheese from the snack tray she'd placed on the table in front of them. "How's your job working out?"

"So far, I love it. Sam was right. My boss is such a nice guy. I think he knows I'm gay, but he doesn't bother me about it at all. I'm rooming with a really good-looking female park ranger. She's about my height but thirty pounds lighter, got long black hair, almost black eyes, and long, killer lashes. She doesn't wear make-up though. Heck, she doesn't need it. She's a part-timer in the summer, but they put her on full time. She's got some crazy hours, that one."

"Does she play for our team?" Halie asked, egging Ronni on.

Ronni's expression shone of complete innocence, as if she hadn't even given it a thought. "I'm not sure. I don't think so though. She's asked me if I have a boyfriend and naturally I said no, but we don't talk that much. Our schedules have been pretty opposite so far."

"Haven't noticed, huh? I find that hard to believe."

"To tell you the truth, my mind's been on someone else," Ronni said.

"Oh yeah? Do tell. Who is she?"

"Someone I ran into that night I ate dinner with you guys last month, on my way to the motel. Her car stalled and I fixed it for her. She has these deep brown eyes, like yours, that drew me in and wouldn't let me go."

Halie blushed. "Thanks for that. Was there a mutual connection?"

"I couldn't say. I wasn't there long enough. I should have asked her to go for a cup of coffee and find out, but at the time I didn't even think I'd be here much longer. For all I know, she might not have even accepted my invitation. She looked like something was bothering her. Maybe that's why I didn't ask. I watch out for her car when I'm out. It has a butterfly sticker on the back bumper. "

"I can't imagine too many people have butterfly stickers on their bumpers. I'll keep an eye out for you too."

Ronni smiled. "Thanks, I appreciate it. It's nice having my best friend back."

"It certainly is," Halie said. "Speaking of which, we're having a couple of friends over for Thanksgiving this year and we'd love it if you could come too."

"Good company, free food and beer, are you kidding? Of course I'll be here." Then in a serious note she added, "Thanks. I wasn't looking forward to spending the holiday alone. My dad's going to my uncle's, but I haven't built up enough vacation time to visit him. Plus, I need to save money right now, not spend it."

"Great. I'm sure Sam will be happy. She really likes you."

"Of course," Ronni said. "What's not to like?"

After dinner, Halie prepped the fireplace and lit the wood. The temperature dropped below the freezing mark. In a way she was glad, since no more kids came to the door in over an hour. Relaxing, she made a bowl of popcorn and sat watching a movie with Ronni and Jake. Not ten minutes later, the doorbell rang. Halie's body jerked as she sat erect.

Jake barked, sprung up, and ran first to the door and then back to Halie.

A concerned expression crossed Halie's face.

"Who'd be out now? I wouldn't even answer it," Ronni said.

After the ringing came a set of rapid taps on the front door. "I better go see anyway," Halie said. "Stay here," she said to Jake. The porch light was on. Halie peered out the peek hole and saw a woman dressed in a pirate outfit with a black hat and feather sticking out, her breath rising in the air in front of her. "It's Felice," Halie whispered. "The woman you met in the photo gallery."

"The one you seemed to not really want to be there?"

"Yeah, that's the one."

"Pretend you're not home."

"I can't. She must have seen the lights on."

"Then go ahead and open it if you want. I'm here, so you don't need to worry. I'll kick her ass ten ways to Sunday if she gives you any trouble."

"I don't doubt that," Halie said. She opened the door.

"Trick-or-treat," Felice said.

"Felice," Halie said, her reply flat. "You're kidding, right?"

"I am. Actually, I brought a treat for you." Felice held up a bakery box. "Devil's-Ghoul cake. I know you like to eat, and I know Sam's out of town, so I thought you might want a little company on a cold night. I can't stay for long, unless you want me to. I've got a party to go to, as you can see," she said. She placed her hand on the plastic hilt of her scabbard.

"How did you know where we lived and how did you know Sam was out of town?" Halie asked.

"I'm still on good terms with certain people in Grand Teton who don't think I'm such a terrible person and who'll talk to me. People who tend to forgive and forget, and give other people second chances. And as I'm sure you're aware, secrets are few and far between around here, even when you don't live in government housing," Felice said. She leaned to her right and glimpsed into the foyer past Halie.

"That may be so, but your dropping by unannounced kind of took me by surprise. Under different circumstances I'd invite you in, but with Sam not being here—"

"You have company?" Felice shot back. "I smelled the fireplace on and saw the lights, but I didn't realize—I mean—I wasn't expecting—"

"Is there a problem here?" Ronni said. She held Jake by the collar.

"No problem," Felice answered. "I stopped by to drop off a cake for Halie and thought she might like a little company for a while, but I can see she's well taken care of." Addressing Halie, she continued, "If you ever decide I'm not such a bad person to be around, give me a call. You can get the number from the college. That is, if you can fit it into your schedule."

"I really think you should leave now," Ronni said. "I'm not fond of your tone. I suggest you keep the cake too. We ate already."

Felice opened her mouth as though she was about to reply. Instead her eyes narrowed. "Enjoy the evening," she said, then turned and strutted down the front steps.

RONNI DROVE OUT of Sam and Halie's driveway and headed to work the following morning. She enjoyed spending time with Halie, but was anxious to get back to her normal routine. She'd planned on working on her Jeep that night after work. But when she reached the end of the driveway, she threw it in reverse and headed back from where she'd left. She rang the doorbell and Halie answered. Halie stood in her bathrobe.

"Hi, what's up? Did you forget something?" Halie asked.

"No. I don't want to worry you, but I think you should take a walk with me to the end of the driveway. It looks to me like someone ran over your mailbox."

Halie took a deep breath. "Let me throw on some clothes and I'll be right there."

The mailbox was leaning into the yard at a forty-five degree angle, and a portion of the fence beyond was broken. "I didn't hear anybody run into this last night, did you?" Halie asked.

"No, nothing."

"Maybe a group of kids pushed it over, with Halloween and all."

"I don't think so," Ronni said. "There's a dent in the post. I'm guessing someone ran into it."

Tears started to well in Halie's eyes. "I'm so tired of this, I really am. We haven't done anything to anyone. Why can't whoever's doing this leave us alone? I don't know how much more of this I can take."

Ronni cradled Halie in her arms. "It's okay. I'll tell you what. Why don't I come back again tonight after work and stay with you? Sam will be home tomorrow. I'll see if I can get off work early if you want."

"That'd be great if you would stay. Don't take off early though. I'll be alright. I have to go to work too."

"Come on, let's go back in the house. I'll see what I can do about temporarily fixing the mailbox and then I'll go. I find it highly coincidental though, that your *friend* Felice stopped by last night and now this morning, the mailbox and part of the fence are mowed down," Ronni said.

"Yeah, that doesn't sit well with me either."

"Are you going to tell Sam?"

"I'll wait until she gets home tomorrow."

WHEN SAM FINALLY got home late Wednesday afternoon, Jake all but knocked her over. He barked and sprang in a circle, knocked over her duffle bag and pushed his weight against her until she kissed and petted him. Then he ran toward his bed and raced back, leaving barely enough time for Sam to get in a quick hug with Halie. "This guy's crazy," Sam said.

"You have no idea," Halie said. "He's been on pins and needles since you left. He stares out the window at night waiting for you. I'm surprised he has any energy at all. I think having Ronni here helped though. He seemed to quiet down when she was around."

"Yeah, I'm glad she stayed with you. It put my mind at ease." Sam walked to the cabinet where they kept Jake's treats. "Let me give him a chew stick so he calms down, and then I can say hello to you properly." After Jake raced off, chew stick in mouth, Sam took Halie in her arms. "I missed you so much," she said.

"I missed you too. I'm glad you're home again. I got worried with the weather. I hoped your flight wouldn't get delayed. It started snowing here around one and within a couple hours, we already had half a foot. I left work early. The forecast called for a foot," Halie said.

"At the rate it's falling, they may have underestimated a bit."

"You should've seen Jake when I let him out. He pounced in the snow off the steps and raced around the yard like a loon, until his footprints crisscrossed the yard in every direction. He practically left no fresh patch of snow untouched."

"Yeah, he loves the first snow of the season. It's funny to watch him when he gets crazy like that."

"So, did you bring me anything?"

"As a matter of fact, I did, but I'll get to that in a minute." Sam pulled Halie closer. She missed the scent of her and enjoyed the feel of her body pressed against hers. She leaned forward and kissed Halie tenderly on the lips.

Halie reciprocated the kiss more timidly than Sam expected and ended it in what felt to Sam as, once again, an abrupt manner. "Let's go eat," Halie said. Then she spun around and headed into the kitchen. "I'm starving and I've got some things I need to tell you."

Under other circumstances, Sam would have found humor in Halie's eating comment, knowing her desire for food takes over almost everything else, but today the comment cut like a knife. She hadn't seen Halie in days. They hadn't been close since before their trip to New Jersey. The slender veil of confidence she bore of their relationship returning to normal was shaken once again. The energy in Sam's body was sucked from her the instant Halie turned and walked away. All she could manage to say was, "I'm taking my bags upstairs." She knew she couldn't go in the kitchen at that moment and eat, as dejected as she felt. She also realized in some way she was part to blame. She could have spoken up. She could have tried charming her partner. She didn't have the confidence though to do more.

Chapter Twelve

"WHEN DO YOU start giving ski lessons again at Alpine Crest?" Cali asked April as she brushed the shiny back of one of her favorite quarter horses stabled at the ranch.

"In a few weeks, why?" April said.

"I thought I might apply for a part time job there this season. I need to stash away some extra cash. There are a few things I wanted to buy that I've had my eye on."

"You have room for another part-time job?"

"The animal hospital cut one of my nights, plus the reduced winter hours here don't help, and I still have weekends free."

"You better hurry then. I think tomorrow's the last day they're taking applications. And you'll need to go in person. They won't hire anyone without interviewing them. What job did you have in mind?" April asked.

"What do they offer, do you know?"

"It's more like, what don't they offer. When I applied a couple of years ago, I went to the job fair they held in town. I recall openings for housekeeping, daycare, guest services, parking attendants, working the ticket office, front desk, maintenance, ski lift operators and ski lift attendants—"

"Ski lift attendant is actually what I was interested in. I get to meet people and be outdoors. I guess they let you ski the slopes for free on your time off too?"

"Yeah, plus you get discounts on lift tickets in the other resorts, and in local businesses and free ski and snowboard lessons if you want them. You might even get me teaching you."

"That would be great. I love to ski. The problem is I don't have the money to spend on tickets," Cali said.

"Not that you'd have much time with your schedule. But if you're really interested, I'd give a call over there today and see if they can fit you in tomorrow. It'd be better than stopping by unannounced."

Cali closed the stall door behind Midnight. "I'll do that, thanks."

SINCE RONNI WORKED late at the garage on her car the night before, she decided to take a break this evening and enjoy a relaxing dinner in town and a movie, per her roommate Tracy's insistent invitation. Tracy was beyond attractive, and Ronni enjoyed her company, but all during dinner, all she thought about was Cali. The time between the present and their meeting that night in the rain continued to grow and despite Ronni's effort searching for her. She was no closer now than she'd been that night. She'd almost resigned herself to the fact that finding Cali wasn't in the cards.

Perhaps worse than the thought of never seeing Cali again was the fear that she would find her and Cali would have no interest in her whatsoever. She couldn't read Cali's assessment of her when they first met. It wasn't like they came upon each under the best of circumstances, and the fact Ronni felt an unexplainable attraction didn't mean that Cali did. Ronni knew she wasn't hard on the eyes, but she could stand to lose a few pounds, and her smoking probably hadn't made a great impression, not that she was trying to impress anyone. She could quit smoking though. That might stack a few more cards on her deck.

"Hello, earth to Ronni," Tracy said.

"Huh, what?"

"Yeah, 'what' is exactly the point. Have you been listening to anything I've said over the past five minutes? You seem like you're a million miles away. Am I that boring?"

"Uh, no. I'm sorry. No, you're not boring at all. I'm enjoy your company and I'm glad you asked me to go out with you — well, not go out, out with you. I mean — you know what I — "

"Forget it. I get the drift. So who is she?"

"Huh?"

"I said, who is she? What, you didn't think I knew you were gay? Pu-lease, I may be straight, but your gaydar or whatever you own that you beam out is quite clear. Besides, why else would your attention not be smattered on me?"

Ronni's expression relaxed and she smiled. "Gaydar? And how do you know about gaydar?"

"I may have a couple of rainbow stripes in me. Hell, I am human, and you have an alluring charisma to you, whether you know it or not. Not that I'm interested, of course, since I'm straight, so don't let it go to your head."

"Of course, no, I wouldn't do that." Ronni wiped her mouth with her napkin before placing it on the table and tapped her belly, pleasantly surprised by her roommate's confession. She sat a few inches taller. "Man, I'm stuffed."

"Me too," Tracy added. "So, spill it. Who is she?"

"Her name's Cali Brooks. You don't happen to know her, do you?"

"Sorry. The name doesn't ring a bell. Why didn't you get her number?"

"Because I wasn't thinking at the time I guess, and didn't see the point. It's not like I lived here. I was visiting friends and riding back to my motel after dinner. It was late and raining. I was tired. I saw her on the side of the road. Her car broke down and I helped get her on her way, but there was something in her eyes and the tone of her voice and the way she carried herself. I don't know. I know it sounds stupid, but I sensed something special about her. I just didn't do anything about it.

And now, months later, all I can think about *is* her and I don't even really know who she is, or if by some miracle I might even be a passing thought in her mind."

"You got it bad girlfriend, I can see that. Well, I know if some tall, handsome stranger rescued me one rainy night, I'd remember them," she said, then winked.

"Thanks for saying that."

"Come on, let's get out of here and rent a movie instead of wasting our money in the theatre. You most likely won't be paying attention anyway. I'll make us a nice, big bowl of popcorn, and you can drift off to wherever you like, and still have company doing it."

"Thanks, Tracy, you're the best."

"You got that right, and don't forget it."

Ronni forced herself to stay focused on the ride home. She knew not doing so could prove fatal. After passing through a traffic light, the vision of what she'd seen seconds before registered in her mind. They passed a convenience store parking lot and Cali's car, or what she thought was Cali's car, was parked out in front. Ronni's heart raced. Her palms sweat. "Hold on," she said to Tracy, then spun the Jeep around and headed back to the store.

"What the heck are you doing? Are you crazy? You're lucky there wasn't a cop around or you'd have gotten a ticket."

"I looked first."

"The heck you did. So what gives?"

"I saw Cali's car in the parking lot of the convenience store we just passed."

"Of course. That makes perfect sense now. If you ever do that again, even though you're bigger than me, I'm going to make you pay," Tracy said.

Ronni pulled into the parking lot. "Sorry, you're right. I shouldn't have done that, at least not with you in the car. The car's gone, but this means she probably lives in the area and wasn't passing through."

"Well that's something I guess," Tracy said.

"You think I'm crazy, don't you?"

"Nah, I've done worse. I think it's nice and I hope you find her. It'd be nice if you didn't kill yourself or anyone else in the process though."

"I said I was sorry. It won't happen again."

When they got to the apartment, Ronni said, "I think I'm going to give up smoking. If I ever do get a chance to meet her again, I don't want it to be with a cigarette hanging out of my mouth."

"Yeah, not a great look, but good luck with that."

"Thanks, I'll probably need it," Ronni said. At least Cali Brooks was no longer a phantom. Warmth rose up within Ronni. Cheeks flushed, her hope of finding Cali was renewed, and now she had a place to start her search.

Chapter Thirteen

A LIGHT SNOW sprinkled the landscape early Thanksgiving morning, then picked up considerably as the day wore on. By noon, six inches had fallen. Halie hoped the weather wouldn't ruin their Thanksgiving dinner. She spent the better part of the morning and the prior evening preparing for the meal while Sam spruced up the house. In addition to making butternut squash soup, a vegetable lasagna, winter salad with walnuts, apples, and cranberries, along with a cranberry-orange balsamic vinaigrette dressing, she made Sam's favorite stuffed mushrooms. She also cleaned and cut string beans which she'd later sauté and top with roasted almond slivers. Last on the to-do list was to cut the spinach and corn quesadillas into slender triangles for appetizers.

Jake barked several times and ran from one end of the living room to the other as an unfamiliar car pulled into the driveway. Cali Brooks stepped from the driver's side of the vehicle first, then April and Corrine got out. Sam opened the front door and waited for them behind the glass storm door. "You sit and be a good boy," she said to Jake.

Sam hugged April first, then Corrine, and shook Cali's hand as April introduced her. "It's so good to see you guys," Sam said, "and to meet you Cali. You resemble your mother so much."

Cali smiled. "Thank you, and thanks for inviting me. My mom told me what you did for her. I can't thank you enough. She might not be here today if it weren't for you."

"You don't have to thank me, it's what I do, and I was glad I was able to help. Your mom is one tough fighter, that's for sure. She gave that mountain lion a heck of a time and probably a major headache judging by the size of the rock she belted him with."

"That sounds like Mom," Cali said.

Jake groaned.

"Okay buddy, you can say 'hello' now, but be gentle," Sam said.

After Jake made his rounds, they walked into the living room where they were met by Halie. Halie's eyes widened. "Hey April, Corrine, and...Cali? Cali Brooks is your tenant?" Halie said.

"She is. You two *know* each other?" April said.

Cali and Halie exchanged glances and partial grins. Halie answered. "As a matter of fact, we do. We met at the Jackson Hole Arts Festival. Cali's a teacher. She bought—is in the process of buying—one of my photographs, and we're working together on a project to help preserve the art program in the school where she teaches. I thought you said the person you were bringing with you today worked with you at the ranch, April."

"I did, and she does," April said. "She also works one day a week at the school, among other jobs. I can't believe you know each other, and Sam knows Cali's moms."

Halie addressed Sam. "How do you know her moms?"

"Hillary Coleman is Cali's mom."

"Coleman's her maiden name," Cali said.

"She and her partner Melanie are the women I rescued on Rendevous Mountain."

"Oh, my god. Yes, the mountain lion attack. That was awful," Halie said.

"I forgot to mention to you that Cali is April and Corrine's tenant, though I only found out by accident who Cali was when I talked with April the other day," Sam said.

"Wow, it is a small world, isn't it? I'm glad your mom's okay now," Halie said.

"Thank you. She's still got some reconstructive surgery ahead of her, but things are pretty much back to normal."

"Thank goodness. That couldn't have been easy for you. Have a seat everyone. I'll be back in a minute." Halie retreated into the kitchen, then returned a short while later holding a platter filled with appetizers. She set platter on the coffee table in front of the sofa. The wood in the fireplace crackled and warmed the room, giving it a festive glow. Sam turned the football game on, toned low, and although she didn't watch constantly, she checked the scores on occasion.

"We're expecting one more person," Halie said as she poured wine into her guest's glasses. "My friend Ronni. She called a few minutes ago to let me know she'd be a little late. She said we should start without her and that she'd get here as soon as she could."

April glanced at Cali. "Are you okay? You look like you've seen a ghost or something."

"Who, me?" Cali said. "No, I'm fine. I—well I—I think I might know Halie's friend Ronni, but then how strange would that be, right? Yeah, I mean, now that I think about it, it would be too much of a coincidence I'm sure we're not talking about the same person, forget it," Cali said.

"Not so fast, you never know. Are we both talking about the five-foot-seven, one hundred and sixty pound, give or take a few, biker chick with a huge heart Ronni Summers?" Halie asked.

"I don't believe it. That's her, though I don't really know her. I mean, she helped me out one night—my car—it broke down—she helped—but that was it. I mean, I don't have her number or anything. Right, well, why would I have her number? It's not like—"

"Aha," Halie responded. "This is very interesting. Am I right to assume you have a butterfly sticker of some sort stuck to the bumper of your car?"

"I do. How'd you know that?"

"Oh, let's just say a little birdie told me."

"WE HAD A great time guys, thanks," April said. "Dinner was fabulous. Oddly enough, I didn't even miss not eating turkey, the food was so good. I'm sorry we're cutting out early, but since Cali's car only has front wheel drive, and the roads look pretty bad, I'd rather not risk it."

"I feel better too that you guys get home safe. Oh, and don't forget your dessert," Halie said. She handed April a doggie bag with a piece of pumpkin pie and coconut cream pie in it for each of them. "At least I know I won't get fat on my own."

"Thanks," April said, "though you've got a long way to go before you have to worry about your weight. I hope we get to meet your friend Ronni soon. I'm sorry we missed her, but she did a nice thing helping that guy out. Guess he's got one more thing to be thankful for this year."

"Yup, that's Ronni for ya," Halie said. "Sam would have done the same thing though, so I can't fault her."

Then Corrine added, "April too, but that's why we love them. Sam, I'll call you Saturday morning and we'll decide then what time to get together, okay?"

"Sounds good," Sam said.

"Thanks again for everything," Cali said to her hosts, and then to Halie alone she added, "We'll talk at the end of the month to see who your first artistic winner is, and in the meantime, would you please say 'hello' to Ronni for me, in the slim chance she remembers me."

Halie smiled. "Oh, somehow I'm pretty sure she remembers you."

RONNI PULLED INTO the driveway over tire marks freshly imprinted in the snow. She realized she must have just missed Sam and Halie's friends. She felt a twinge of disappointment and hoped she was still welcome now that everyone else had gone. She hadn't seen Halie in almost a month, and Sam longer than that. As she shut the engine off, her stomach growled. She hoped Halie saved her some food since she hadn't eaten all day.

After Jake almost knocked Ronni down and got his share of affection from her, Sam and Halie greeted Ronni with open arms and hugs. Ronni was dressed in black khakis, a white turtleneck under a dark green cable sweater and black boots. She brought two bottles of wine, which Halie cradled in one arm.

"So what happened?" Halie asked. "I know you woke up late and then got tied up on the phone talking to your dad and then your mom, but what happened with that guy on the way over?"

"I passed a Nissan Sentra that veered off the road into a snow bank.

I knew if I stopped I'd be even later. I almost left him there, but I couldn't do it. I knew he couldn't get out on his own, so I hooked him up to the Jeep and pulled him out. He must have run over something in the road though, because his front tire was flat too."

"Poor guy. Lucky for him you came along," Sam said, then she excused herself to go outside to clear snow. Ronni offered to help, but Sam rejected her offer, suggesting instead she eat and relax, two words Ronni was more than thankful to hear.

Once Sam was out the door, Halie grabbed Ronni's arm and pulled her part way through the living room until she followed her into the kitchen. "Have I got news for you," she said.

"Oh, yeah?" Ronni inhaled what she thought was the smell of baked mushrooms and Parmesan cheese. "God it smells good in here. I think I could eat a horse."

"No horse at this establishment, but I think you'll like what's on the menu. Why don't you sit and relax so I can feed you."

"Yes, Mom," Ronni replied in a voice of amusement.

Halie reheated a bowl of butternut squash soup and placed in front of Ronni, and before her friend downed half of it, she brought out a plate piled high with a sampling of all the food she'd prepared, including a few stuffed mushrooms and a couple slices of the quesadillas. Then she placed a side bowl of the winter salad with mixed greens next to Ronni's plate.

"Holy cow! You expect me to eat all that?"

"Oh, I don't think you'll have a problem. Leave room for dessert." Halie opened one of the bottles of wine Ronni brought and poured each of them a glass before sitting at the kitchen table next to her. "Now, for the important stuff I've been dying to tell you. You're going to kick yourself hard when you hear this."

Ronni shoveled a large piece of lasagna into her mouth before Halie finished speaking, so she gestured with a twirl of her hand to indicate Halie should go on.

"The woman you've been dying to find, the one with the butterfly sticker on the bumper of her car—she came here with April and Corrine today. She was their guest—their new tenant—April's co-worker. I had no idea."

Ronni nearly choked as she attempted to swallow the food remaining in her mouth in one gulp. "What? Are you kidding me?"

Halie didn't comment, but her expression told Ronni she was not joking.

"I don't believe it. How could I be so lucky and unlucky in the same day? I guess I'll have to chalk one up for no good deed goes unpunished," Ronni said.

"Oh, I wouldn't say that," Halie countered. "She appeared quite taken by your valor, and knowing you, even if you knew she was here ahead of time, I'd bet money on it that you'd have helped that guy anyway. It's how you're wired."

Ronni pouted. She didn't want to admit Halie was right. "Maybe." The thought of only minutes having separated her from finally meeting Cali again was difficult for Ronni to process. If she hadn't worked late, or got up out of bed sooner, or hurried getting ready a little more, she might not have run into the guy who ran off the road and she'd have had the pleasure of looking into those warm, trusting, brown eyes she'd lost herself in on that rainy night in August. As Ronni drifted to that moment, she envisioned Cali Brooks' inviting smile. "I have to see her. I can't stand it anymore. The thought of her drives me crazy."

"You may have to wait a while. In addition to working at the ranch with April and part time teaching at the elementary school, she's taken on another part time job as a ski lift attendant over at Alpine Crest Ski Resort." Halie filled her friend in on Cali's teaching job and how they'd met at the Art Festival, never having a clue this was the person Ronni was after. She finished with, "and she'll be working at the resort this weekend, including tomorrow. When's the last time you went skiing?"

"I'm supposed to work tomorrow too, but maybe I can convince my boss to let me work a half day—start early, help clear the snow—and then go. I'm off Saturday, but I don't know if I'll be able to last another day, especially knowing what I know now."

"I wouldn't last, if I were you," Halie said.

"Unfortunately, it's been so long since I've stepped into a pair of skis, I'm not so sure I'd make it down the hill in one piece, but you read my mind. At this point, I'll do anything to get to see her. I need to know if we have chemistry and a chance at something that might be great, or if I misread my feelings, or have blown them out of proportion over all these months."

"I doubt you blew things out of proportion. She's quite charming, smart, funny, entertaining—"

"Okay, okay, stop rubbing it in. I'll do it. If I can't get off tomorrow, then I'll go Saturday. Besides, how hard could learning to ski again be? They say it's like riding a bike. Once you learn, you never forget."

"Do they now? I never heard that, but if that's so, then it appears you have your day laid out for you."

A moment of silence followed as Ronni finished the remainder of her food. She watched Halie, who appeared deep in thought, as her own thoughts shifted from Cali to her best friend. "Dinner was better than fantastic. Thanks so much for saving me some. I'm stuffed."

"I'm glad you enjoyed it, but you haven't had dessert yet. I haven't either, so if you're up to a piece of pie, I'll join you."

"Well, since you put it that way, I suppose I could squeeze in dessert," Ronni said. She leaned back and slapped her round belly.

Halie stood and meandered toward the refrigerator. "Good, because watching you eat made me hungry again." She placed the pies on the counter and took two cake plates from the cabinet. "Pumpkin or coconut?"

"How about a thin sliver of each?"

"That's what I like to hear, but I'll ignore the words 'thin' and 'sliver.' Coffee?"

"That'd be great." Ronni watched as Halie prepared the coffee. "Hey, I wanted to ask you a question, but you don't have to answer it if you don't want, because it's probably none of my business, but I worry about you."

"What? Why so? There's nothing to worry about. Ask away, I don't have any secrets."

Ronni fidgeted with her desert fork. "Is everything okay with you and Sam?"

Halie was quiet for a moment. "We're okay, why?"

"I don't know. I picked up on something in the sullen stare Sam tossed your way tonight before she walked out the door to shovel. I thought it might have to do with the trouble you guys have been having with the vandals. I can't figure why Sam would hold that against you though, but her expression in the foyer indicates she does."

"It's not like that. I think my actions, or inaction as the case may be, frustrates her sometimes and she doesn't know what to do about it, and I don't know how to make things better. It's not something I do on a conscious level, at least I don't think so. I love Sam. I don't mean to hurt her." Halie poured the coffee and brought the plates of pie to the table. She sat and broke off a piece of pumpkin pie.

Ronni remained silent as they ate. She only commented on how good the pie was, waiting for Halie to elaborate on her own.

"I haven't exactly been very loving and attentive to her lately, which she hasn't been used to and probably can't understand, and I haven't exactly come clean as to the reason why," Halie said.

"Why not?"

"Because I'm not entirely sure I know why I'm reacting the way I am either. Everything sort of hit me at once. Recovering from my accident, the move, starting my career over, losing my friends, the reality of the danger of Sam's job and the fact that every day she walks out the door there's a chance I can lose her. We had a good chat a few months ago, before our trip to visit her mom. I thought after that talk I was back on track, and I felt wonderful, but then the hammer fell with Coco and the house being vandalized. I don't know how to explain it, but I feel violated. And I don't know if they're after me or Sam or both of us, but it's unnerving. I can't relax. I feel like someone's always watching us, even though I'm sure they're not. Sam doesn't appear that bothered. She's used to dealing with this sort of thing, but I'm not. And I know she wishes she could make the unease go away for me, but she can't and I can't pretend everything's okay just to make her feel better. It's strange, but the closer I attach to Sam emotionally, the more distant I've become physically, especially now." Halie paused again before continuing. "I think I'm afraid of losing her, and it scares me to death. I can't picture my life without her in it anymore. She's everything to me."

Ronni polished off her last piece of pie and quietly set the fork on top of her plate. "Have you told her how you feel?"

"Some of it I have, but not the 'afraid of losing her' part. Her job's in law enforcement. That's not going to change and I don't want her contemplating changing her job to ease my worries. And if I told her, that's exactly what she'd do. I know her and I don't want her to change for me. She loves her work. It's a huge part of who she is. It's funny how that part of her work never bothered me when we first met."

"I hear what you're saying, but any one of us could die any day or at any time for the stupidest of reasons, completely unrelated to their job. There's a million ways something can happen, but I think the worst thing you can do is withhold love when it's so precious to begin with and our time on this earth is so short. If you love Sam that much, and it's clear she loves you, you shouldn't shut her out. If you do, you risk the chance of bringing to reality what you fear most. I'm sure Sam has her own fears related to the possibility of losing you. Has she been distant with you?"

"No."

Seeing the tears welling in Halie's eyes, Ronni shifted to a lighter tone. "See, that's why I'll be strapping on the skis this weekend and slogging it up the mountains in search of my love. It's worth the risk."

Halie grinned. "Thanks for listening. I think talking about it helped. You're right, of course, everything you said."

Ronni puffed out her chest. "Yup, when I'm right, I'm right."

Chapter Fourteen

BY MORNING THE main roads were clear and the side roads were passable, even without four wheel drive. The road crews did an honorable job keeping up with the snow overnight. This time of year tourism centered on the skiers, and the state and county crews knew the importance of keeping the roads accessible. The ski resorts would be lapping up Mother Nature's present to their cause today.

As Sam headed down the stairs from the bedroom, Jake in tow, she smelled coffee brewing. She gave Halie a peck on the cheek. "Morning."

"Morning."

"Mmm, that smells good. You made breakfast already?"

"I did. I heard you moving around up there so I figured I'd whip us up some French toast and eggs. We're both going to have a busy day, so we may as well be prepared for it," Halie said.

"True, thanks." Sam planned on meeting Corrine for Christmas shopping and to help her pick out a saddle for April, while she hoped to get fashion shopping help for Halie's presents in return. Halie, on the other hand, agreed to meet Colin Mitchell at Alpine Crest Ski Resort and photograph him in action on the slopes.

Sam let Jake outside onto the snow-covered deck. The tree branches hung white with the new powder. The morning was pleasantly quiet. Sam closed the door behind Jake and stood behind it watching him as he bounded through the snow like an antelope. When Halie finished by the stove and sat, Sam sat next to her and sipped her coffee. "That tastes great," she said. She held the mug in one hand and cradled it with the other. "What time are you meeting Colin?"

"Nine o'clock by the main ticket booth."

"You know I'd rather you didn't go, right?" Sam said.

"I do, but it's a good opportunity. He's not only paying for my day of skiing and my time, he'll pay for any shots he likes too. I'd be a fool to let this opportunity slip by."

"I know, but I still don't like it."

"Besides, aren't you meeting Corrine today anyway?" Halie asked.

"I am. It's not about not wanting you to go because I want you here with me instead, it's about the danger and the possibility you'll like taking these action shots, expand your business base, and then I'll never see you."

"That won't happen. What are you getting at the store?"

"I'm not saying, but if we have time I think I'll see if I can get Jessie and Katelynn metal detectors as one of their presents. What do you think?"

"I think you're crazy, but I also think they'll love them because those kids are so much like you," Halie said.

"You think so?" Sam said. "I think they are too, and I'm proud of it."

"You're too much. Come on. See if you can get Jake inside and then let's get going. I guess you plan to finish shoveling too, so if we don't get moving, neither one of us will get to where we need to be on time."

"I APPRECIATE THE offer Sam, but I'll pick you up," Corrine said on the other end of the line. "You're the one who's doing me the favor. I've got one house to show this morning and then I'm free. Since I don't know exactly how long it'll take, this way will be better. As soon as I'm done I'll swing by. See you in a little."

By ten thirty Sam and Corrine were on their way, traveling along Highway 22 headed toward Wilson. As they neared the Teton Pass, they saw brake lights and traffic backed up. "Shoot," Corrine said. "I wonder what's going on up there."

"Probably an accident. My guess is someone went faster than they should have around one of those turns. Whatever the holdup is, I hope it doesn't take too long to clear, and I hope no one's hurt," Sam added. Like everyone else, she hated sitting in traffic.

"I can't wait until Christmas to surprise April with the new saddle for Lady Jane. She deserves it. Every year she talks about getting a new one, and every year she doesn't. I'm glad you agreed to come with me, since I have no idea what I'd be looking at."

"I don't mind. I love shopping for stuff like that. It's shopping for clothes that I despise. Speaking of which, if we have some time I could use a little help with Halie's presents in that category. Hardware stores, furniture stores, sporting goods, tackle shops—no problem, but clothing stores? Not a fan."

Corrine chuckled. "You're just like April. You two are unbelievable. I think she'd rather shovel horse manure than go clothes shopping."

"And I'd join her. I shop online for most everything I need. But you see the way Halie dresses. I mean, I love her style, but I don't have the first clue about fashion."

"I'm sure we'll have time. Plus, we should get fabulous deals today. It's the fringe benefit of sucking it up and shopping with the masses on black Friday."

Another fifteen minutes passed with no movement in either direction. Suddenly, and with uncertainty in her voice, Sam said, "Did you feel that?"

"Feel what?"

"I felt a vibration. I think it was a tremor. That's it again, it's getting—"

Corrine's voice cracked, "I feel it now too."

Seconds later, Sam heard it, first in the distance, and then growing louder, a sound similar to that of an approaching freight train. Corrine and Sam exchanged glances. Sam shifted her attention up the mountain pass. A cloud of white bore down on them. Corrine reached to open the driver's side door.

Sam grabbed her arm. "Don't! Stay in the car! You'll get yourself killed if you—"

"I'M NOT DOING it. It's as simple as that. The trail is clearly marked 'Dangerous-Off Limits,' so why would you want to go down it?" Halie was adamant and furious at the same time that Colin would suggest a reckless idea such as taking a restricted trail. She'd put up with his controlling manner all morning, but he was pushing it too far. The money wasn't worth it.

"Because I can," Colin said without hesitation.

"Because you can doesn't mean you should."

"There's no fun in doing anything if you don't take risks. It's the thrill of danger that makes the ride exciting and worth doing. Besides, we'll get more awesome pictures. This powder's untouched."

"I don't get you. If you wanted untouched powder, why didn't we go backcountry skiing like you'd originally planned?" Halie didn't hide her growing annoyance. She stood on top of the hill and argued while an icy wind pounded against her and chilled her bones, regardless of the many layers of clothing she wore underneath her ski suit.

"No one sees me backcountry, whereas here, plenty of people can see me. Let's cut through the needless tension. Why don't we take a break and have a nice hot cup of coffee or cocoa and then start fresh?" Colin suggested. His eyes held a mischievous glimmer.

Halie would have welcomed a cup of coffee at that moment, but she understood what Colin was trying to do, and she wanted no part of it. "If starting fresh means taking that trail, then I'm out."

Colin clenched his teeth. "Whatever. You're fired."

Before Halie could respond, Colin popped off his skis and walked toward the restaurant at the top of the hill. "Asshole," Halie grumbled under her breath. Who needs him anyway, she thought. If nothing else, Sam would be glad she'd have more time on her hands now to spend with her. Of course, Sam wouldn't be home if she left now. She'd still be with Corrine. Halie pushed the end of her jacket sleeve back and checked the time on her wristwatch. Another hour and a half and April would be finished with her last lesson. She figured it would take her twenty minutes to get down the hill anyway. She could check in with April, and see if she wanted to have lunch with her and maybe finish off the day on the slopes together. Halie wasn't in the mood to ski alone. If April was busy, she'd pack up and go home. She'd seen April's car in the parking lot on her way in, and parked next to it this morning. The trail she was on would lead her toward the ski school anyway. She glanced behind her once more to see if Colin came to his senses and changed his mind, but he was nowhere in sight. In disbelief at his stubbornness, she pushed off with her skis and began her descent.

RONNI CALLED SAM and Halie's house several times that morning, but got no answer. She was eager to talk to them, especially since she now believed she knew who their menacing vandal was after he'd brought his car into the shop. White paint residue clung to the damaged bumper, which could have come from Sam and Halie's fence, and the color of the car matched a paint chip she'd saved from off their mailbox pole the day after Halloween. Before leaving work, she left Sam and Halie a voice mail message pleading they call her as soon as they got in. She had one additional item to occupy her thoughts now as she headed for Alpine Crest Ski Resort, though meeting Cali remained in the forefront.

Ronni was nervous and not sure what she'd say when she'd meet Cali again, but was excited by the prospect at the same time. She wished she'd taken the chance to get to know her better on that rainy night when they'd first met. After getting her rentals straightened away, she carried her skies to an open spot at the base of one of the hills and set them on the snow. Her trepidation of getting back on skis for the first time in over a decade did not deter her from her goal as she scanned the area map. "Wow, there's a ton of trails to cover. This is not going to be easy," she said aloud to no one. She'd asked the woman at the ticket counter and a man in the ski rental if they knew what lift Cali worked at, but neither one could help her. Well, I guess I'll start in the middle and work my way over to the one side and if that doesn't work, pray I have enough energy left to work my way over to the other side, she thought before she stepped into her skis and did exactly that.

AFTER TWO HOURS of non-stop skiing, and half a dozen ski lifts later, Ronni bent over to stretch her back. Her legs felt like Jell-O. She contemplated taking a break when she spotted Cali helping a skier onto the chair lift at the last trail on the left side of the mountain. Her heart raced and her face flushed as she pushed forward and got on Cali's lift line. Calm yourself Ronni—deep breaths, deep breaths. This is no big deal. You're fine. You look good. Stay calm. The line snaked along, but at the end, she didn't pay attention, and when a young man next to Ronni told her to "move it along" she realized a good six feet were open between her and the front of the line. Embarrassed, she shoved off with her poles and pushed with her skis. As her eyes connected with Cali's, she smiled and lost her footing. She ran straight into Cali and knocked her over.

Ronni lay still for several seconds before she moved or spoke, her eyes locked on Cali in a heated dance. Her breathing quickened.

"Hey, get a room already," someone from the line yelled.

Ronni snapped back to reality. Cheeks flushed, she excused her clumsiness several times as she helped Cali to her feet. "I'm so sorry. I — my legs are tired — I wasn't paying — "

"It's okay. I can't believe you're here." Cali's tone was welcoming. She directed Ronni to the side, away from everyone as her counterpart took over. "Is this a coincidence, or were you trying to find me?"

The rose color in Ronni's cheeks turned even redder. "I haven't skied in years. You wouldn't catch me dead on these hills if it wasn't for a good reason. No, I'm definitely here to see you," Ronni said, relieved once the words were out. She scanned Cali's face nervously to pick up on her expression. The response was that charming, warm, inviting smile Ronni remembered from the night she'd helped Cali with her car.

"I'm flattered. No one's ever gone to so much trouble to find me. You seem a bit shaky though. Do you want to sit down and have a cup of coffee or coco? I'm on break for a half hour."

"I'd love to. You read my mind."

Ronni was fairly certain their half hour passed, but Cali hadn't made an attempt to leave. Ronni was surprised how easy she was to talk to and how smart she appeared to be, and she was now certain the fluttering she felt on their first meeting was no fluke. She was definitely attracted to Cali and her body didn't hide the fact. She felt an energy flow through her she hadn't felt in years, and by the way Cali was paying attention to her, she thought she may be feeling the same thing. Once her nerves settled, Ronni talked with Cali with unusual ease, as if she'd known her for years.

"My time's up. I better get going. Would you walk with me outside?" Cali asked.

"I'd love to," Ronni said.

As they exited the lodge from the second floor and walked out on the deck, Cali stopped and leaned over the railing. She pulled a pen out of her ski jacket pocket and took Ronni's hand. On her palm, she wrote her phone number.

The soft fingers touching Ronni sent a charge through her body and to her core. Every stroke of the pen against her skin triggered tremors within.

Cali searched out Ronni's eyes when she finished. "Call me," she said in a seductive tone, her eyes drawing Ronni in.

Before Ronni was able to answer, she felt the deck vibrate from under her. Others must have felt it too as their attentions shifted and they eyed one another in confusion. Ronni realized that Cali had grabbed her hand. She saw a group of teenagers point up and to their left, then heard Cali whisper, "White Dragon."

AT THE BASE of the hill, Halie checked her watch. Ten minutes before eleven o'clock. She was familiar with April's schedule since she'd taken skiing lessons with her last winter. April would be getting her group rounded up to head outside now. Five minutes later and she'd have missed her and they'd be on the slopes. April would be too busy to talk to her then. Halie snapped off her skies and leaned them against the rack in front of the ski shop which doubled as a ski school. The building was situated on the far left side of the mountain near the base, about a quarter mile from the condo development at the farthest end. There were a couple of short runs with t-lines and one that went higher up with a chair lift, both to the left of the ski school, not far from the trail Halie had just descended. Behind the two-story building towered the mountain covered in pine trees, for as far as Halie could see. Inside, the building was filled with ski and snowboard equipment and apparel. The school was built with a small room in the rear of the building where everyone met and where those without their own equipment got fitted with rentals.

Halie bent over and unbuckled her top boot snap. As she stood, she heard the loud thundering of what sounded like a train approach. Then she saw a mass of snow high upon the mountain slide toward her at ferocious speed. She bolted into the ski shop. "Everyone out! Everyone out, now! Avalanche! Get out the building and run to your left! Out of the building to your left!" she yelled. Halie raced to the back room where she knew April would be. She was there with half a dozen or so kids. Halie knew they'd only have seconds. She feared they wouldn't make it out in time.

April's eyes met the fear in Halie's. She immediately corralled the kids together. "Out, let's go!" April yelled. She led them out the back room and toward the front door. The kids were in varied stages of dress, and running with ski boots on didn't help their situation. Halie followed close behind, with another woman behind her. The thunderous roar became overwhelming as Halie's heart beat so fast she thought it would jump from her chest. They wouldn't make it. She realized that now, but at least they tried. As they neared the circular wooden sales counter in the middle of the store, Halie felt the hairs on the back of her neck rise. "April, everyone, duck in behind the counter, now!" she commanded. She pushed them from the rear the same instant she felt hands on her own back push her. The sound of wood splintering and glass shattering surrounded her as she fell forward.

Chapter Fifteen

BEFORE EVEN REGISTERING the snow that entered through the broken passenger side window or the pounding in her brain, Sam shoved her hand through the window opening and thrust upward with all her might. She shifted up onto the car seat for more leverage. Within seconds, she felt her fingers free of the snowpack and saw a stream of sunlight filter through. If nothing else, she concluded they'd now have a shaft of air to breath until they could dig themselves out or until someone located and rescued them. She forced herself to slow her breathing and get a grasp on the situation. Her taut muscles relaxed. Her next thought was of Corrine.

Sam leaned toward her friend. "Corrine, are you okay? Corrine, for God's sake please say something."

An unrecognizable mumble drifted from Corrine's lips before consciousness came to her and her head sprang forward, eyes wide open. "What happened? What's going on?"

Sam placed her hand on Corrine's knee. "Take it easy. We got hit by the avalanche. We'll be okay. We're close to the surface. I found an opening and we've got air. Are you hurt?"

Seconds passed before she responded. "I don't think so. I probably can't say as much for the car though."

Sam was glad Corrine hadn't lost her sense of humor. They were going to need it. Sam surprised herself at how quickly she reacted after they came to a stop. She'd learned about what to do in avalanche situations, both as a victim and a rescuer, but she never thought she'd have to apply her knowledge as a victim in real life. Sam recalled the moment the car slammed into the guardrail and rolled countless times before it stopped. She understood time was of the essence and that snow could set firm in seconds, but at that instant she had no idea how deep they were buried or how far down the mountain they slid. Once she saw sunlight, she knew they had a chance.

She was also aware that science was on their side and the plausibility of not being buried deep was a good one. Similar to how larger objects in sand or salt move to the top when shaken up, Corrine's car would act the same way, which is why Sam yelled at Corrine to stay in the car. That and she knew the car frame would provide additional protection. "I'm going to try and dig a bigger hole for us to get out of. If you feel okay, go ahead and check around in the car and see if you can find anything we can use that might help us.

Corrine undid her seatbelt. She slithered into the back of the vehicle. "There's an ice scraper around here somewhere."

"Great. That might help, and if it doesn't, I can push it through the hole and wave it back and forth until someone sees it. How do you feel?"

"I feel like I'll be donning colorful bruises around my shoulder and ribs. How about you?" Corrine said.

"Overall, I think I'm okay. Maybe a little of the same that you got."

"Guess I won't be getting April that saddle for Christmas now."

"We'll get out of this, I promise you, and we'll still go get that saddle. It just won't be today," Sam said.

RONNI STOOD AS if in shock while people scattered from the deck at the lodge, some screaming, other's yelling for their kids. Ronni heard the words "I gotta go," from Cali, felt her release her hand, and caught sight of her running across the deck, but Ronni didn't react. Her legs wouldn't move for several seconds, and once she did chase after Cali, she was slowed by her bulky ski boots and the sea of people pushing to leave the slopes or find loved ones.

Ronni drove forward against the crowd, attempting to get back to the lift line she'd found Cali on, but snow blocked the way. As she searched for Cali and an alternate route around the snowpack, she heard sirens from the parking lot and helicopters overhead. Ronni traveled south along the side of the snow slide for a distance before giving up and heading back toward the parking lot. From there, she saw Teton County Search and Rescue field personnel being organized and deployed onto the slopes and what appeared to be a staging area set up. Ronni headed toward the staging area. She passed rescue personnel carrying shovels and collapsible probe poles.

The closer she got, the more devastation she could see. She breathed deep. She saw a debris field of splintered wood and broken off branches from pine trees, rocks and dirt, and a mangled snow cat lying on its side, pushed from where it sat into the parking lot. Part of the parking lot was engulfed with snow as well, several cars half covered. And although the condos farther off to the left of the avalanche's path remained untouched, the ski school was almost completely swallowed up, with only a portion of the second floor visible. The upper floor of the structure was severely damaged and shifted from the floor below.

"Oh my God," Ronni said aloud. Although she still wanted to find Cali, she knew she was okay, and now felt the need to seek out someone from the rescue team to see if there was anything she could do to help. The staging area appeared chaotic. Twice she said, "Excuse me" to a rescue member, only to be pushed past and unanswered. She clearly understood why. Time was certain to be of the essence here. She didn't know how long buried victims had under the snow, but she imagined not long. As she stood, waiting to get someone's attention, a second team of rescuers arrived with medical and evacuation equipment, as did members from Alpine Crest Ski Patrol, Wyoming K-9 Search and

Rescue, and sheriffs and fire departments.

Ronni approached a man who was flagging off what appeared to be an entry/exit gate or check point for the rescuers. "Excuse me sir, is there anything I can do to help?"

"I'm sorry lady, I appreciate what you want to do here, but there's still a threat of another slide. Unless you're trained medical or rescue personnel, you'll need to clear the area." As the man spoke, rope-off points were already being set up to keep all non-rescue and non-medical personnel at a safe distance.

Feeling helpless, Ronni headed to the parking lot, hoping her Jeep was not one of the vehicles covered in the avalanche, though fairly certain it wasn't, based on where she'd remembered she'd parked. While she exited, media vans and TV station helicopters found their way to the accident. Ronni was overwhelmed. The scene appeared a disheveled mass of confusion. When Ronni finally found her Jeep and plopped into the seat, she turned on the engine and sat, thankful she and Cali had avoided the avalanche, and hopeful anyone else affected would be okay. She stared at the phone number penned on her hand. As the heat cranked in the Jeep, Ronni realized how tired she was as her eyelids felt heavy. She put the Jeep in gear and merged with the rest of the cars exiting the parking lot. A few seconds later, she pulled into an empty space and dialed Cali's number.

CALI RAN ALL the way from the lodge toward where she saw the avalanche descend. She prayed the path was in the woods only and not covering any of the trails, the townhomes, or the ski school. She also knew the likelihood of that would be slim. Already the sound of sirens and helicopters flooded the air. Snowpack blocked her way to the ski lift where she worked, increasing her worry.

She scanned the length of the debris field and headed north. A short while later, she was able to cross. From there she saw the debris line blocking her way was narrow, perhaps a sliver off the main slide, but the trail below and the lift line she worked were intact.

Further west however, a wider debris line cleared trees all along the mountain, all the way into part of the parking lot, covering the ski school to the extent only part of the top was visible, but clearly it had shifted from the base. Cali's heart sank. Her heart pounded faster. From her vantage point, she saw people scattering everywhere, most making their way out of the ski area. She saw rescue crews gathering near the base of the mountain and in the parking lot.

She knew staying on the mountain was dangerous and decided to head to where the rescuers were. There was no way down to the ski school from where she stood anyway, and the last thing she needed to do was start another slide. As she headed back the way she came, her cell phone rang. At first she thought to let it ring. Then she thought, what if it's April?

"Hello?" Cali said. Her voice shook.

"Hi, Cali? It's Ronni. Are you okay?"

"Yeah, I'm fine, but the devastation...have you seen it?"

"I have. It's awful. I tried finding you, but couldn't. Then I tried to help, but they wouldn't let me do that either," Ronni said.

"The ski school...it looks bad. April was teaching today. I work with her at the ranch. She's a friend of Sam and Halie's."

"Oh, God," Ronni said.

"Where are you?"

"I'm sitting in my Jeep in the parking lot. Where are you?"

"I'm on my way to the parking lot. I was going to see if they'd let me help, since I'm an employee." As Cali talked, she saw rescue personnel already begin their ascent up the mountain, leaving flags in certain places.

"They won't let you. Not even employees. I was told outright if I wasn't medical or rescue personnel, I couldn't be here. I think we're more of a risk than help at this point."

"I'm going to try anyway. I can't leave knowing April's here," Cali said. "I'm going to call her as soon as I get off the phone with you."

"Do you want me to meet you?"

"No. Maybe you can get a hold of Sam though, or Halie and let them know. See if they've heard from April."

"Okay, be careful." Ronni hung up and dialed Halie. She got no answer. Then she called the house phone and left a message.

HALIE'S HEART BEAT swift and fierce as she strained to see through the darkness, adrenaline coursing through her veins. The thunderous, crashing, sickening sound of the avalanche that collapsed the world around them had passed, followed now by multiple children crying and sobbing. She attempted to move her limbs. Nothing appeared broken. "April, are you okay? How are the kids?"

"My shoulder's hurt, but otherwise I think I'm okay. Kids, call out your names to me, one at a time, please." After the last child called out her name, April took a deep breath. "They're all here, Halie," she said, before adding in a whisper, "Justine didn't answer. She was behind you. I don't think she made it, but don't say anything. The kids are scared enough.

"It's so dark in here I can't see my hand in front of my face," Halie said.

"Hang on a minute," April said. "There should be a flashlight or one of those lamps with the battery pack around here. We had a few located around the store in the event of a blackout, since we don't have generator backup, and we've experienced blackouts before. I'm pretty sure they kept at least one by the cashier's counter."

"You search your end and I'll search mine." Halie extended her arms to the one side and with great care, gingerly reached out until she felt wood and shelving. She slid her hands over the bottom of the top shelf, from one side to the other, then repeated the process on the shelf below. Her hand traveled over what felt like a candy bar or two, plastic bags, a pair of scissors, some other odd shaped object she had no idea of what it was, and then felt the rectangular battery pack with a light mounted on top. She felt for the button to turn it on, depressed it, and lit up the space that was their shelter. The sparse sanctuary separated them from life and death. "Looks like you were right."

"I found one on this end too," April confirmed.

As soon as Halie flipped on the light, the cries from the kids subsided into sobs and whimpers. They sat huddled between two semi-circular cashier counters, the ceiling above them caved in on an angle approximately six feet above, with enough room for five or six of them to stand erect at the same time. Then she shone the light to the space between the counters, from which they entered and to the space on the other end. The side they entered was completely compacted with snow. On the other end, the light carried into another pocket of space, but not far and then darkness once again. Halie met April's eyes. They locked with an unseen connection and understanding of the situation, but held a determination and awareness needed so as not to scare the kids.

"The glass cover on this lamp is cracked, but it works," April said. She held the battery in her hand like a precious diamond ring. "We'll keep this one for backup if we need it. Can everyone move all of their body parts? Fingers, toes, arms, legs?"

The kids each responded in turn that no one was hurt.

"Great. That's a big plus. Someone's definitely looking out for us," April said.

When Halie watched the kids move their limbs and turn their heads left to right, up and down, she recognized another familiar face besides April's. "Tommy Weston, is that you? It's Ms. Walker, from the gallery where your mom works."

Three children sat between her and Tommy, and another four between Tommy to April. Like April, Halie knew they needed to keep these youngsters occupied and focused on anything but their current situation. Remaining calm would conserve oxygen.

Tommy breathed in and halted his sobbing. "Yes ma'am, Ms. Walker ma'am."

"So your mom finally broke down and let you take skiing lessons, did she?"

"Only after Grandma helped me pester her until she gave in." A momentary smile crossed his face before receding. "Maybe I should have listened to my mom. Now we're in big trouble. Are we going to die?"

"No, were not going to die," Halie said. She wrapped her arms around the kids sitting near her and watched April do the same. "April and I are going to see if we can get us out of here. And if we can't, then we'll sit and wait to be rescued." She unzipped her jacket. "You see this object hanging around my neck?"

Tommy mumbled that he had, and so did the other kids.

"Well, it's a transceiver. It sends out a signal to rescue crews that tells them exactly where we are, so it's just a matter of time before they come get us. In the meantime," she eyed the two candy bars on the shelf and reached for them, "we can play a few games, and the winner will get a piece of one of these chocolate bars, okay?"

The kids nodded and April smiled at Halie.

"That sounds like fun," April said. "Why don't you guys think of something to play while Halie and I see if we can find us all a way out."

After pushing against the shattered boards above them and crawling through the few open spaces that seemed as though they might lead somewhere, April and Halie realized in short order they were encased in a cement-like snow covered enclosure with no escape and would have to wait for help to find them.

"Let's test our cell phones," Halie whispered, "though I highly doubt we'll get reception under all this mess." They pulled out their phones. Neither got a signal.

"It doesn't matter," April said. "Rescuers wouldn't have gotten us out any quicker."

"I know, it's just—"

"I hear you, but it is what it is. Let's get back to the kids before they worry."

"Okay, no go on us finding a way out," April informed the kids. She sat in her spot again, "Which means we'll wait until they rescue us. Anyone come up with any ideas on what game they want to play?"

"We don't have any games," one of the girls said.

"Yeah," echoed other responses. "I didn't bring my Game Boy."

Halie was thankful for her recent visit to New Jersey. Had she not met Jessie and Katelynn, she'd have no idea what they could do either, since her nephews only played video games, rode bikes, and played sports. "Well, you guys are lucky because I have a fun game that doesn't need a board or batteries. It's sort of a word game. You guys interested?"

April lifted an eyebrow. "I'm curious."

"Me too," one of the girls called out.

"Great, so this is how we play." Halie gave everyone the basic fundamentals as they formed a circle on the floor. She was thankful she and the others wore ski clothes, the cold intensifying as they sat. "I'll start us out with names of animals. The game moves to the left. The first person who misses yelling out an answer, doesn't answer right away, or messes up on the beat, sits out the game until only one person's left. We'll start the first round slow, and then we'll pick up speed. The last

one remaining gets a piece of the candy bar." Halie set the rhythm, just
as she remembered Sam's niece Jessie had, with a mix of slaps on the
thighs, clapping of the hands, and snapping of the fingers, to the beat:
slap, slap, clap—snap, snap, "sheep."

To her left, the next girl followed Halie's lead. Slap, slap, clap—
snap, snap, "donkey," and on it went. Halie was surprised how good
the kids were at the game and had trouble keeping up with them as the
speed of the game progressed and she was the first one out. Everyone
laughed. She was thankful the distraction was working.

As Halie listened to the kids, the sounds of their voices faded and
her thoughts drifted to Sam. She thought about the first time she saw
the handsome ranger in Chief Thundercloud's office, and the
unexpected reaction her body felt when she first shook Sam's hand and
stared into those emerald green eyes, and felt the wonderful sensations
all over again. She recalled the tense and precious moments they shared
during her assignment at the park last summer. There were so many
special moments, now that she had time to think about them, and she
remembered their first kiss, a kiss that melted her heart and left her
lightheaded. She remembered the first time they made love.

She wiped a tear from her cheek. She thought of all that Sam did for
her in the short time she'd known her and all the caring and selfless
things she did for others, and she longed to hold her in her arms and
breathe sweet words in her ears, and love her fully and not let her go.
She had wasted precious time by not showing Sam how much she cared
for her. Having escaped death once, she should have known better.
She'd never let anything get between them again, never let her work or
fear control her, and resolved to make up for lost time if she was lucky
enough to be given another chance.

Halie hadn't initially noticed Tommy moved from his spot until she
felt the tug on her arm. Only three players remained in the game. April
was one of them. "What's up?" Halie said.

Tommy whispered so only she could hear. "I wanted to tell you, in
case we don't make it out of here, that I had nothing to do with the stuff
Brian did to you guys. I told him you were good people and that he was
being a jerk, but he wouldn't listen. He made me swear not to tell Mom.
I wanted to tell her, I did, but I couldn't. I'm sorry."

Confusion etched itself across Halie's face. "Tell her what?"

"About Coco, the stuff with the house, the car, your fence—all of it.
It wasn't all Brian's fault though. Since Dad left, he's been angry *a lot*,
and he's been mad about all the time Mom spends at work. I think he
blamed you. But his friend Toby Hodgeman was the one who pushed
Brian to do stuff he didn't want to do, and Toby was the one that spray-
painted your garage door, at least that's what Brian told me. Brian
shouldn't have let him do it though, and I told him so."

"You did? That was very smart and brave of you to stand up to
your brother. Don't worry about Brian though. I'll have a talk with your

mom. You did the right thing."

Tommy inclined his head, apparently relieved to have the burden his brother placed on him lifted from his shoulders. He returned his attention to the game as Halie's hand touched his arm.

Of all the people she thought might have been the ones harassing them, Brian wasn't even on her radar screen. She partly understood what drove Brian, though his actions remained wrong, but what puzzled her most was how Brian's friend, someone so young, someone who didn't know them at all, could hold such hatred for them. Had his parents filled him with that much hate? Was it his teachers or relatives? He must have learned it from somewhere. The thought saddened her.

SAM HEARD THE muffled sound of sirens and hum of large engines, which she guessed might be snow removal equipment from Wyoming DOT. The cold quickly seeped through their clothes, making their wait for rescue that much more uncomfortable.

"I smell gas. It's making me nauseous," Corrine said.

"I know. I smell it too. We're going to have to find something else to try and dig free with, or at least dig a bigger hole for air. The plastic ice scraper's not cutting it."

"Yeah, but what?" Corrine said. A minute later she said, "I've got it. What about the wrench for the spare tire?"

"It's worth a shot. Where is it?"

"It's in the hatch area, under the pull up carpeting—in with the spare."

"I'll get it," Sam said as she crawled into the back and leaned over the seats into the rear of the SUV. She stretched out as far as she could to pull up the rug and compressed cardboard flooring and withheld a gag. She felt lightheaded and hoped she wouldn't pass out from the fumes.

"Did you find it?" Corrine asked.

"Yeah, I got it. It's just a matter of getting it out."

When Sam returned to the front of the vehicle, she thrust the metal bar from the tire jack into the snow, which was hard and compact. Small chunks broke free. She realized her effort was going to be futile, but kept at it.

"Hurry Sam, I feel like I can't breathe. My heart's racing. I can't stand this. I don't think we're going to make it."

"You're fine Corrine, try and relax. You're giving yourself a panic attack. We have air, and I can see light. Help is on the way, you have to believe that. I won't let anything happen to us, okay? I promise."

"If I could catch my breath, it might not be so bad," Corrine said.

"Corrine, sit back and focus on nothing except the air flowing in and out of your lungs. Every time your thoughts drift to something else, redirect them."

"I'll try."

"Good." While Corrine worked on calming herself, Sam plugged away at the snow. After several more minutes, her arms felt the strain. Suddenly, she heard voices. "I think someone's coming."

Corrine opened her eyes. "Oh, God, I hope so," she said.

"We're down here!" Sam yelled. "Down here! Two of us!" Even with the shaft air and sun they had leading to the surface, Sam found her voice muffled, as if her yells merely bounced against padded walls. Then she turned to Corrine. "I hope someone heard that. Are you okay to dig for a while and then we'll switch places again? I need a rest. It's like chipping away at cement with an ice pick."

"Sure. I'm okay now. Thanks for the chat before. I'm sorry I lost it."

"It's okay. Under the circumstances, I think you're doing pretty darn good."

Sam and Corrine traded places, and several minutes later, Sam heard the rescuers above them. They called down and Corrine answered. Soon, firefighters armed with shovels were digging them out. Once a large enough opening was made, they got Corrine out of the passenger side of the vehicle first. Sam helped by pushing her as they pulled. Sam was next. As soon as they had her on top of the snow pack, she was wrapped in a blanket. "Thanks," she said to the fireman who pulled her free. "You don't know how happy I am to see you guys."

"Feeling's mutual, trust us," he said.

Sam knew exactly what he meant. There was nothing worse than arriving on the scene of an accident and losing the victims before you could rescue them. Once outside the car, Sam had a chance to look around. She realized how lucky they were. They'd rolled about a hundred and forty feet down the side of the mountain before a tree stopped them. Short of the pain she felt throughout her body, she and Corrine suffered only minor cuts from the broken glass and some symptoms due to the gas fumes, though the fresh air helped to quell the nausea. After a few more minutes, firefighters assisted them via rope up the hill. The farther up the side of the mountain they came, Sam got a clearer picture of the devastation and other cars partly buried and partly visible. Her legs wobbled slightly from the sight and the climb, but she continued on, as did Corrine.

Sam watched rescuers in probe lines make their way across the mounds of snow that covered the highway and runoff below. She recognized them using the three-hole-per-step approach as they moved across the snow pack. Those on the line stood hand-to-hand. They probed once outside their right foot, then in the center, and then outside their left foot. Flags were placed in areas that needed additional attention, and K-9 units followed a safe distance behind, so as not to disturb unsearched areas.

As Sam observed and wished she could help, not used to being the victim and not the rescuer, they were escorted to the staging area. From there, they were taken to the hospital to be checked out and treated, in spite of Sam's numerous protests.

HALIE AND APRIL spent the last half hour in silence, trying to conserve air, several rounds of their word game played out. They had tired out the kids, most of whom were asleep or close to it. The chill had seeped into their bones. Halie became increasingly aware of the thinning air, her breathing labored. She pushed fear aside and focused instead on the commotion above them. She whispered to April, "Do you think the rescuers will get to us in time?"

"I'm beginning to wonder that myself, though I hope so," April said.

"Do you think Sam and Corrine heard about what happened? I wonder if Sam's up there trying to get us out," Halie said.

"I don't know, but I'd have to think the chances of that are slim if they were out shopping. I wish they were though. I can't think of anyone I'd rather see than those two right now."

"Me too," Halie said.

In the silence that followed, she struggled to stay awake, and watched April do the same. April's head bobbed forward as her eyes closed, then snapped up again. Halie didn't want to sleep. In her mind, if she fell asleep, she'd have given up. Part of her knew she might not wake again and she couldn't let that part win. She missed Sam so much and prayed she was among the search crew looking for them, even if her thoughts were similar to April's.

When she took in the young, innocent faces around her, anxiety fastened its hold once again. Her heart ached. They had to make it out, and soon. They had to.

A handful of snow dropped on Halie's head in concert with a creak in the make-shift ceiling. Halie realized she must have dozed off, and so had April, though she was the only one who awoke to the noise. The flashlight April found dimmed to a barely orange glow, the other one went out long ago.

When the creaking stopped, the ceiling dropped another foot. Halie's heart raced with fear. Did they survive this long only to be crushed by the collapsing ceiling? Could life be so cruel? As her throat tightened and anxiety level rose, she heard the faint sound of voices and her heart raced for a different reason. Soon she heard more voices and the sound of shovels and the buzz of chain saws.

When the noise stopped she yelled, waking the others. "Down here! We're down here!" She coughed, the air was so thin. "There are nine of us," she managed. Then she heard the muffled buzz and whine of chain saws start up again and cut through the wood above them before a rush of fresh air filled her lungs.

BOTH SAM AND Corrine tried reaching Halie and April on their cell phones to no avail as they waited to be treated at St. John's Medical Center.

"I don't understand why Halie's not picking up," Sam said. "It's not like her. I know she's with that Colin guy on the slopes, but I'd have thought she'd have left her cell phone on. She knows I worry about her."

"That is strange. Although I know when I call April sometimes, if she's in the middle of a ski lesson, she doesn't call until she's on a break. The odd thing is, she should have been on break by now." A few moments of silence followed. "You don't think the tremor that caused the avalanche on Teton Pass could have affected the ski area, do you?"

"No, the areas are too far from each other. There's no way the two are connected. Please, don't make me worry more than I already am," Sam said.

"Sorry, but when I'm sitting around doing nothing, I let my mind wander. I can't believe how long this is taking. If these wounds were more serious, we could have bled to death by now."

"Who knows how many people were injured at the Pass, and since we're not that bad off, I'm sure that's why we've been stuck waiting," Sam said. She viewed the flat screen TV in the far corner of the room, which aired a closed captioned CNN program that had cut off for a commercial. "I haven't seen anyone else brought in lately, so I figure they should take us soon. I think I'll give Ronni a call and see if she can pick us up. She should be off work by now."

Before Sam finished dialing the number, CNN returned on the air with more breaking news. The newscaster reported, "As the search and rescue continues at the site of the second avalanche to hit Teton County today, more pictures are pouring in from the devastation at the Alpine Crest Ski Resort. The number of people recovered has now climbed to—"

"Holy—Corrine—Jesus, did you hear that? Halie and April. Oh, my God. What if that's why they're not answering their phones? We gotta find a way to get over there. Now!"

Corrine stood, her face pale as if in shock. Suddenly, as Sam grabbed her arm to leave, another group of people, mostly kids, were brought through the door.

Sam stopped in her tracks. Halie led the kids through the door. "Oh, my God. We just heard the news. Thank God you're safe. You both look awful," Sam said, as she gently hugged Halie.

"What happened?" Corrine said, holding onto April.

"It's a long story. But before I get into that, what are you both doing here?" April asked.

"We got stuck in the avalanche at Teton Pass."

Halie held her hand to her mouth. Tears streamed from her eyes. "An avalanche at Teton Pass? I can't believe this. It's been an unbelievable day," Halie said. "I have to sit."

Sam helped her to a chair. April sat also, but kept hold of Corrine's hand.

"We're okay," Corrine said. "The car's not—but the EMT's insisted we be checked out."

"Us too," April said. "Today was the scariest day of my life. I didn't think we'd make it. I'm so glad to be here."

As soon as April finished, Cali walked in, followed by Ronni.

"Please," Sam said, "No more. Tell me you two are okay."

"We're fine," Ronni said.

"What are you both doing here? How'd you know we were—"

"We're fine and never mind that now. We're your rides home," Ronni said.

LATER THAT EVENING, Sam and Halie sat together on their sofa, facing the fireplace, unable to unwind from their terrifying and draining day. Sam rested against the cushion by the armrest, and Halie leaned into her shoulder. They held hands in silence for some time until Halie spoke.

"I'm not sure after everything we've been through today that this is the right time to bring up this conversation, but then we never know when we'll get another chance."

Sam's eyes met Halie's and she squeezed her hand tight, but said nothing.

Halie relaxed and continued. "I'm sorry that I've been distant with you, and I'm even sorrier that I keep telling you things will change when for one reason or another they don't. When I was trapped under that snow today...I did a lot of thinking. I promised myself that if or when I got out of there, I'd doubly show you how much you mean to me and never let wasted time come between us again."

Sam was about to reply when Halie interrupted. "Hold on—there's more. That's what I planned on telling you, what I thought I resolved in my mind, but I can't. I don't want to make the same mistakes I've made before and hurt you all over again. I'm not sure the solution is as simple as I thought it was earlier."

"I don't think it's that simple either, though I wish it were, but I'm glad we're discussing it," Sam said. "I've thought about what's transpired and think maybe we need to make more time for each other. We don't go out often like we used to and we don't talk about our problems or try to deal with them together. I don't remember the last time we sat in front of the fireplace and held hands like we are now. I miss it." Sam watched the flames flicker and rise. She soaked in their warmth, a comfort.

"I miss it too," Halie said. "I had similar thoughts. I think we can't hold things inside. We need to discuss things that are bothering us rather than bottle them up. I promise I'll be open with you from this moment forward, no matter how difficult or uncomfortable the subject matter might be for either of us. In the long run, we'll be stronger for it."

"And I'll do the same, I promise."

Halie smiled. "And if that doesn't work, we'll see a relationship counselor. I'll do whatever it takes. You're too important to me and so is our happiness. I love you."

"I love you too."

Halie leaned toward Sam and kissed her gentle on the lips, several times. "I don't know about you, but I think this day caught up to me. All of a sudden it's a struggle to keep my eyes open.

"Me too," Sam said. "Plus I'm not sure if I have any coherent thoughts left."

"How about we go to bed and you hold me tight until we fall asleep?" Halie suggested.

"I'm all for that," Sam said. "It's finding the energy to make it up the stairs that I'm worried about."

Chapter Sixteen

WEDNESDAY AFTERNOON, FIVE days after the avalanche, Cali walked into Nature's Vision.

"Hey, thanks for stopping by," Halie said.

Cali made her way across the wooden gallery floor. "Are you kidding me? You don't have to thank me. I'm the one who's thankful for everything you're doing for us, especially after all that's happened to you. How are you? And Sam?"

"We're fine. Thanks. It's not something we'll ever forget, but things are getting back to normal."

"I'm glad. Even for me, not being directly affected, it was scary. You're so helpless. Anyhow, on to brighter topics. Do we have our first winner?" Cali asked.

"Not just a winner, but a winner who's painting sold the first day I displayed it."

"I don't believe it."

"Believe it. I'm thinking maybe I'll put the top two works of art up next month, instead of one. I also thought it would be better to limit the payment the kid's parents got on their behalf to twenty percent of the sale instead of fifty percent, and then give the school the other eighty percent, but then also give the kids a framed certificate," Halie said.

"That's a great idea, but who'll pay for framing?"

"The gallery will. I'll cut the suspense. Your first winner was Jennifer Paulison."

Cali clapped her hands like a child on Christmas. "That's fantastic. Hers was my first choice too. She's one of our third graders. She has self-confidence issues, so this certificate should do wonders for her. I can't wait to give her the good news."

"I'm glad." Halie proceeded behind the counter and brought out Jennifer's certificate and two checks. "Here you go," she said as she handed the items over to Cali. "By the way, this isn't my business and you don't have to answer, but have you seen Ronni since we were all together at the hospital? Have you guys talked since or gotten together?"

Cali fixed her eyes on the front window of the gallery. "No, but it's only been a couple of days. I've been super busy anyhow. I'm sure she'll call."

RONNI PACED IN front of the telephone mustering the courage to dial, but her nerves up to this point prevented that simple action from happening. Ronni fought with the voices in her head. Why hadn't Cali called? Was she expecting her to call? What if she was the only one who felt a connection and Cali didn't? But then again, she did get her phone number. Ronni recalled the warm, tingling sensation she experienced when Cali took her hand on the deck at the ski lodge and wrote her phone number on it. After that, everything got crazy. True she'd called her to tell her when they found April and Halie, and they met at the hospital, but when they parted, Cali didn't mention that Ronni should call her.

Lost in thought, Ronni hadn't registered her roommate traipse by, barefoot and in her pajamas, scarfing down a slice of cold pizza until she heard "What's your problem? Call her already for heaven's sake. You're killing me already."

"She might not be up yet. I don't want to wake her."

"Pu-lease," Tracy said. "If I'm up, then she's definitely up. Besides, if an avalanche can't get the two of you together, what will it take? It's not like you won't have plenty to talk about. You know you want to. Suck it up and make the call."

Ronni relaxed and smiled at Tracy. "You're right. I'm being stupid. The worst she could say is no."

"Of course I'm right." Tracy bit off another huge piece from her slice. "Well? What are you waiting for?"

"A little privacy would be nice."

"Oh, you kill me, really you do. Fine," she said, and headed into her room. "But if you don't call her, I'll be sure to make you as miserable as you've made me these past few days."

ANGELA'S RESTAURANT WAS quiet for a Thursday evening during the holidays, which Ronni preferred. She was glad she didn't have to yell over other patrons to talk to Cali. Soft Italian music played in the background. They sat at a small table against the wall and not far from the fireplace. A candle and a vase of fresh pine branches intertwined with red berries adorned their white linen table. The smell of garlic bread wafted through the linen napkin that kept their bread warm. Ronni's stomach growled.

A grin etched the corner of Cali's mouth.

"Sorry about that," Ronni said, her cheeks turning crimson. "Bread?"

"Bread would be great, and don't worry about it. I'm starving too. If your stomach hadn't growled, you'd have heard mine chime in."

Ronni appreciated the ease and kindness Cali exuded. "Thanks for saying that," she said. She broke off a piece of bread and placed it on Cali's plate.

Cali's eyes held Ronni's. A comfortable silence followed until Cali replied, "Thanks for calling and inviting me to dinner tonight. I want you to know I'm happy to be here with you. I've never been to this restaurant before. It's quite nice."

"The food's supposed to be fantastic. My roommate recommended it," Ronni said.

"Excellent food is a bonus, but spending time with you is even better."

Ronni swallowed hard, her heartbeat quickened. "I agree...about spending time with you," she managed.

"I'm sorry I didn't get to say much to you at the hospital. It was such a crazy day. I should have called you after. The whole thing kind of shook me up."

"I know what you mean, and I wasn't sure if I should call or not...if you wanted me to," Ronni said.

"Of course I wanted you to. Please don't think I make a habit of writing my phone number on other people's hands."

The two women laughed. After the ice was broken, their conversation lingered well past their meal and dessert as Ronni explained in more detail what happened to Sam and Halie, from what they told her, and Cali chimed in with April and Corrine's corroborating versions of that tragic day. Then they talked about their families, jobs, and future aspirations. Ronni couldn't get enough of Cali. She didn't want the night to end, but knew it soon would. She drove slower on the ride home than she did to the restaurant, and when she pulled in April and Corrine's driveway, she shut off the engine and said, "I'll walk you to the door."

"You don't need to do that, but if you want to, I won't stop you," Cali said.

Ronni's face lit up. "Great. Don't move." She got out, strutted around the rear of the car, then opened the door for Cali. Once Cali was out of the Jeep and Ronni shut the door behind her, she added, "It feels strange walking you to the door, knowing April and Corrine are home. I feel like I'm back in high school, sneaking around with my date."

Cali laughed. Her breath floated upward in the bitter cold. "I know what you mean, but my living arrangements are temporary. April and Corrine have been so great to put me up like they have. I admit though, I'm rather experiencing the same sensation, though back in high school my first real date was with a guy, and he turned out to be a complete jerk. I don't even know why I agreed to go out with him. I think I was still in denial about being gay. Other than him walking me to the door when someone else was home, this date, thank goodness, is nothing like that evening."

Ronni stood at the top of the steps. She fidgeted from one foot to the other, more from nerves than the cold, uncertain how to end the evening. "Well, I better let you get inside before you freeze to death out here. I had a nice evening," she said.

"I did too." Cali took Ronni's hand into her own. "I noticed you haven't lit a cigarette once tonight. Why's that?"

Ronni thought she'd lose consciousness at Cali's touch, and her question sent a bolt of embarrassment through her, yet she knew she needed to answer. "I gave up smoking."

Cali's eyes bore into Ronni's. "Just like that, for no reason?"

"I, uh, well—no, not for no reason." Ronni's cheeks warmed again. She was thankful the light given off from the holiday decorations wasn't bright enough that Cali would notice her blush. "I stopped for you," she managed after an awkward silence. "I thought that in case I was lucky enough to meet you again, I didn't want my chances with you ruined if I smoked. I came to the conclusion during our first meeting that you didn't like smokers."

"Interesting," Cali said.

The tone sent shivers along Ronni's spine. She wanted nothing more than to kiss Cali in that moment, to feel the softness of her lips and tenderness of her touch, as she imagined so many times during those sleepless nights since they met.

Cali stepped closer, her line of sight focused on Ronni's lips.

Ronni clutched onto the invitation sent. She tilted her head and leaned in for a kiss. She kissed Cali gingerly at first, then again with greater urgency. Ronni heard the beating of her heart throb in her ears, her desire overtaking her when Cali parted her lips and explored her mouth with her tongue. Ronni eagerly met Cali's advances. All thoughts were focused on the woman before her while the world stood still for that moment. When their mouths separated, Ronni took a deep breath. "I'll take that as a yes that it would be okay to call you again?"

"You better take that as a yes, or I did something wrong."

Chapter Seventeen

A LIGHT SNOW was forecast for the first Saturday in December, but so far the weather was fine, partly cloudy and no snow. Sam was glad. She had plans she didn't want the weather ruining. When she heard car doors slam shut and saw Jake head for the front door, she joined him.

After warm hugs were exchanged, a bag of bagels handed over, and jackets taken and placed into the foyer closet by Sam, Cali asked, "Whose idea was it to have us all over for breakfast?"

"It was Sam's," Halie responded, "and Jake's of course."

Cali laughed. "Of course. Well, I wanted to say thanks. It's so nice to be here again, and so good to see you all." With her last words, her eyes drifted to Ronni.

The glance didn't go unnoticed, as Sam held Halie's eyes with her own before she focused on Cali. "You're more than welcome, and we're glad you could come," Sam said. "Why don't you guys go ahead and sit at the table while we wait for Corrine and April. I'll take the bagels into the kitchen. They smell so good. I'm not sure how long I'll be able to hold off. The garlic bagel's calling my name."

"Lucky me," Halie said, as Sam disappeared into the kitchen.

Two minutes later, Jake sprang up and ran to the front door barking seconds before the doorbell rang. April and Corrine stood outside on their stone steps.

After sturdy hugs were again exchanged, they all settled back around the dining room table.

"How much food did you bring?" Halie asked. She held two bags of donut boxes. "First these guys pick up enough bagels to feed a couple families and then you guys bring enough donuts and coffee to feed an army."

"Well," April started, "The way I see it, you can't go wrong if you overestimate. Besides," she paused, "we all know how much you like to eat."

Halie gave April a playful slap. "Very funny, but other than Cali, I've seen you all do a pretty good job of putting it away yourselves."

"Guilty," Ronni replied, tapping her belly. "No, seriously though, I'm so glad we're all here too. What a difference a couple of weeks make."

Corrine reached for a sesame seed bagel. "I'll say, and how lucky we all were. Other than a few scratched up faces and April's sore shoulder, we did okay."

"I read they rescued the guy Halie was skiing with, Colin Mitchell, the one she was hired to photograph, though they think he may have been the cause of the avalanche above the ski school," Sam informed everyone.

"I thought the avalanche was caused by the tremor?" Corrine said.

"Only the one by Teton Pass that we got caught in. The other they're blaming on him. He was skiing in a restricted area, and restricted for good reason. Halie said they argued about it on the mountain that morning, and when she wouldn't go with him, he fired her. When she left him, he went into the lodge, but when he came out, he must have skied the restricted trail anyway."

"That's infuriating," Corrine said.

"You can add thoughtless and asinine to the list of words describing him. He called from the hospital during the week to apologize to Halie. We were surprised to hear from him. He sounded remorseful, but unfortunately, he'll have to live with what he did the rest of his life. Lucky for him not more people were killed. Three in total, including at the Pass, but lots more injured," Sam said.

Halie's facial expression grew more serious as she set her cup of coffee on its saucer. She addressed April. "The woman behind me in the ski school, Justine. Did you find out if she made it?"

"No, she didn't," April said, "but she was also very ill. She shouldn't even have been at work, but she said it helped to take her mind off things. She wasn't being paid, she just hung around. She couldn't do much, but she liked talking with me and the kids, and other people. Justine had lung cancer—they didn't give her much time. As sad as losing her is, her dying quickly may have been a blessing in disguise for her. I miss her though. She always cheered me up, when I should have been the one cheering her up. That's the kind of person she was. The kids loved her too."

"I think most things happen for a reason," Cali said, "even if we can't understand why. It's possible God sent the White Dragon for a purpose."

"When the avalanche hit and we were standing on the deck at the base lodge, I heard you whisper 'White Dragon' but I didn't think anything of it at the time. What's that all about?" Ronni asked.

"Since the Middle Ages, in Europe there's been an old riddle passed around from generation to generation—'What flies without wings, hits without hands, and sees without eyes?'—the answer is The White Dragon—the avalanche. My mom's partner told me about it many years ago when I was still a kid. It stuck with me for some reason. An avalanche exemplifies the powerful forces at play in nature and solidifies the fact that nature and White Dragons have and will continue to demand our respect," Cali said.

"Respect Colin certainly didn't show," Halie said. "The name's perfect. It was a White Dragon, the way it swooped over us. I think though that this dragon may have realized what happened and sat above us, above our group of kids at Alpine Crest, and held back the weight of the snow until rescuers came. I think it protected us from being crushed."

"It very well could have," Cali agreed. "I also read in the paper that an avalanche breaker existed at the bottom of the mountain in front of the condos and the ski school. Without it, I don't think anyone wants to ponder what the outcome would have been."

Cali barely got her last word out before Jake jumped up, ran toward the front windows, and barked incessantly.

"I believe that's my cue to make more coffee," Sam said.

"What are you talking about now?" Halie asked.

"You'll see."

A CARAVAN OF vehicles led by Halie's co-worker Susan Weston made their way in front of Sam and Halie's property.

"What the heck?" Halie said as she neared the front door.

Sam put her arm around Halie's waist. "This was all Brian's idea. He organized the whole thing. Susan told me about it. Tommy told Brian what happened during the time you guys were buried, and he felt so bad about what he did to us, he wanted to fix it in some way. He called our garage door guy and is having the side of the garage door that his friend Toby vandalized replaced. He's paying for it from his job at the ranch with Charlie and money from his savings. He got everyone we know together. When other people from town heard about it, they wanted to be here too, to show their support and make a statement that they don't tolerate hate in this town either."

"I—I—can't believe it." Tears streamed down Halie's face. She wiped them dry with the back of her hand.

Sam kissed the side of her face. "Things have a way of working themselves out. We just have to be patient."

Halie turned. "You all knew about this didn't you? That's why you brought enough food for an army, isn't it?"

The facial expressions which followed, along with avoided eye contact, gave them away.

"I knew something was up, but I couldn't figure out what. What about Brian's friend Toby?" Halie asked.

"The sheriff met with him and his family. He'll get a healthy taste of community service sprinkled with sensitivity training administered through a troubled youth program," Sam replied. "It's so strange. Before all of this happened, I helped rescue his dad from Phelps Lake, where he'd injured his ankle. The guy was arrogant and critical of me at first, but warmed up rather quickly after he realized the predicament he was in and that he had no choice but to rely on me. I wonder if he filled his son with hateful thoughts early on in his life. I could see that in him. It's funny how things happen sometimes."

"That is strangely ironic," Ronni said. "His dad's confiscating his car, so maybe something did rub off on him that day you found him. He's going to let us fix it at the shop, but he's not giving it back to his son until he completes his training and every hour of service the judge sentenced him for."

"You don't think that'll make Toby even more mad and resentful against us though?" Halie asked.

"Not a chance. He'll work at the Jefferson Hill Healing Center. They handle long term and acute care AIDS patients, including children with AIDS. He doesn't know how lucky he is to live the life he's living, but he soon will. I suspect he'll get to hear some interesting stories too, stories that will put real faces and souls behind the bodies he sees. His false ideas will be tested," Sam added. "Brian will take the sensitivity training as well."

"That's good. I guess we better stop standing around then and greet our guests," Halie said. A smile stretched from one side of her face to the other. "And get them fed," she added. "As for you," Halie said to Sam in a hushed tone while everyone else put their jackets on and headed out the door, "*you,* I will pay back later. You better conserve your energy. You're going to need it."

"No doubt," Sam said.

Another title from Regina A. Hanel:

Love Another Day

Plagued by nightmares and sleepless nights after a tragic loss, Park Ranger Samantha Takoda Tyler longs for a calm day at Grand Teton National Park in Wyoming. But when she's summoned to the chief ranger's office and introduced to Halie Walker, a photojournalist working for The Wild International, her day is anything but calm. When she's assigned to look after Halie, their meeting transforms into a quarrelsome exchange. Over time, the initial chill between the women warms. They grow closer as they spend time together and gain appreciation for each other's work.

But Sam's fear of loss coupled with rising jealousy over an old lover's interest in Halie grinds their budding relationship to a halt. Halie finds that anywhere near Sam is too painful a place to be, and Sam is unable to find the key to open the door to a past that she's purposely kept locked away.

With fires raging out West and in the Targhee National Forest, Sam works overtime, helping fill the staffing shortage. She misses Halie and wants to take a chance with her. Before she gets the opportunity to explain herself, Sam learns the helicopter Halie is on has crashed. Ahead of an oncoming storm, Sam races to the rescue. Can she save the woman she loves? Or will the past replay, closing Sam off from love forever?

ISBN: 978-1-935053-44-6
Available in both print and eBook formats

Other Yellow Rose books you may enjoy:

The Game of Denial
by Brenda Adcock

Joan Carmichael, a successful New York businesswoman, lost the love of her life ten years earlier. Alone, she raised their four children, always cherishing her deep love for her wife. Her memories of their life together come back even stronger as one of their daughters prepares to marry. Joan and her four adult kids fly to Virginia to meet the groom's family and attend the ceremony at the small horse farm owned by the mother of the fiancé.

Evelyn "Evey" Chase, also a widow, has secrets in her past, and her memories of her dead husband aren't pleasant. She's concerned about meeting her future daughter-in-law's family, certain that she and her three kids will have little in common with the wealthy New Yorkers. Besides, the thought of two women in a relationship bringing up a family together makes her uncomfortable, even though her daughter-in-law assures her that lesbianism is not hereditary or catching.

When the two women meet they are drawn to one another in a way neither anticipated, and the game of denial begins. Evey fights her attraction and doesn't realize the effect she has on Joan. Joan tries to shake off her feelings, seeing them as a betrayal to the memory of her wife. Besides, isn't Evey Chase straight? After Evey and Joan share an intimate moment at the wedding reception, they are both emotionally terrified and Joan flees. Will Joan overcome the feeling of betraying her former mate and stop denying her desire to be happy again? Can Evey finally face her past in order to accept the love of another woman and the desire to live the life she had once dreamed of?

ISBN: 978-1-61929-130-0
Available in both print and eBook formats

Jess
by Pauline George

Jess is a modern day lesbian Lothario who was so hurt from an emotionally damaging relationship that now she doesn't let anyone get close. She protects herself by keeping her relationships short and sweet. When Jess's sister Josie challenges her to get to know a woman before she jumps into bed with her, Jess is intrigued. How hard can that be?

Although she's a serial monogamist, Jess has deep-seated morals that will be tested to the limit by her carefree acceptance of Josie's challenge. When she falls for her sister's best friend Katie, she suddenly finds her life upended, and she's left wondering if she actually has what it takes to have a lasting and fulfilling relationship. Is she destined to spend her life bed-hopping? Will her ever-growing attraction to Katie be the catalyst for romance, or will Katie's indecision about her life prove to be Jess's downfall?

ISBN: 978-1-61929-138-6
Available in both print and eBook formats

It'sElementary
by Jennifer Jackson

Tolerance and acceptance are growing in society, but don't tell that to a parent of a school-aged child. Teachers are supposed to be straight, wholesome, and good examples for the children they teach. This is why one vague rumor about a slightly effeminate teacher at Baxter Elementary resulted in a mob of angry parents demanding his removal. Victoria was a first hand witness to the carnage, which is why she vowed to never let her personal life mingle with her professional life. It was a good plan. That is until a most-certainly-not-her-type, absolutely adorable, first-year teacher got under her skin. And, when a confused and desperate parent targets her protégé, Victoria must decide which is more important: her career or love□

ISBN 978-1-61929-084-6
Available in print and eBook formats

The Gardener of Aria Manor
by A.L. Duncan

Janie O'Grady is a woman quite adapted to her life and circumstances as they are, living in New York City during the Great Depression. A hint of cynicism clouds the cold winter streets and keeps the rum runners strange bedfellows to the Irish mob's bounty in and out of speakeasy's, daring to brush shoulders with the neighboring Italian mobs. At a moment where Janie fears for her life she is presented with circumstances which seem like a harsh nudge from the heavens to decide her own destiny.

Feeling there is no other choice, Janie makes the fateful decision to change her identity and move to the Devon countryside on the coastal shores of England, as a Head Gardener to a 17th century manor, where déjà vu and the intrigues of a past life and murder mystery over shadow her life in the big city.

This tale invites you to peek into the pages of one woman's life and follow her incredible story of self-discovery of a very different kind; where looking back at one's past includes connecting the threads of passions and desires of a life lived before. A life lived where one's odyssey must wait to complete the circle in the next life.

ISBN: 978-1-61929-158-4
Available in both print and eBook formats

Strength In Numbers
by Jeanine Hoffman

Bailey ran out on her best friend, Jay, years ago but wants to make amends if she can. Sharon has buried herself in work for so long she isn't sure she knows how to do much else. Riley, a one-time LPGA golfer, has traveled and played the field while competing on some of the finest golf courses of the world. And, then there is Jay whose heart was broken by Bailey so many years ago — she hasn't fully trusted anyone since. All four women have things to face about themselves and the others. Fate brings them together to face a crisis none of them ever expected. Their lives will turn upside down, and the outcome can only be determined if they will believe that there is *Strength in Numbers*.

ISBN 978-1-61929-051-8
Available in print and eBook formats

OTHER YELLOW ROSE PUBLICATIONS

Brenda Adcock	Soiled Dove	978-1-935053-35-4
Brenda Adcock	The Sea Hawk	978-1-935053-10-1
Brenda Adcock	The Other Mrs. Champion	978-1-935053-46-0
Brenda Adcock	Picking Up the Pieces	978-1-61929-120-1
Brenda Adcock	The Game of Denial	978-1-61929-130-0
Janet Albert	Twenty-four Days	978-1-935053-16-3
Janet Albert	A Table for Two	978-1-935053-27-9
Janet Albert	Casa Parisi	978-1-61929-015-0
Georgia Beers	Thy Neighbor's Wife	1-932300-15-5
Georgia Beers	Turning the Page	978-1-932300-71-0
Carrie Brennan	Curve	978-1-932300-41-3
Carrie Carr	Destiny's Bridge	1-932300-11-2
Carrie Carr	Faith's Crossing	1-932300-12-0
Carrie Carr	Hope's Path	1-932300-40-6
Carrie Carr	Love's Journey	978-1-932300-65-9
Carrie Carr	Strength of the Heart	978-1-932300-81-9
Carrie Carr	The Way Things Should Be	978-1-932300-39-0
Carrie Carr	To Hold Forever	978-1-932300-21-5
Carrie Carr	Trust Our Tomorrows	978-1-61929-011-2
Carrie Carr	Piperton	978-1-935053-20-0
Carrie Carr	Something to Be Thankful For	1-932300-04-X
Carrie Carr	Diving Into the Turn	978-1-932300-54-3
Carrie Carr	Heart's Resolve	978-1-61929-051-8
Sky Croft	Amazonia	978-1-61929-066-2
Sky Croft	Mountain Rescue: The Ascent	978-1-61929-098-3
Cronin and Foster	Blue Collar Lesbian Erotica	978-1-935053-01-9
Cronin and Foster	Women in Uniform	978-1-935053-31-6
Pat Cronin	Souls' Rescue	978-1-935053-30-9
A.L. Duncan	The Gardener of Aria Manor	978-1-61929-158-4
Verda Foster	The Gift	978-1-61929-029-7
Verda Foster	The Chosen	978-1-61929-027-3
Anna Furtado	The Heart's Desire	1-932300-32-5
Anna Furtado	The Heart's Strength	978-1-932300-93-2
Anna Furtado	The Heart's Longing	978-1-935053-26-2
Melissa Good	Eye of the Storm	1-932300-13-9
Melissa Good	Hurricane Watch	978-1-935053-00-2
Melissa Good	Moving Target	978-1-61929-150-8
Melissa Good	Red Sky At Morning	978-1-932300-80-2
Melissa Good	Storm Surge: Book One	978-1-935053-28-6
Melissa Good	Storm Surge: Book Two	978-1-935053-39-2
Melissa Good	Stormy Waters	978-1-61929-082-2
Melissa Good	Thicker Than Water	1-932300-24-4
Melissa Good	Terrors of the High Seas	1-932300-45-7
Melissa Good	Tropical Storm	978-1-932300-60-4
Melissa Good	Tropical Convergence	978-1-935053-18-7
Regina A. Hanel	Love Another Day	978-1-935053-44-6
Regina A. Hanel	White Dragon	978-1-61929-142-3
Jeanine Hoffman	Lights & Sirens	978-1-61929-114-0
Jeanine Hoffman	Strength in Numbers	978-1-61929-108-9
Maya Indigal	Until Soon	978-1-932300-31-4

Jennifer Jackson	It's Elementary	978-1-61929-084-6
K. E. Lane	And, Playing the Role of Herself	978-1-932300-72-7
Helen Macpherson	Love's Redemption	978-1-935053-04-0
J. Y Morgan	Learning To Trust	978-1-932300-59-8
J. Y. Morgan	Download	978-1-932300-88-8
A. K. Naten	Turning Tides	978-1-932300-47-5
Lynne Norris	One Promise	978-1-932300-92-5
Paula Offutt	Butch Girls Can Fix Anything	978-1-932300-74-1
Surtees and Dunne	True Colours	978-1-932300-529
Surtees and Dunne	Many Roads to Travel	978-1-932300-55-0
Vicki Stevenson	Family Affairs	978-1-932300-97-0
Vicki Stevenson	Family Values	978-1-932300-89-5
Vicki Stevenson	Family Ties	978-1-935053-03-3
Vicki Stevenson	Certain Personal Matters	978-1-935053-06-4
Vicki Stevenson	Callie's Dilemma	978-1-61929-003-7
Cate Swannell	A Long Time Coming	978-1-61929-062-4
Cate Swannell	Heart's Passage	978-1-932300-09-3
Cate Swannell	No Ocean Deep	978-1-932300-36-9

About the Author

Regina lives in the mountainous suburbs of Northern New Jersey with her partner of twelve years. She's earned Bachelors' degrees majoring in accounting and biology, with a minor in German. She's also a Certified Public Accountant and works for the Federal Government protecting the taxpayer's interests. In addition to writing fiction, she loves the outdoors and enjoys hiking, kayaking, reading, watching football, and trying out new vegetarian recipes. *White Dragon* is Regina's second novel. Her first novel, *Love Another Day*, won a 2012 Alice B. Readers' Lavender Award certificate.

VISIT US ONLINE AT
www.regalcrest.biz

At the Regal Crest Website You'll Find

- The latest news about forthcoming titles and new releases

- Our complete backlist of romance, mystery, thriller and adventure titles

- Information about your favorite authors

- Current bestsellers

- Media tearsheets to print and take with you when you shop

- Which books are also available as eBooks.

Regal Crest print titles are available from all progressive booksellers including numerous sources online. Our distributors are Bella Distribution and Ingram.

CPSIA information can be obtained at www.ICGtesting.com
Printed in the USA
LVOW06s2049270514

R8487700001B/R84877PG387073LVX16B/7/P